ONE MISTY MOISTY MORNING

SUSANNA M. NEWSTEAD

PASTMASTERY PRESS

Cover art and design by matthewryanhistoricalillustrator.com/
Photography by Valerie Drew valadrew@yahoo.co.uk
Editing by Gill Whatmough

Published by PastMastery Press
Medlar House
Hanover Drive
Brackley Northants. NN136JS UK
sue@pastmastery.com

ISBN 978-1999905972

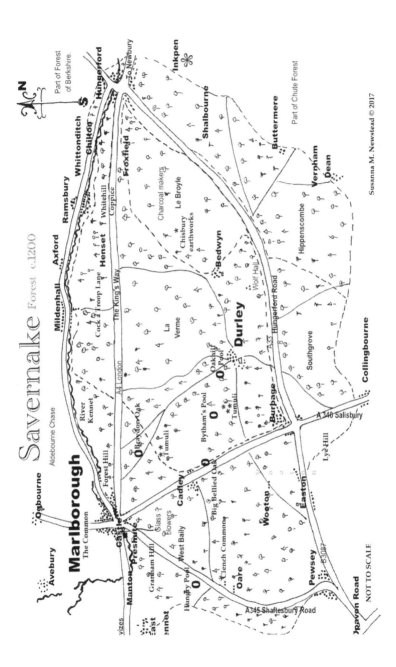

Savernake Forest c.1200

Susanna M. Newstead © 2017

NOT TO SCALE

Marlborough and Savernake Forest c.1200 (1)

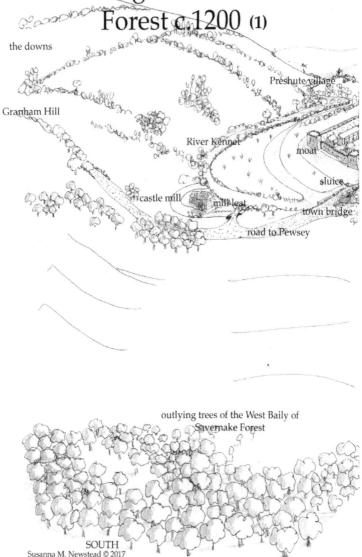

the downs

Preshute village

Granham Hill

River Kennet

moat

sluice

castle mill

mill leat

town bridge

road to Pewsey

outlying trees of the West Baily of Savernake Forest

SOUTH

Susanna M. Newstead © 2017

Marlborough Town and the forest c.1200 (2)

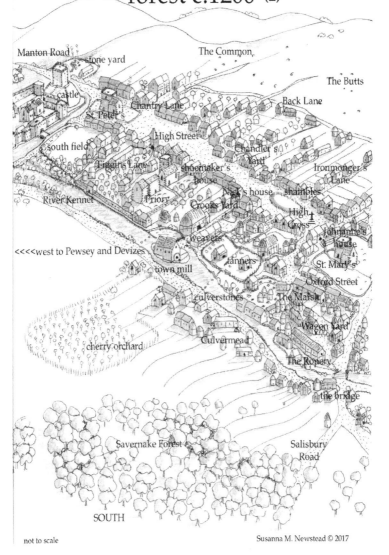

Manton Road
stone yard
The Common
The Butts
castle
Chantry Lane
Back Lane
St Peter's
High Street
Chandler's Yard
south field
Ironmonger's Lane
Tiggins Lane
shoemaker's house
Nick's house
shambles
River Kennet
Priory
Crooks Yard
High Cross
Johnanne's house
weavers
<<<<west to Pewsey and Devizes
tanners
St. Mary's
town mill
Oxford Street
culverstones
The Marsh
Wagon Yard
cherry orchard
Culvermead
The Ropery
the bridge
Savernake Forest
Salisbury Road
SOUTH

not to scale

Susanna M. Newstead © 2017

Marlborough and the forest c. 1200 (3)

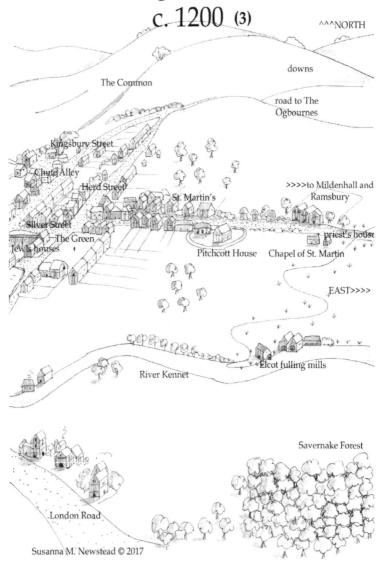

^^^NORTH

downs

The Common

road to The Ogbournes

Kingsbury Street

Chute Alley

Herd Street

St. Martin's

>>>>to Mildenhall and Ramsbury

Silver Street

The Green

Jew's houses

Pitchcott House

Chapel of St. Martin

priest's house

EAST>>>>

River Kennet

Elcot fulling mills

London Road

Savernake Forest

Susanna M. Newstead © 2017

ONE MISTY MOISTY MORNING

One misty moisty morning, when cloudy was the weather,
I met with an old man a-clothèd all in leather.
He was clothèd all in leather, with a cap beneath his chin,
Singing 'How d'ye do and how d'ye do and how d'ye do again'.
This rustic was a thresher, as on his way he hied,
And with a leather bottle fast buckled by his side.
He wore no shirt upon his back, but wool unto his skin,
Singing 'How d'ye do and how d'ye do and how d'ye do again'.
I went a little further and there I met a maid
'A-going, a-milking, a-milking sir' she said.
Then I began to compliment and she began to sing,
Singing 'How d'ye do and how d'ye do and how d'ye do again'.

PART OF AN OLD ENGLISH FOLK SONG

Chapter One

The blackbird was singing amongst the orchard blossoms and I was walking about with my dogs, joyfully whistling and mimicking him and confusing the poor creature. Eventually he flew off with a 'chuck, chuck, chuck' over the hedge and scuttled across the roof of John Brenthall's house, the first house in the village, close by the lane leading to the road to Salisbury. Here lived my chief wood warden and the man who knew everything there was to know about my forest.

John came out of his door and waved. "It promises another fine day, m'lord.

He was a serious man with dark hair and complexion; the sort of face which would need to be shaved by dinner time were he to have shaved at dawn. His limbs were loose and supple and his eye unfailing. John was the best tracker in the forest and knew every byway and green lane.

"Aye John. A good day to be out in the forest."

It was a misty morning with a slight damp in the air and a cloudy sky but the sun would burn it off and we should no doubt be warm enough later to strip to our shirts.

I whistled Mildred, my year old wolfhound, and Ben another of my dogs, two years old and given to me as a present by a neighbour. My little white gazehound Holdfast, was doing something of her own at the other side of the orchard. She would come when she felt like it. My older hound Mildred's mother Jocasta had chosen to stay with Tostig my groom in the stable that morning.

Peter Brenthall, John's fifteen year old son came out of the door, a crust of honeyed bread clamped between his jaws. Performing the action of a foot being jammed into a boot, he hopped on one leg.

He was followed by a yearling wolfhound, who jumped up at him excitedly. This was Mildred's brother Maxime, the dog I had given to Peter on his birthday last year.

"Down!" said Peter through his crust of bread and Max backed off and ran with John to the road.

"You are doing well with Max, Peter," I shouted, "he is so excitable, it can't be easy. Mildred on the other hand is as cool as cream."

At her name Mildred looked up at me and placed her rear end down on the turf. I felt for her wiry head.

A startled wren went whizzing and rattling over the orchard, set up by Holdfast's quartering of the hedge.

"Difference between dog and bitch sir," said Peter authoritatively.

We became aware of the clopping of a horse on the chalk path which ran from the forest to the village. Out of the trees came a man on a brown rouncey. When he saw us, he speeded up and bounced along until he was almost level. He was not a natural rider and was clinging on for dear life.

"My Lord Belvoir," he said out of breath.

"Good morning Grist," I said, recognising the bearded man in front of me as one of those employed by Nicholas Barbflet, the town reeve and master of the corn mill in the centre of Marlborough.

"What brings you to Durley?"

"This, sir," he said, fishing a piece of parchment from the front of his tunic.

I took it and he dismounted with an ungainly wobble.

Turning away I broke open the letter.

'To the Most Gracious Lord, Aumary Belvoir, Warden and Constable, Greetings from Nicholas Barbflet

This morning at Cowper's yard, we have discovered a murder. Might you come at your earliest convenience and take charge of the investigation? Nothing will be touched until you arrive. The coroner will not be called until you give us leave. There has been no hue and cry.

Myself as Witness Nicholas Barbflet Town Reeve.

Upon the nineteenth day of May in the seventh year of the reign of our

10

esteemed monarch John.'

Just like Nick. Straight and to the point. However, I did ponder on the manner of the wording. He had not said, 'we have discovered a body,' as most folk would.

When I got to Marlborough, I understood why.

*****

I stared down into the barrel.

"You have looked everywhere?"

"Aye we have. Nothing here," said Nick.

I looked round the cooper's workings. It was situated in Crooks Yard close by the lane to the town mill.

Here were made many items, not just barrels, but buckets, small bowls and some large metal containers. The fruits of the cooper's labours were scattered over the yard.

One barrel in particular held a rather gruesome consignment.

I looked around for the cooper who owned the yard, a man called Durwyn Cowper.

"You the first finder, Cowper?"

"Aye, sir."

"Tell me in your own words what happened."

Cowper put his hands into the front of his leather apron and rolled on the balls of his feet.

"'Twere early. Just light. I knew that this barrel should be filled up with ale by Annie Brewer up the road, yesterday. 'Twas one of our new ones. It were rolled back down here and I stored it overnight ready to go to the mill tomorrow."

"Why did it not go straight to the mill, Cowper?"

"It were too late and the mill gates were closed. They'd all gone home. All but Bullard and Menier and his lad. They'd be in the mill eatin' supper."

11

"Ah I see. Is this the only barrel for the mill?"

Nick interrupted, "We have three a week, this is Wednesday's ale. A bit late."

I nodded.

"Go on, Cowper."

"So me and my lad, Drew, we rolled the barrel - 'taint far of course - down to the mill. Only we never got far."

"I suppose you heard...."

"Aye we did. So we righted it and before it ever got outta the yard, we took off the clevis...," he stooped to pick up a metal band, "and prised off the chime."

This was apparently the wooden rim of the barrel which held the top in position.

"Forced open the head, this is the top plate... and found... *that,*" he grimaced.

I peered down again and noticed out of the corner of my eye, the town doctor and my good friend Johannes of Salerno, creep in through a small gap in the gate, closed then and guarded by Hal of Potterne, my senior man at arms.

"I can see why no hue and cry was called Nick."

Barbflet nodded.

"Mind you sir. 'Twas not the first time it had been opened surely," said Master Cowper.

"Oh...?

"Someone had taken it all off before and replaced it," said Master Cowper.

Johannes came up behind me. I pointed into the barrel.

The doctor was a big man, tall, over six foot, near to 45 years of age. He had shoulder length brown hair, scrupulously clean and shining, with just a hint of grey at the temples, which was tied back in a queue and he was clean shaven, contrary to current fashion, which dictated that men wore beards, as I did myself. His eyes were an amber brown, clear and direct of gaze. He tipped his head over the barrel top and drew back quickly.

"Well.... No one I hope, has had a taste of this ale?"

12

The cooper looked decidedly green. "No sir… well - you wouldn't would you?"

"No, but if you had delivered it to the town mill as requested, and the cask was broached in the normal way… someone would have taken the first sip," said Johannes with a cheeky grin.

Nicholas wiped his sleeve over his forehead. "God's wounds, Johannes. That would probably have been me."

I turned to look at my friend. "Well that is the strangest gruit I have ever known added to ale Nick," I said, smiling broadly.

Gruit is the mixture of herbs and other plants added to ale to give it a particular flavour.

We all four stood round the barrel and silently peered in.

There, floating almost at the top, was a man's head.

Ha, ha Paul my scribe! I have surprised you again. You might have guessed though, eh?

"Well, let's have it out then," I said.

Everyone looked around as if it was never going to be their job to fish out a severed head from an ale barrel.

Eventually Master Cowper took a leather cloth he had in his apron pocket and spread it on the ground.

Johannes sighed and rolling up his sleeves he fished for the head in the ale with two hands and laid it on the cloth. The ale streamed away.

Two brown eyes, dimmed by contact with the liquid, stared up at us. We noticed a hooked nose, bushy eyebrows and a tanned complexion. Long brown hair going grey was kept back by a leather cap which was tied tight beneath the chin.

The head kept falling to the side and in order to examine it properly, Johannes had to keep hold of it.

13

With his usual calm the doctor started to make a detailed study of the decapitated man. First he turned the head and looked at the back.

"The cap remained on the head when he met his death. No evidence of any head wound. No blow to the back of the head rendering him unconscious.

An outdoor man by his tan, in his... fifties would we say? Good teeth. The beard is not well kept though, as if he normally kept it cropped but could not do so at the time of his death. No fat on the cheeks or chin. A thin man - we are looking for a thin body. The head has been severed from the body but not cleanly. There is evidence of a chopping action here, see."

"Jesu forfend!" exclaimed Nick, crossing himself. "I hope the poor man was dead before they did that to him."

"We cannot tell the manner of his death, for we need the body."

Nick sighed and stood up straight. "I suppose I shall have to order a search of the town and environs. I was hoping to keep it quiet a little longer but...."

"Aye, we must I'm afraid. And we need to see if we can find out who the man is. None of us here know him?" I asked.

All shook their heads.

"Put word about, Nick. Has anyone lost someone? Has a man not returned home? Has a neighbour been missed? Ask the priory if any of their guests are missing."

The priory of St Margaret of Antioch lay a few yards down the High Street. They had a large guest house where travelling folk or people who were sick or on pilgrimage might rest before setting out on their journey again.

"Can we look at the river? I'll lend you men from the castle for that. Look into every outhouse and store, every barn, every privy. The rest of him must be somewhere."

"What shall we do with...?" asked Cowper nodding towards the head.

"Sad to say, Cowper, we must return him to his intoxicating liquid so that the coroner may see him. Then we shall see about setting him out somewhere where this bit of him," I pointed to the head, "... can wait for the rest to be found."

14

*****

Ah Paul. Welcome back my scribe. I am just reading aloud what we wrote earlier. I'm sorry I fell asleep on you. I am an old man of seventy three summers and am apt to do that at the drip of a dewdrop. My body is worn out but my mind is as active as a dancing deer.

What? You went for something to eat in the kitchen? Well, that is fine. You cannot be expected to scribe all day on the meagre fare which the priory feed you, can you? You are a growing lad. It's good of the prior to lend you to me now and again, I know. I expect he realises I will feed you up.

Now today, we are going to write about a murder which I examined in my role as Constable of North Wiltshire, in 1206. In the previous year, King John, God assoil him, had made me the person responsible for investigating all suspicious deaths in my part of the county. I'd had quite a bit of experience digging about, sifting information and solving crimes and John always mindful of the law, wanted to do his very best to bring justice to all and not only to the wealthy. John was ever interested in the little man and he had a huge appetite for the law and law making. Say what you will about him, but he had a brilliant mind and was father to much of the legal machinery in place in the courts today, you know.

Pardon Paul? Ah yes. I suspect that is true. I do expect that his name is mud at the priory in the town. No abbey, priory, monastery or cathedral will speak well of this much maligned king. He taxed them to beggary for his wars to recover his lands on the continent. They will not think or write kindly of him.

You are writing for me because I can no longer hold a pen and we are speaking about events which happened over forty years ago. Many chroniclers wrote about John after his death - some of them a long time after he died in 1216. They were less than fair, I know. All we can do is try to make our own record a kinder, truer one - he really was not the complete monster he was painted. But - we digress. Shall we pick up where we left off and write about that murder which was reported to

15

me on the morning of April 15th 1206?

*****

We laughingly called this the year of the six babies and the six murders. 1206. Six people brutally cut off from life and six babies born to take their places in the world. There was my own Simon, my son and heir born on April 5th. Shortly afterwards Richard Marshall, my head groom, was gifted with a son by his wife Mary. On May 12th, sweet Janet Peddler was safely delivered of a girl and a boy – twins, and on the morning of May 14th, Geoffrey Reeve, Johnathan Reeve's little lad came lustily into the world. Sadly the little girl child born to the Sylvestres did not survive the night of May15th. Their second tragedy.

The winter of 1204/5 had been harsh and long and sadly it was to be the death of many of the older and more vulnerable folk of my demesne: Durley a village of some hundred or so souls, deep in the Forest of Savernake close by the town of Marlborough, in the county of Wiltshire. I was also responsible for many of the outlying villages and cotts and the trades of the forest.

I, Aumary Belvoir, was the hereditary warden of that forest which I held for our monarch John and now at last, after eighteen months of marriage, my wife Lydia had given me a son. An heir to follow me in the wardenship.

Lydia was my second wife. Cecily had been my first love and she had been murdered some years ago along with my five year old son Geoffrey. This had been a huge blow to me and the birth of my second son in September 1206 was a cause for great celebration. By my first wife I also had my daughter Hawise, who was nearly seven and the light of my life.

Most of the vacant houses, left by the deaths of their occupants in the winter, were repaired and occupied again. Young Johnathan Reeve took up the house left by old Tom Giffard and installed Philipa, his new wife, there.

Martyn Pedlar and his wife Janet were living in the house of her first husband and had plenty of space to expand their household, even though they were new parents in their middle age.

Richard had rebuilt the house near the little river which had once belonged to two of my tied peasants, Edith and Edmund Brooker, both now deceased and lived there with Mary.

Only Martyn Carpenter's house remained empty now. He had been the village's chief wood worker and had been killed in an accident in that dreadful winter of 1205, when the land had been locked up with ice and snow from December to April. I had been wondering who I could install there now as I had made my way down the steps of the manor and out through the gate. Tostig, one of my grooms, had been courting a lady from Wooton, a village a few miles west. She was a few years older than my groom but this did not seem to matter. Alison Dexter and Tostig Frith had been thrown together last spring, when I was investigating the murder of a man of Wooton and I wondered if this was the couple I would shortly be installing in my vacant cottage. These were the simple thoughts which exercised me that spring morning in 1206 until I was forced to consider the matter of the head in the barrel.

*****

The coroner came and went. He was not much interested, he said. Find the rest of our mystery man and then he would convene his jury of twelve men over fourteen years of age to establish the cause of death and record it in his books.

The head was once more taken from the barrel. The priest of St. Mary took charge of it and stored it, dripping, in a box in the crypt of the church for the day when it might be reunited with the body. The ale was poured away, the barrel scoured.

The town was searched. Nothing came to light. No body could be found. No one was missing. We stayed that night with my friend Johannes and bedded down, not for the first time, in his comfortable parlour. He had been born in Oxford but had taken the name of the place he had learned his doctoring, Salerno in Sicily, the very best place in the world to learn the art of medicine, he told me. He was a very wealthy man, having made his money as a young man, soldiering in the Holy Lands with our previous king, Richard. Now he was giving back to the inhabitants of this little downland town.

Hal and I settled ourselves on two thick straw paliasses and went yet again, over the circumstances of the finding of the head as Johannes, Hal and I had done, earlier that evening,

"Why would anyone want to put an 'ead in a barrel o'ale?" asked my old friend, chief man at arms and sparring partner Hal of Potterne. He was a grizzled veteran of the wars of John's father, Henry the Second. He sported a long grey forked beard which he kept brushed to perfection, wore it in imitation of his Viking ancestors, he said and he was rightly very proud of it.

"I mean… it might not a'bin found."

"Sooner or later it would. As it decomposed in the ale, someone would have found it - even if they only opened the barrel to find out what was wrong with the taste of the ale and why it was making folk so sick."

Hal sniffed. "Don't bear thinkin' about, do it?"

"No indeed."

"I've 'eard o'rats falling into ale tuns but never an 'ead. Do you reckon we 'as to open every barrel of summat in town to see if the rest 'o 'im 'as bin diced up like an onion and stored somewhere else?"

"That is a good thought, Hal. I'll ask Nick tomorrow to let it be known that anyone who has taken delivery of a barrel - any barrel, say, in the last three days, should open it and look, if they haven't already. You could be right. The poor man might be in pieces. We might not be looking for a complete headless body."

"You reckon sir, the body is in the forest somewhere? It's a big place. We might never find it."

"It's not impossible, Hal." I yawned, "we just need to know how the head got to the cooper's yard and into that barrel without anyone being seen."

"Busy place, the town. Who's goin'a notice a man with a sack, or a pack or

18

a saddlebag?"

"And the yard is locked of an evening."

"And the barrel lid was fixed. That's no quiet job."

"Ah yes," I sat up. "Tomorrow we ask around. How many houses are there close by the yard? Someone must have heard something."

Soon we were snoring and the matter of the head in the barrel passed from our minds. Luckily I did not dream of it.

*****

Our questioning the following day revealed nothing. No one had heard anything. No unusual sounds had come from the yard in the middle of the night. Not a peep. If it had, no one was telling. The same could be said for the ale brewster up the street. The head was not in the ale when it left her brew house. It had been returned to the cooper's because the mill was closed. It should have been delivered the next morning. I questioned the coopers who worked with the master in the yard. The three apprentices, Drew, Fiddler and Wariner lived at the High Street house and bedded down at the home of the cooper. Mistress Cowper vouched for them. They were all asleep in their beds, in her attic, she said protectively, when the deed must have been perpetrated. In order to go out at night, they would have to pass through the sleeping room of the Cowpers and they had not.

The journeyman cooper, whose name was Alfred Easton, lived with his wife at the top end of Kingsbury Street where they rented two rooms. He too had been in his bed.

Master Cowper had been until late, at the new ale house on the High Street, called the Green Man. He had had a deal of ale and had fetched up at his cottage at the junction of Crooks Lane and High Street after midnight. He had been lucky to avoid the watch and to have been fined for breaking the curfew but there were plenty of folk who were about after dark and I knew that a blind eye was turned to many of the goings on. His wife swore that he came home rather the worse for wear that night and went straight to bed. She'd waited up for him. There was no doubt he was a little fragile that morning. Even though no woman could testify for or against her husband, I had no reason not to believe Mistress Cowper. No help there.

I was all ready to pack up and go home and get my foresters out in the trees to look for what remained of our decapitated man when I was called to meet with my only witness to the murder - the strangest witness I ever *did* meet and one who could *tell* me nothing. Nevertheless it transpired that she was certainly the last creature to see our decapitated man alive and had without doubt witnessed the whole thing. The problem was, Isabella, (as we later found out her name to be), could not speak. She could growl and howl and thrash about on her chain and that is how we found her, tied to a tree, hungry and thirsty and very bemused.

My witness was a bear.

Chapter Two

I had just mounted Bayard, my roan gelding, and turned his head to the opening of the cooper's yard when a young lad, breathless and sweating, careered around the gatepost.

His eyes scanned the place and he made directly for me.

"Sir. Are you the Lord Belvoir? The one who...," his breath ran out and I never did find out what it was he thought I did.

"I am." I dismounted. The lad was about ten with a shock of almost white hair worn long to the shoulders. I recognised him but could not at that moment put my finger on where I had seen him.

He blew up his fringe. "I run all the way from..." more deep breaths, "from the West Baily, sir. Me Da, he wants me to take you to him."

Now I remembered. This was the son of Aldo Swift the glassblower, who had his glass kilns in the western part of the forest.

"And why would he want you to come and fetch me...?" I searched for the lad's name....

"Osric, sir," said Hal. He knew everyone in the forest. "Aye, Osric. Why the hurry?"

"He's afraid she'll do some damage sir. Come quick. He don't want to hurt her but he don't want no hurt done."

I looked round at Master Cowper and the others but they just shrugged.

"Very well Osric... lead the way."

Hal took the boy up on his saddle and we trotted out of the yard. We made directly for the hill where marched row upon row of old forest trees, ash, beech, holly and oak.

The glass blowers had made themselves a new road; a track through the trees which went down the hill from their camp directly to the river from whence they took their gravel and sand for the making of glass.

Up this track we went and once in the trees, Osric jumped down and forged ahead on foot, calling to us to hurry.

We came out into the clearing where the wooden huts of the glass blowers had been erected.

Aldo Swift came up quickly and took his son under his arm. "Well done lad." Hugged in this way, Osric wriggled off, embarrassed.

"Now go and get a drink."

Aldo tugged his forelock. "Sir Aumary. Thank you for coming. This way."

"On foot or shall I ride?"

"Foot, sir. It's not far and the horses might spook her - or she them."

I left Bayard with the glassblowers. Hal dismounted from Grafton and we followed the chief glass man into the trees.

As we walked I attempted to get some idea of what this summons to the forest was all about but we threaded our way so deeply into the undergrowth, ducking under branches and carefully negotiating the briars and blackberry bushes which abounded in the understorey here, so what I heard was very fragmented. I decided to wait until we stopped moving.

We had been walking for only a matter of heartbeats when I heard a terrible growly, grumbling, a wailing and moaning.

"God's cods!" said Hal, crossing himself, "who's that then?"

"Not who Hal" said Aldo, "what."

We both looked alarmed.

"There are fewer wolves in the forest now," I said, "than in my father's day, and they are a poor sort of creature, mostly nocturnal. What might make that...."

We came out into a sunlit clearing.

There, tethered to an oak by her ankle, standing on her hind legs and a little over six foot high, was a dishevelled brown bear.

*****

She was howling and thrashing and once she saw us, she came down onto her four feet and tried to reach us. She came up short on the chain attached to her leg.

"Poor beast," said Hal. "I wonder 'ow long she's been there?"

I watched her carefully. She sat at the extreme end of her chain and growled low in her throat.

Her hair was brown, long and matted and in places a little patchy. Her ankle had been rubbed raw by the chain and it looked very sore. Her head was round with small ears tipped with amber hair. When she opened her mouth to moan, I noticed that she had few teeth left. The claws were light in colour and wickedly long. Her eyes were intelligent, soulful and sad and I noticed that one of them was weeping and sore as if it had been damaged, maybe by a whippy briar. I noticed that her nose bore an old pink scar where, I supposed her previous handler had had a ring through her nose. At least her present bearward was kinder for there was no trace of it now.

"Aldo, can you run back and fetch water and if you have it, something she might like to eat. I have a feeling she is very hungry and thirsty." He ran off to do my bidding.

I approached the bear slowly.

"Now then old girl..." I said, for I did think this was an old bear, not a fit and fast youngster.

"Let's see about getting you freed from this tree."

Hal hopped from one leg to the other. "Sir, you can't mean to let 'er go. I mean there's no tellin' what...."

"I do not think this bear will be any trouble, Hal," I said.

Say again Paul? How did I know? Haha! I had seen the like of her before, at fairs and festivals, always accompanied by their bearward. The man

23

who looked after them.

"This Hal, if I am not much mistaken, is a performing bear. And an old one at that. She will be used to doing the master's bidding."

"God's ditties, I 'ope yer right," said Hal.

I smiled, approaching very quietly and carefully.

"There are no wild bears here now, though I think up in the north of the country there were a few in my great grandfather's time. They come now, I think from the frozen countries to the north of us. They are taken from the wild when young and are trained to do tricks and behave like a human. They can be quite tame."

"You get any closer and we'll see just 'ow tame," whispered Hal.

"The bearward wants you to think the creature is fierce so that it makes him seem clever and brave but in truth, they are no more dangerous than a large dog or a mettlesome horse, when trained."

I stretched out my hand and fondled the rough fur at the base of the creature's neck. The bear extended her head and turned it, just as one of my dogs might do when I fondled their ears.

"There old girl. Now you stay just there and I'll see how you are fastened."

The bear watched me walk around the tree with sad brown eyes. The end of the chain was fixed to the ground with a metal spike and wrapped around the tree trunk. I wiggled the spike and it came free, then I unwrapped the chain and let it fall. The creature made no attempt to run away. She sat at the base of the oak and watched us carefully. Much as we had watched her.

Aldo returned with some water which he poured into a dish. The bear stood on four feet and took the water gratefully. We topped it up four times.

"My son is coming with some meat. All we have is rabbit I'm afraid, and a little fish."

"She will love that I'm sure. Oh..." I had remembered something. From my purse, I took a little apple which I had stored there and forgotten about.

I gave it to the bear's mouth and tossed it in. She opened her teeth, what she had left and crunched happily.

"Sorry old gal, I have no more."

Osric now approached with great trepidation. He would not come near the beast. I took the meat from him and again tossed it to the bear. She picked it up deftly and hungrily bit into it. That demolished, she started on the trout.

"Poor beast, she is starving. We shall need more than this to appease her hunger," I said.

I looked back at Aldo.

"How did you find her?" I asked.

"The wailing, just as you heard," he answered. "We wondered what the devil it was. A few braver sorts came to look and there she was. They came running for me and I sent Osric to you."

"You did well. How did you know where I'd gone?"

"One of the lads that came back to the camp from town said he'd seen you go into the cooper's yard."

"Ah."

"In truth, I didn't know what to do, but sir, this is your forest and a beast like this found in it… well I just thought you ought to know."

"Thank you, Aldo."

I scratched my head. "What is she doing tied to a tree, alone? Where is her bearward?"

I walked around the clearing. I was aware of the bear following me slowly on all fours and Hal, his hand on his sword pommel, following the bear.

I turned back to Aldo. "Lend me some men Aldo, I'd like to make a search, just a few yards around the clearing."

He ran off to find some men. Osric, with a quick look over his shoulder at the bear, ran off after him.

"She likes you sir," said Hal smiling. "She's following you."

I smiled. "Company, Hal. All her life she has been used to company and suddenly, here she is tied up in a strange place with no one. No water, no food. For goodness knows how long."

"And missin' the person who looks to 'er?"

"And I fed her. I'm a friend now."

"Well… I wouldn't go as far as to say that," said my old retainer, with a chuckle.

I caught my lip in my teeth, "So where is your master, old bear eh?"

I scanned the undergrowth. "He would never have tied you up like that unless he intended to come back to you pretty quickly."

"Think 'es gone into town, sir?"

"No, Hal. He would take the bear. Never pass up a chance at money. He'd make her perform. Earn his night's lodgings and food."

"Who's gonna lodge a bear, sir?"

"Someone with a barn perhaps, someone who can attract a crowd to toss pennies to a dancing bear. Market day maybe?"

"Master Green at the Green Man, sir?"

"Perhaps."

"They 'ave a yard at the back an' a coupla outbuildings."

"It's a thought, Hal. It's market day tomorrow. Maybe there would be a performance there."

"Oops off she goes, sir," said Hal quickly as our bear suddenly loped forward on all fours, passed me and crashed her way through some new ferns and brackens. The chain dragged behind her.

Her snout upwards, she tested the air like a dog scenting a deer and was off again, though not really at any speed. We followed.

Hal thought to grab the chain but I called out, "No leave it Hal, she is going somewhere that's for sure. She knows where she is going."

We did not need to follow far.

Another clearing surrounded by mature birches and oaks, the understorey made up of holly and bracken, with the leaves of the woodbine and wild columbine trailing up the branches and the new unfurling leaves of the cow parsley dotted here and there.

Our bear came to a halt at the side of this clearing just beneath the gently arching bough of an old beech. I came up beside her and patted and stroked her terrible wiry fur.

She gave out a huge roar which made all the pigeons of the forest lift up at once. I hunkered down.

Hal picked up the end of her chain which was about eight feet long.

"What's the matter, girl?" I said.

The bear tossed her head as if she were shaking it for a 'no'.

I looked around the clearing. Just in front of us, the bracken had been trampled down.

I stood and walked towards it.

"Ah," I said, "Yes, my girl. Now I see why you are so upset."

Hal came up beside me leading the bear who hung back a little.

We looked down. There was a pair of feet sticking out of the undergrowth. We pulled one small ankle boot each, the sort that starts as one piece of leather tied round the lower leg and eventually moulds itself to the shape of the foot.

Out from the bush came a man, clothed completely in leather.

Clouds of flies rose up as we dragged him and there was a fearful smell.

"Well, looks like we have found our headless man, Hal," I said.

The bear roared again.

*****

The man was indeed clothed in leather. His boots, as I have mentioned were pulled over tight leather breeches which were patched and scuffed. His long sleeved cotte, which had also seen better days, was leather and tied with lacings at the front. Under this he had a worn and rather grey wool shirt. Close by we found a small pack with the sort of items a man might need who was much on

27

the road. To the top of the pack was roped a carefully folded supple short leather cloak. A little way off in the centre of the clearing we found a stout staff which would aid a man walking a long distance. We were in the process of searching round the body when Aldo found us.

"We shall not need your men now thank you, Aldo."

He nodded, unperturbed. "Shall I send a hurdle for the body sir?"

"Aye Aldo. That would be useful."

"The coroner sir?" said Hal.

"The coroner be damned. He can view it when we take it back and reunite it with its head."

We were not supposed to move a body before the coroner had seen it but I would take charge of proceedings now. If there was to be an amercement for moving it then I would pay the fine or I would argue against it being levied at all.

I looked back to the bear. "What on earth are we to do with her?" I said aloud.

*****

After scouring the ground about the body for any clues (we found none, only the blood where the man's body had been parted from his head), we roped the remains to a hurdle and two of Aldo's men dragged it, decently covered with an old blanket, down the hill.

We followed them into town. I called into Johannes' house and shouted into the kitchen that we had found the body.

Agnes, his little housekeeper came out, looking puzzled.

She was a mute dwarf and she, Johannes and I communicated by writing and in sign language. She lifted her arms and her shoulders.

This meant, I think, "What are you on about?"

I laughed. "Can you tell Johannes please, that we have found the body, Agnes. He will know what I mean. And can he meet us at the cooper's yard?"

28

She nodded animatedly.

I turned Bayard and clopped up the road.

We waited for Johannes as he fetched the head from the priest at the church of St. Mary.

He came quickly through the gate and Hal once again shut it with a clang.

The doctor offered the head to the neck and pronounced it a perfect fit.

Then we set about trying to find out how the man had met his end.

"Well, that is easy. Here; see."

I craned my neck to look where Johannes pointed at the body. Sure enough, there was a slit in the leather, to the rear, high up just where the spine drew down the back.

"Someone who knows that if you pierce a man here, his spine will be severed and he will fall and be unable to move his arms or legs."

"So the spine is broken."

"To all intents and purposes, yes. Like a man who falls and breaks the column of his back. He no longer moves his limbs."

"So the man was alive but could not move."

"That is my guess, yes."

"Awful."

"I have seen it once before in my life," said Johannes. "When I attended a joust - oh no, I was not taking part...."

The horror on his face made me laugh.

"It was an unlicensed joust on a field just outside Oxford. Many folk... I think Earl Marshall was there for one... came to compete. I saw a man unhorsed and his spine severed just below the neck."

"He survived?"

"Aye, after a fashion. He could not move at all, had difficulty breathing and eventually he died, but it did not kill him immediately."

"So our bearward is lying in the forest helpless and then his head is struck off?"

29

"Struck to a point yes." Johannes did not need to continue. The thought of what had happened, was terrible.

"His body is then hidden, his bear tethered and the head is brought into the town and ends up in a barrel of ale."

We have to ask... what for? Gods! Johannes. What a tangle!"

I know what you are about to ask, Paul. What did we do with the bear?

Well, we asked a couple of the men from the glassblowers camp to gently lead her to Durley. At first we had no volunteers but when they saw how docile she had been with Hal and I and when a couple of silver pennies jingled in my purse, they took on the job.

I told them they were to find John Brenthall and his son Peter and give the bear into their keeping. Tell them the story of her finding and the discovery of her bearward. Feed her as much as she would eat, water her and tether her carefully to a tree, perhaps in the orchard. I would see to her on my return.

The body of the bearward was laid in the church, his head reunited with the rest of him, this time in front of the altar and prayers were said for his soul. He would be interred in St Mary's churchyard later next day. Once the coroner had seen him of course.

No one had remarked that a dancing bear had been performing in the town and there is no doubt if there had been such an occurrence, folk would have spoken about it for days. So our bear and her warden had not been coming from Marlborough but to it. This made it even more difficult to understand why someone should wish to kill the bear man and hide his head in a Marlborough cooper's barrel.

I asked around before I left. Did anyone know of a performing bear locally? Had anyone seen such a thing in another town? Of course they had, but it was not our man in leather and it had been a few years ago.

We left the town a little disconsolate and no further on with our conundrum.

*****

We made haste to get home as I wanted to be sure that the bear was safe and as happy as she could be, tethered to a tree in our orchard.

As we approached the village we heard a terrible yelling and shouting and the bear growling and made quickly to the source of it. My heart fell to my boots for the sounds were coming from the orchard.

As we rounded the church I could see that the bear was romping free around the trees and that a couple of Peter's bee skeps had been overturned.

Peter and a few of the village folk were chasing the bear, who looked as if she had half of one of Peter's woven basket skeps in her hand.

I dismounted at the turn by the church and ran over the grass, leaping the low hedge of blackthorn and hawthorn which we had planted around the field. This was growing but was not yet tall enough to call a proper hedge. I yelled at Hal to go to the manor and fetch food.

People looked back over their shoulders as they saw me approach and they slowed down to a stop. The bear looked back too and sat down to tear the woven straw piece of bee hive she had managed to filch.

Peter came running up.

"Sir, the men who left her didn't tie her properly and she got free. She made straightways for my bees and tore into one of the hives."

"The smell of honey no doubt. I had forgotten that it is said that bears like honey. Now we know it's not just an old tale," I said, smiling. "I'm sorry for your hive, Peter. I should have known that an orchard full of bees is not the place for a bear."

The bees were furious with the thief and some of them circled her but she batted them away unconcerned and dipped her head to gorge on the comb she had found. It was only small as it was the very beginning of the season and Peter did not raid his hives over winter as many did, destroying them and having to build up again. He left them enough to survive on.

"This hive is ruined now. The bees will die or flee. I gotta stop her getting to the rest."

"Leave her to me. I think she will trust me. I need a peace offering. Once she has eaten her fill of honey and there is very little for her, I'll offer her something else tasty and hope that I can lead her away and tether her again somewhere else."

"Dad has some fish ready for her in the house. I'll go and get it," said Peter and he ran off leaping the growing hedge and disappearing into his house across the road from the orchard.

I approached the bear slowly. Suddenly I heard a voice close beside me.

"Well, Isabella. We meet again," it said, "Good to see you but, where's your Da?"

I turned. There was Martyn Peddler who lived in the village with his wife Janet. He would be off soon with his pack, to tramp the highways selling his wares up and down the villages and towns of southern England from Cornwall to Kent, though truthfully since he had married and was a new father, he travelled less far.

"Peddler," I said. "You know our bear by name?"

"Aye, sir. And she knows her own name too. Whatever is she doing here?"

"Ah... I will tell you. First I must pacify her and get her somewhere safe. I thought the hay barn might be a good place. There isn't too much hay left at this time of year but she will be snug there until I can decide what to do with her."

Peter ran up with some fish. Martyn Peddler took it from him and approached the bear making soothing noises and using her name often.

The bear took the fish and dropped the now finished and destroyed comb. Peter dashed forward to retrieve it and ran off to inspect his hives and the damage done.

Martyn took hold of Isabella's chain. "C'mon ol' Izzy," he said, "let's get you somewhere safe."

She lurched along behind the peddler and we walked together down the lane past the church, rounded the corner of the manor wall and went into the

32

haybarn through its large double door. Isabella followed meekly, crunching on her trout.

"Isabella?" I mocked. "Rather a...well, grand name for a bear isn't it?"

"Ah well... y'see Godfrey named her after the old Queen - John's first wife, sir."

"Isabella of Gloucester?"

"Aye that's her. Course it was a while back that."

"Seventeen years by my reckoning since John married his first Isabella. I went to the wedding. It was held at Marlborough castle and my father took me. Mind you then he was just plain Count John. I was about fourteen, I think."

"Be about right."

We had reached the barn and we wrapped the chain around one of the timbers which held up the roof. Then we set about banging the metal stake which held Isabella's chain into the hard packed earth of the floor. She sat down comfortably next to Peddler on the hay and I sat at the other side.

"So she is as I thought, an old bear?"

"He didn't have her from a cub. He got her from another man. Said she was about five then."

"So she might be twenty-two or so now. She is looking a little grizzled round the mouth."

"Aye, maybe." Peddler looked up at me. "So where is Godfrey then?"

"First tell me how you know the man," I said.

Martyn Peddler stretched out his legs in front of him. "You meet all sorts a-travelling the roads as I do, sir," he said. "I think I first met Godfrey Barend, ooh, about ten years ago. He mostly travels the pilgrim routes. Glastonbury, Canterbury, St. Albans, Walsingham. Course I din't go that far up and stayed down south. I meet him most often on the route from Glastonbury to Canterbury."

"You would travel together?"

"Yeah. When we met we'd do business together. He with his performing bear and me with me goods. Pilgrim places have rich pickings, sir."

"I'm sure they have. So many folk coming and going and with nothing to do."

Martyn laughed. "You might say that." He looked at me, all jollity gone. "Is he dead then sir? Godfrey?"

"Aye I'm afraid he is." I told him the story of finding the head in the barrel and then the body in the forest.

"He shook his head. "He were a rogue make no mistake, but he didn't deserve that."

I asked him if he might quickly, before tomorrow was too old, go into the town and formally identify the man Godfrey Barend.

"Aye, I can do that for him. At least he can be buried with a name."

"Do you know if he has any contacts in this part of the world? No one in the town seems to know him. Other bearwards have come and gone but none as distinctive as Godfrey."

"Aye," he chuckled, "no one would forget him with his leather and all. I'd never been this far north before I fetched up at Durley so I can't help you there."

Martyn Peddler had been found with a nasty head wound and was left for dead in a pool of blood on the road into Durley in the hard winter of 1204. He had completely lost his memory for a while but once he had been nursed back to health by his now wife, Janet he had decided to stay for most of the year in the village and work his fields with her. He now only went peddling in the kinder summer months.

"What was the man like, Martyn?"

"Like? Well. What you mean is, was he the sort of man who was likely to end up head severed from his body and in a barrel?"

I chuckled. "I suppose that is what I mean," I said honestly.

"He was, as I said, a rogue. Not completely honest but not bad neither. He would take advantage of a situation as soon as look at it."

"Such as?"

"Well, I remember him filching a pie that was set out on a table to cool.

Swore blind that he hadn't had it. 'Musta bin Isabella here' he said to the good wife baxter who baked it. Course she wasn't going to argue with a bear, was she?"

I laughed. "Ah, that kind of rogue."

"No one would chop off a head for that kinda thing now would they?"

"Who can tell, Martyn?" I said.

"He was good to Isabella - plenty of bear men are not. As good as he could be. No one ever gets rich trailing a bear around the countryside. He fed her well - days when he didn't eat himself she got fed. I remember that."

"Wouldn't do to keep her hungry anyway, would it? She might get nasty."

Martyn looked me squarely in the eye. "Izzy? Never. As meek as a lamb she is. Though course we don't want folks to think that, if we are doing tricks and stuff, now do we?"

"No. She was pretty hungry when we found her and you're right. She was not aggressive at all."

"There you are then. Godfrey was content to wander the road, a bed in a barn here, a performance at a manor there, a meal at the side of the road where ever. He didn't ask for much. Makes it all the more odd he ended like he did."

I stretched my arms above my head and yawned. "Well, we must look to other reasons why men are killed."

"You mean he might a fallen foul of someone on the road?"

"Ah no, his purse was still in his pack. Only a few pennies, true, but still money. He was not robbed."

Suddenly I felt Isabella at my side, leaning heavily on me. She was a great weight and to avoid being crushed, I shifted myself upright. The bear leaned into the hay, curled up her legs and snuggled onto her side.

"Aw bless her. She's tired," said Martyn rising and dusting himself of hay.

"We'll leave her. I'll look in on her at close of day and ask Wyot the gatekeeper to look to her in the night."

I went to the large door in the barn and closed it, putting down the huge oak beam which served as a lock.

Martyn and I wandered out of the other door into the fading sunshine. Hal was lounging on a bench outside.

"All well, sir?" he asked.

"Yes Hal. Isabella is asleep."

"Isabella sir. You named the beast already? You know what they say. You name a beast, you keep a beast."

I smiled. "No fear of that, Hal. No, she had a name already and we now have a name for the man who owned her."

Martyn came out of the barn and fixed the doors together with its rope.

"Godfrey, Hal," he said "Godfrey Barend I knew him. Used to travel with him sometimes."

"Ah."

We all three walked towards the hall steps.

"Hal, tell me, what makes a man kill another? How many reasons can you think of? It's not robbery for it was no theft. Not in self defence either."

We ascended the steps and went into the hall where I fetched a jug and three cups from the pot board.

We pulled out the bench and sat.

"Jealousy or envy," said Hal.

"Hmm... that likely Martyn?"

The peddler took a gulp of ale.

"Don't think so. Nothing to be jealous of m'lord."

"Argument over land?"

"Had no land."

"Argument over a woman?"

"Had no woman but Izzy."

"Argument over money?"

"That might be the case if we could find out what kind of money," I said, sipping my ale.

"You mean like debt or summat," said Hal.

"That likely Martyn? You knew the man?"

"Hard to say. He did dice now and again. Who doesn't?"

"Hmmm"

"But it still doesn't tell us why his head turned up in the barrel o' ale, does it?" said Hal sagely.

"Now that to me smacks of revenge." I said, tipping up my cup.

Both men turned to me.

"Why would you want to poison ale destined for the mill; for that is what the head would have done?"

"But it's two separate things," said Hal, "The 'ead bein' in the ale and the murder of Godfrey."

"Ah, but is it?" I said.

We all looked down at our cups, imagining a head floating in the ale which had been sloshing around in my fine pewter jug.

None of us could finish our beaker.

Chapter Three

I could not sleep that night for wondering what I was going to do with Isabella the bear. She could not stay with us and how was I going to find her a new master?

I rose early and went out to the haybarn to see her and take her some apples.

I was not the earliest riser, for Peter was in the barn, in the half light, feeding her stale bread dipped in lard.

"She is so tame sir," he said when I entered and startled, asked him how long he had been there.

"Since just before dawn sir. Wyot let me in," he said. "And I have managed to get her to do some of the tricks that her bearward had taught her."

I smiled. "How did you get her to do that?"

"Simply by working out what it was he must have said to her to make her do things. Like I would with Maxime."

"So if you say 'sit' she sits, eh?"

"Well, no sir, not quite like that but if I ask her to give me a paw she will do that. I have rewarded her with little sippets of bread and dripping. She loves them."

"What else will she do for bread and dripping?"

"If you ask and tap her side, she turns right and left. And she will dance if you tap her legs. Course she has to be standing for that."

"Peter, you are a natural bearward. Good luck in your new job," I teased.

Peter chuckled. "I don't think so. Dad wouldn't let me anyway."

I undid the chain which kept Isabella held to the beam "Shall we take her for a morning wander round the meadow? She has been here all night and I see no evidence of any... ahem...."

"Dung sir?"

"Aye Peter, dung."

*****

I rode into Marlborough very early and clattered into Nicholas Barbflet's yard, close by the town mill. The gates were open.

There were few workers visible there at this early hour and they were busy with the sluice gates to the mill race. One of them told me they were expecting a large consignment of rye grain. Some of this had been grown on the poor soils of the flat plain further south and it was now being carted up to Marlborough for milling. Rye was not as popular as corn of course, but this early in the year it was a good crop and provided folk with a source of flour for bread.

I watched as the men manoeuvered the gates into position and the mill pond filled with water. The river beyond began to shrink as water was drained off.

I was so engrossed in their work and in the rushing of the water, that I did not hear the cry of 'milk- fresh milk' which rang out around the enclosed place of the yard. At last as they came closer I heard them and I looked back. There were two women with buckets suspended on rope harnesses from their shoulders. Our fields around Marlborough were mostly given over to sheep as the ground was fit for little else, the soil being poor and thin. However towards Manton and Preshute villages, the river valley, prone to flooding and so much more lush in grass than the uplands, were just right for dairy cows.

Early some summer mornings these dairymaids would milk their cows in the fields where they grazed and carry the produce the short distance to the town. Folk came out with buckets and jugs, dishes and flasks and the maids would fill them and take money.

"Milk sir, warm and fresh from the cow?" asked one maid coyly as I leaned on the wall which surrounded the mill pond.

I was going to shake my head but instead peered into her pail. The milk looked appetising and creamy. It was a long time since I had taken milk fresh

40

from the cow. Indeed it was most unusual, for folk usually made cheese with their milk and most milk hereabouts, was from goats or sheep.

I fished out a small pewter cup which I always carried in my purse and dipped it into the pail.

The maid took some money from me. The millers now crowded round and did the same. Some of them filled jugs and took them into the mill house.

The girl eyed me from top to toe.

"I haven't seen you here before, sir." She licked her lips suggestively.

"No, I don't really belong here," I said "I am a forest man who has business with the town reeve."

The girl leaned against the wall as I sipped my milk. It was delicious.

She wore a netted cream coif which caught back her brown hair severely from her face. Her dress was a red brown. Over this she wore a long open undyed linen apron which hung down free front and back, caught at the waist with a workaday tan belt secured with a horn buckle. I noticed that the shoulders of her dress were padded, to allow for the weight of the buckets she carried. Her face was thin and her nose snub but the whole was not unpleasing to the eye.

"How often do you come into town with your milk, lass?" I asked. "I likewise haven't seen you before. Not that I am too often in the town."

"We used to come once a week in the summer but now with the market we come on market days too, since the king has seen fit to give us two days a week more to sell."

"Ah yes. The new market."

King John had confirmed the charter in 1204 giving the town the right to hold two markets a week, one on a Wednesday and another Saturday, as well as a fair in August.

"Where do you live then?" asked the maid as I turned back to lean over the wall and look into the rapidly rising water.

"Durley village in Savernake," I answered absently.

"Oooh, that's a long way." She swayed her hips, adjusting the buckets on

41

her shoulders. "You must have more milk for that's a long walk," and she held out her hand for my cup. "Here."

"Oh no... not at all," I said. "I rode. I set off very early this morning."

I wiped my cup on a square of linen I also kept in my scrip and put it away. "And no more, thank you."

She looked peeved, then smiled. "You rode?"

I nodded over by the wall of the yard where Bayard stood contemplating the grass tantalisingly just out of reach.

"My horse."

The maid's eyes grew round.

Then Nick came out of the mill and hailed me. "Aumary, m'lord Belvoir. 'Tis mighty early for the Lord of Savernake to be out in the town!"

The maid blanched and backed away.

"Audre," he said. "Morning to you."

Audre bobbed a curtsey to Nicholas, taking care not to spill her milk.

She was about to turn and flee when I had a thought.

"No mistress, please stay, I'd like to ask you something."

She turned slowly and through narrowed eyes she gave me a look which said "What can someone like you possibly want to ask someone like me?"

"You come very early to the town? I notice your buckets were quite full when you arrived here. Is this your first stop in Marlborough?"

"Second," said Audre in a flat tone. "We do the cooper's yard first. Up there"

"Ah," I said. "I thought you might. And did you do the cooper's yard on Wednesday?"

She furrowed her brow. "Last Wednesday?"

"Yes."

"We couldn't make them hear us early. 'Twere all locked up. We don't go in the yard; just to the gateway."

I nodded. "And when you returned from the Mill Yard here?"

"It was still locked and we heard voices from inside so we never bothered

42

and went on to Angel Yard and the tanners, sir" she added. "Same there we wait at the gate."

This would have been when Master Cowper was finding the head and had secured the gate.

"Where do you live, Audre?"

"Preshute sir," she said.

"And which way do you come into the town with your milk of a morning?"

The girl gave a slight glance at her silent partner some distance away from us who had been waiting and listening.

"Normally we come by the river bank and across the bridge then into town but the last few times we came a different route."

"Why's that?"

The girl licked her lips.

"On account... of the bear, sir."

"Bear Audre?"

She thought that we did not believe her so she appealed to her friend.

"There was a bear wasn't there, Berry? Honest to God."

"Aye a big brown brute with monstrous teeth and...," said the second dairy maid.

"Was there a man with the bear Audre?" I interrupted.

"A man? Aye. We were afraid of the bear it's true but we were just as afraid of the man. He was...."

"Frightening," said the other girl.

"And he looked at us strange like. He was all dressed in leather like some foreign soldier." She shuddered. "Why would anyone want to be dressed all in leather in this weather?"

I turned to Nick who had now come up and with his fingers in his belt, was watching and listening carefully.

"Nick, can you get someone to write down what the girls can tell you? Where they saw the bearward? When? How often? What was he doing? Get them to describe him... in their own words and then get them to sign their words, however they might."

I strode over to Bayard, "I'm for the doctor's house and then I'll be back."

Johannes was breaking his fast on some sort of porridge, when I entered through the open kitchen door. He spooned the stuff into his mouth as he listened to the latest information on the head in the barrel.

"So the bearward was seen on the river path?"

"It's likely yes."

"He then must have gone up Granham Hill and entered West Baily that way," said the doctor.

"Why would he miss the town? There are surely good crowds there for a performing bear. Especially on market days."

"Hmmm."

"Anyway, I came to ask you, how long do you think the body had lain in the forest without its head?

Johannes finished his gruel and laid down the dish and spoon.

"Hard to say, but no more than three days and it cannot be too long for I do not think the bear would have survived without water. Though what do I know? I am not an animal doctor. A man may survive a week without water, I am told, but I have never put it to the test."

"It has not rained. So she could get no water that way," I sighed. "Talking of not being an animal doctor, when you have time, can you come out to Durley and doctor our bear? She has a sore and weeping eye and her poor ankle is rubbed raw with the chafing of her gyves. I want to try to make her a kinder harness."

"No doubt Judd Saddler could do that for you."

"I'll go up there later today. Will be the strangest harness he ever makes I warrant."

We both chuckled.

"I'll come out after noon. It's market day tomorrow so I have to be back. Many people come in from the country to be seen on market day and I get very busy."

He stood and re-tied the leather thong which kept back his hair.

"Your bear... will she let me doctor her? I mean am I putting myself in danger saying I'll treat her? One swipe of her large paw and...."

"She is as mild as a lamb and as gentle as a doe, Johannes. Have no fear." But I did cross my fingers behind my back as I said it.

*****

Back at Nicholas' mill, I sought him out in his office at the rear of the mill building. The dairymaids had gone, he said and would fetch up in Chantry Lane later, where there were other worker's yards, before they went off to either fill up their pails again or go home.

"You took their stories?"

"Aye I did. They are on that table."

I picked them up and scanned the neat writing. Both accounts were signed with a cross.

"Master Bullard's writing, I see." Nick nodded.

Bullard was Nicholas' clerk. He wrote a fine clerkly hand and kept the books and accounts for the mill.

I sat down on a stool in front of Nicholas' table and stowed the papers in my scrip.

"You know that I was in Normandy when you were elected in 1204 Nick?"

"Aye I remember it. With the King I heard."

"I was. I am sorry to have to ask this but when you were elected, were you a popular choice? Who were you up against? I missed all the news at the time, of course."

"I gained more votes than any other. That's how I became reeve."

"I know but, was there any dissension at the time? I know that after two years at the helm, you have more than proven yourself and Marlborough men like and respect you... I do know that. But then - that year; did any oppose you?"

"There were three other candidates. Master Henry Glover, out on...."

"London Road, yes. I know him."

"Master Metier the Goldsmith up on Silver Street and Master Fletschier."

I nodded.

"I might have been elected by the town but the king had to ratify the decision. Without that seal of approval, my title means nothing."

"How often must the reeve be elected?"

"Every two years. This year we shall start again though I am hopeful of holding onto the job."

"I have no doubt you will succeed again for you are a popular fellow. Who runs beside you this year, Nicholas?"

Nick folded his hands before him on the table. "Master Metier will try again, I'm told. Henry is too busy with his new young wife and Master Fletschier gained so few votes last time he will not stand again."

"Dented his pride eh?"

"You know the man, Aumary, know what he's like."

I laughed. "Indeed I do. He is one of the suppliers of arrows to the castle and I buy some from him for my armoury at Durley. Who else?"

"Luc Mason."

"Do I know the man? I can't recall him."

"Has a yard out on the Manton Road."

"Ah yes, he is building the new houses for the Widow Partridge."

"That's so. Yes. And lastly Eustache Tylor"

"The tilemaker out on St. Martins?"

"That's him. I'd also heard that Warin Fuller from Elcot was in the running but I am unsure if they will allow a man who lives in Elcot to run for town reeve."

I stored all these names in my memory.

"So who might have a grudge against you Nick?"

"A grudge?" He was quite taken aback.

"So, if not one of your fellow candidates, who else might you have annoyed?"

I looked into his eye. "Last year when we had the trouble over the Jews up in Silver Street, you caused a few townsmen to be locked up for a while and you fined them."

"No more than did you at the castle with your soldiers Aumary. In fact, your case is a harder one. Four men hanged and the rest shamed publicly."

I shrugged, "The ringleaders were hanged. The rest got off lightly. I would not have hanged them but de Neville is boss...."

"And you tell me you have no grudges borne by any of those who are still amongst the garrison? No desperate need for revenge from the loved ones of those you hanged?" asked Nick.

"Soldiers know when they are beaten. And I made sure there were no loved ones to be angry."

Nick's face grew serious. "You think that the head in the barrel - because it was destined for the mill - was meant to harm me and my workers? You think it may be one of my fellow candidates or one I punished for the raid on the Jews?"

"I can think of no other explanation, though why the poor bearward should have been singled out, I cannot imagine."

"Perhaps it was a case of he was there and no one was there to see and...."

"No, there is a significance to the bearman, of that I'm sure but I just can't see it. Yet."

Nicholas was called away then. Some problem with the consignment of grain and so I made my way down the High Street until I reached the priory. Close by, my friend Gilbert Cordwainer, master shoemaker, had his workshop and home.

Master Cordwainer was an avuncular man, now in his early forties, with a large round tanned face, thick brown hair and a permanent grin.

I knew him well for he had made my boots and shoes since I was a lad and could first walk in them, firstly as a journeyman, then as his own master. His house, workplace and shop were next to the priory entrance and there is no doubt he benefitted from being in such a spot. No pilgrim or visitor, secular or clerical could pass by into the priory without first casting their eyes over his wares.

He was now one of the ten men on the council of Marlborough, headed by Nicholas Barbflet, and a church reeve at the newly built church of St. Peter at the western end of the town, close by the castle. He was a mine of information about the town and its goings on.

I pushed open the shop door and called. "Ho! Gilbert!"

His beaming face appeared around the door jamb of the workshop, a room at the back.

"Ho! My Lord Aumary. Come in, come in. It's good to see you."

"And you, Gilbert."

He ducked under his counter and brought out two leather cups and a flagon of Bordeaux.

"How is your brother-in-law's new business in the wine trade doing, Gil?" I asked, as he poured the wine into each cup.

Gilbert sucked his teeth and sighed. "Be better if the pesky Frenchies weren't proving so damn awkward." He lifted a cup. "Your good health and I hear congratulations are in order. You have a son, I'm told."

I sipped the nectar. "Aye. I have. Simon Johannes, born the day...." I stopped. This was painful for me, "the day Simon died."

"Aye. God rest him."

Simon had been a friend of both Gilbert and myself.

"And you named your littlun' for him. That was kind."

"It's a good name. He will live on."

"Aye...." We lapsed into silence. Then, "So what are the Frenchies up to now then?" I asked.

"Oh, their usual tricks. Last year, they tried to invade - you remember - well of course you do, for you had to muster the men didn't you, in your role as constable."

"Aye I did. But the king changed his mind and we never set out."

Gilbert scoffed into his cup, "Hubert Walter's doing."

"Well, to be fair on the matter of battling to regain Normandy, John was guided by several of his top men - not just Hubert the Chancellor."

"Well, Hubert's dead now, God take him to his bosom, and the Frenchies are running roughshod over Angevin lands."

"And this affects the wine trade?"

"It's all about safety. Getting the wine from Bordeaux to Bristol. There are French pirates in the channel, I'm told. Will put up the price no doubt. And the king is levying greater taxes on imports."

"Best stick to our own jobs then, Gil and leave the dangerous stuff to your brother-in-law, eh?" I said, savouring the good red wine; unusual for I normally drank the more plentiful whites.

"Just when I was getting a taste for the really good stuff!" scoffed Gilbert.

"Oh I'm sure that a special arrangement will be made to carry on the wine trade in spite of hostilities. Too advantageous to both parties, France and England."

"Aye well, Will was always a complainer," said Gilbert. "He's not himself unless he has something to worry about and if he hasn't, he has to make it up." Gilbert looked round quickly. "Oh... don't tell Grace I said that will you."

"My ears were deaf," I whispered.

I sat back on the stool, leaned against the wall and perched my cup on my chest.

"So what can you tell me about the candidates for the town reeve's job, Gil?"

Gilbert paused his cup halfway to his lips.

"Come July, there'll be... ooh, five combatants I think. Unless some drop out."

"Henry Metier? I know him, but not well. "

"No one does," said Gilbert. "Quiet as a cat with cream. Moneyed, yes, but won't get his hands dirty."

"Ah. Not a favourite then?"

"You know who the favourite is. Metier's a good man but too distant."

"Indeed I do and Nick's the man I'd vote for. It's good to know I have him at my back when I'm on castle business. So what about Luc Mason?"

"Good man but not bright enough. He'd be well out of his depth."

"Hmmm. And Eustache Tylor?"

"Bad lot. Too easy to bribe. Be there for what he could get, not for the good of the town."

"Warin Fuller?"

"Ah. You heard that he is making a bid, eh?"

"I did but it's said he will be disqualified."

"He'll have to move to the town to be considered."

"You're pulling a face Gilbert - what else is there about this man?"

There was a slight hesitation as Gilbert put down his cup.

"I don't say he wouldn't make a good reeve, I just don't like him and that's a fact."

It wasn't often that Gilbert took a dislike to someone and said so."

"Whyever not?" I asked, chuckling.

Gilbert lifted the cup to his lips again but before he could answer, his wife Grace spoke from the stairwell, "Because m'lord, Gilbert and Warin had a... a falling out some years ago," she said.

"Oh?"

"Over me. Usual story. One girl, two men wanting to marry her."

She came up to Gilbert and put her hands on his shoulders.

"I didn't marry the richer but I did marry the better man," and she kissed the top of his head.

*****

Leading Bayard by the reins, I walked up to the saddler's yard and shop which lay off Chandler's lane, a little track which ran from the High, up the hill to Back Lane.

Once I had given Judd all the information I could about Mary Marshall, Richard's wife and Judd's sister, who now lived in Durley, we fell to talking about a harness which might fit the bear Isabella.

Judd puzzled a little over how he was to make such a thing, but eventually he said he'd give it some thought.

"We didn't see the bear in town, sir."

"No and that I don't understand Judd."

"Perhaps it has something to do with the fair. You know, our big fair in August."

"The one becoming known as St. Mary's?"

"Aye, sir."

"Why would that be?"

"Perhaps the man was saving his performing bear for the big fair then. Would make a deal more money."

"Nothing to stop him doing both, Judd."

"No. 'Spose not. Mind you, I have heard that the town council was saving up to get a bear in for the fair. Attract more folks, see - a nasty vicious bear. Perhaps the bearward was told to push off 'cos - like you say- his bear was too soft and old."

I looked up quickly. "Who was in charge of this fund, do you know Judd?"

"No sorry sir. I expect the reeve would know though."

I thanked him and left.

Deep in thought, I walked Bayard up the High Street, nodding to folk I knew. I would call in once more to the doctor's house before making my way back to Durley. Perhaps we might travel together.

Suddenly and without warning there was a deep boom as if all the hammers of Thor had been dropped at once. It was no thunder though.

Bayard was startled by the noise though he soon recovered. Other beasts on the roadway began to panic and run. Some folk about on the High, turned their heads towards the southernmost side and looked up into the sky where smoke was billowing. I followed suit and realised that the bang had come from the riverside, down at the bottom of Crooks Lane.

The town corn mill.

Ordering Bayard to stay put (and I knew that he would), I raced for the other side of the street and ducked into the entrance of the lane.

People were coming out and going in and I managed to lay hold of Durwyn Cowper who had stepped out of his gate to look down towards the river.

"Keep folk back, Cowper. On my order. None to pass you going to the mill, unless they can be of use. I will go and look." I yelled, walking backwards. "Any man disobeying will spend the night in the lock up. Use your men too."

I could hear the flames now as I closed in on the town mill. They rose high in the sky and centred on the part of the mill where the grinding of the corn took place.

I told any uninjured man or woman I found to get to the river with any utensil they could find and form a bucket chain, or take water from the large mill pond. I had experience of this before, as on my own manor at Durley I had drilled my folk to run to the water sources as soon as any fire was detected, and to pass buckets of water down the line to the fire. There is no doubt it worked and we had saved our church and one of the village houses, by our prompt action. Fire in a town of houses made mostly of wood and thatch could be devastating.

I found Henry Bullard the clerk, wandering around in shock, shaking his head.

"I cannot hear you m'lord," he said as he banged the side of his head with his palm. "Deafened by the blast!"

"What happened? Is there anyone in the building?" I mouthed.

He managed to read my lips and shook his head again. "I was at the back, came out the side door. Most damage has been done at the other end. Don't know who was there."

I grabbed a passing boy who had a nasty cut to his head, "Is there anyone left in the building?"

He looked at me with dazed eyes. "The millers were at the grain sir. I was at the other end fetching some sacks, walking back to the stairs."

"Have you any idea where your master is?"

He shook his head and stumbled off. I saw a woman running up. Obviously his mother, for she folded him to her bosom, crying "Algar" and hurried him away to one of the closer houses of the lane.

Three men came out from the burning building. One was screaming as his hair, beard and cap burned about his head. He threw off the cap, burning his hands.

I ripped off my cloak and smothered the man, wrestling him to the ground. His wails subsided to a dull moaning.

I leapt up and approached the other two. "Grist!" I recognised the man who had brought me the summons to the Cooper's yard. "Who is left inside?"

Grist too, it seemed, had been deafened for he shook his head and screwed up his eyes. However he had heard me.

"The master, sir, two men, Menier and Wheeler; the rest I'm not sure."

I grabbed Grist and the nearest able bodied man and dragged them back into the mill with me. I noticed a door had been blown from its leather hinges and was lying flat in the path. I looked up. It had been blown through the upper wall where there was now a large gap.

"We search. Now!" But we had to wait a while for the flames to die down a little as water from the river was sloshed onto them.

Blackened timbers stood out everywhere. The heat was enormous. The blast had been concentrated on the end where the actual grinding was done and on the first floor. The fire was fierce but short lived and the water was having an effect.

I called out, "Nick! Menier!

"Henry!" shouted Grist, "Edwy!"

I heard a moan and made for the source. A man lay on his side with a gashed head and bleeding hands but he struggled up and made for the door hole and as he passed me I said,

"Good man."

"Thomas Milward sir," said Grist.

The timbers above me creaked and cracked, the fire crackled and hissed but we ploughed on up what was left of the stairs.

The man I'd grabbed, who I later knew as David Waterman, yelled "watch out!" as a slide of wood and tiles came rippling into the space left by the beams holding up the roof. We all backed off and walked round the debris coughing.

Someone had thought to stop the water wheel outside and everything had come to a halt. When we gained the upper floor, the huge thick grinding stones were cracked and splintered and half was thrust through the wall. There was dust everywhere. We coughed and moved through the fog. There was a trickling of water from the great wheel which was visible through a hole punched in the outer wall. Here the fire had flickered out to a few isolated patches.

The two millers, Menier and Wheeler, were lying some distance from what was left of their grinding apparatus.

They had, it seemed, taken the brunt of the blast. They lay on their backs a few feet apart and had been blown away from the source of the eruption. One man lacked an arm and the other both hands. We found them later, mangled a few feet away. Their faces were bruised, battered and bloodied. Menier, whom I thought perhaps had been the closest to the blast, was unrecognisable as a man. His chest was blown apart and was open to the air, his face destroyed.

David Waterman turned away and retched. He looked about to faint.

Grist just stared in shock. He'd known these men well.

As gently as I could I said, "Waterman, run for the priest at St. Mary's, then for the doctor. You know his house? The one behind the high cross?"

He nodded and turned to go. "He can't help them though can he, sir?"

"No. But we must find your master and he might be able to help him."

I stepped over the debris and yelled out loud "Nicholas!"

There was no answer.

I continued my search and made for the office right at the back of the building. The roof had partly collapsed and some of it was open to the sky. I pushed the door and it stuck and screeched and there was a further fall of timber and a settling of beams.

"Nick!"

The main beam of the room had come down almost flat, for the wall holding it was practically gone. Underneath it, trapped by the legs, I found Nicholas Barbflet, alive but unconscious.

I poked my head from a remaining window and found some lads still bailing water from the river.

"Help, here!" I cried. "Crawl through the hole there."

The main beam, as it had fallen, had gouged a hole, big enough for a man to jump up and slide through. One man sloshed up the bank and with the help of the other, squeezed through the gap, trailing weed and tadpoles in his wake.

"Take the end and lift on three," I said.

Now another man had come into the room. I saw it was Master Tanner, whose yard abutted the corn mill. He would have come over the riverside path and entered the yard from the East. Immediately he grasped the beam and on three, we pulled up and the miller pulled Nick free.

There was a little further settling but in the main no more damage.

Nicholas groaned.

It was obvious there was some harm to one leg and perhaps the other knee, so we could not get him out by carrying him, legs and arms.

I looked around. On the table, at the untouched end of the room, was a large knife. I took it up and set about enlarging the hole in the wattle wall made by the falling beam. Finally it was big enough for the man from the river to go back outside and take Nicholas by the shoulder. I held Nick's hips and together we got him outside onto the narrow strip of grass between the mill building and the river.

Master Tanner, then took the burden of carrying Nick, over his shoulder round to the front of the building.

I checked for anyone else living, collected Grist who had done the same and then followed through the door at the front of the mill.

Johannes was leaning over Nicholas feeling around for damage.

"The other two are dead, Johannes."

"Sure?"

"Heads mashed to a pulp."

"Ah. Do we know what happened?"

"No but we shall find out."

I scrubbed my face with my hands. When I released my eyes, I saw Nicholas' wife Felicity come running down the lane. I went up to meet her. Master Cowper had eventually let her through, for their house was on the High Street at the end of the lane.

I grasped her as she passed and swivelled her round. "Felicity, he lives and is in good hands. Go to the house and prepare him a bed. The doctor will see him and then we shall know what must be done." She nodded rather absently.

"What happened, m'lord?"

"I don't know. Some sort of conflagration. I don't understand but I shall get to the bottom of it. I promise."

"He looks...."

I knew that Felicity and Nicholas were a devoted couple. "He is alive and we both know he is a tough man. Doctor Johannes will mend him."

Again she nodded and I felt her relax. She smiled at me.

With one look back, she walked up the lane to the house and ran the last few paces towards her house staff who had gathered at the top of the lane to look.

A door was procured - not difficult, for many had been blown from their hinges - and Nick was carefully laid on it.

As Johannes passed me he whispered. "Alive and fighting. A cracked leg and possibly a crushed knee but I'll know more later."

I touched his shoulder. "Do your best. He's a good man."

Johannes nodded and followed the door with its burden.

I went back to the mill.

"What can we do, sir? asked Grist.

"Bring out the dead and...." I looked over my shoulder as the priest of St. Mary's came bustling down the lane. "And let Father Torold deal with them. If they have family, they need to be told."

"Menier was single sir, with an old father but Wheeler has a family out at St. Martins."

I nodded.

"Here is Master Gallipot the apothecary, I'm sure he will help the less injured. Can you organise that, Grist?"

"Aye sir, I can."

The bodies were brought out, the millers gathered up and their wounds treated. It was surprising that more of them had not been killed or injured. Most of the injuries were inflicted by flying debris.

Ten men worked the mill and its outbuildings, plus the boy I'd seen and Bullard. All were accounted for by the end of the afternoon. I took as much information as I could from those who had been close when the blast happened. Only one man could tell me anything of real interest.

This was the poor man whose hair had been on fire. He was the oldest master miller and had been on the uppermost floor of the mill when the floor, wheel and stones were ripped apart.

The poor man sat, by the mill leat wall: his scalp and hands burned and his forehead red raw. He was bruised head to foot where debris had struck him and he had a small gash on his leg, where something had torn through the stuff of his leggings. Master Gallipot had patched it up. The large thick apron he wore had saved him more damage I think. His clothes were scorched and peppered with holes where hot ash had rained down on him. He was about fifty with a thin face and sunken cheeks.

Master Apothecary had slathered a grease onto the man's burned hands and face. There was a terrible smell of burnt hair about him.

He sat with his head down and knees up, sniffing now and again.

"Good man, have you not a home to go to?" I asked, squatting down beside him near the wall?

He tried to rise but I pushed him down.

He looked up at me with red rimmed eyes. "Thank you sir." He ran his sleeve over his nose. "Thank you for saving my head."

"It was an action I didn't think about, one I just - did" I smiled. "I'm Aumary Belvoir," I said, holding his shoulder.

I touched his arm....

"Surely you'll want to be away home?"

"This is my home, my Lord Belvoir. I live here."

"Is your part of the mill habitable?"

"Yes, still. It's that bit there," and he pointed to the western end which was untouched by fire.

"Then I think you should go home and rest. Is there anyone...?"

"My son lives with me. Lived with me. He is... was.... My name is Menier sir."

I sighed, "Henry was your son?"

"Aye sir. Dead."

"I am so sorry for your loss... um...."

"Edmund, m'lord, Edmund Menier."

"I grieve with you Edmund."

"He was only twenty four and just out of journeymanship...," and despite his painful skin he covered his face with his reddened hands and wept.

"He was taken quickly Edmund," I said when he had recovered a little. "He had no time to suffer."

"Aye... things like this are always so quick."

"Like this?"

His sad face stared up at me and I noticed both his eyebrows were gone. It gave his face a permanently shocked look.

"Dust blast sir."

"This is what happened here?"

"It is always a hazard in a flour mill sir. But we thought... we ... we thought we had ensured it would not happen by having good ventilation."

"It happens often?"

"No, not often but if precautions are not taken...."

"If you are feeling well enough, can you tell me exactly how such conflagrations... such blasts can arise?"

He shifted himself and tried to lift from the ground but his poor hands prevented him. I pulled my riding gloves from my belt and made him put them on. Then I gave him a hand and pulled him up.

"Flour sir is a very sticky stuff. You must have noticed that when you...," he looked down. "

"Go on."

"No sir, you will not have noticed for I suspect that you never handle flour in its raw state." He paddled his arms painfully against his side and clouds of fine white dust flew up into the afternoon air.

"It sticks to you sir. Us millers, we are always full o' the stuff." He smiled. "It's a very fine dust, very fine indeed and when the enclosed space, like a room where the grind stones are working, becomes saturated with it - you can see it floating around in the air - a stray spark will ignite it and...."

He looked stricken again and I let him weep.

"It will ignite and fire ensues?"

"Something we call over pressure, happens sir. The flames are so fast that one hardly knows they are there until...."

"Until you feel the heat?"

"Aye and then there is a wind which comes with it. It's a pressure, see and it can knock a man from his feet, lift off a roof and break apart a wall."

"I noticed much debris... does this pressure also push things into the air?"

"Men are hit by flying objects, wood, tiles, metal, bricks. It's lethal sir."

"What might be the thing which ignites it?" I asked.

"Friction, sir... in our case, the friction of the grind stones. One wrong move and the whole room will become an inferno."

I stood and looked out over the peaceful rippling of the mill pool. Goodness! I had never thought of milling as a dangerous job.

"You say that you and Master Nicholas had tried to prevent this happening?"

Menier hugging himself and shivering a little in shock, sniffed again.

"Aye sir. We had learned by other's mistakes."

"Oh?"

"Mills like ours have been around for centuries. Milling flour for the folk to make bread. Over the years there have been a few accidents and Master Nick, he went to talk to some of those who had survived the blasts at other mills."

"What did you do?"

"This is an old mill sir. Fifty years maybe. But we have kept it repaired and when we repaired last, we made sure we made enough ventilation - we keep the door open for example and have ventilation holes - that means little holes for the draught to get in and out- in the walls. "

"How"

"Drilled them into the lath and plaster, sir, and we installed some louvres in the tops of the walls."

I must have looked puzzled for Menier said, "Come I'll show you."

I followed the man round the corner of the mill to the easternmost end. This was where most of the damage had been inflicted. Nick's office was on the river wall to the South but the millstones and the apparatus for collecting the flour was housed at this end.

Now it was a sorry mess of charred plaster with great holes torn in the wall. I looked into the hole. The great wheel, dripping and green, was splintered and askew on its pin.

"See here, sir." Menier pointed up. "With a pull of a cord those windows open. And there are holes where the outside draught can mix with the suspended flour inside and not...."

Menier rubbed his eyes with my gloves.

"What is it Edmund?" I asked.

Edmund peered more closely at the wall.

"Holes, sir. There should be holes."

"I see them Edmund... there's one and another... there."

"Aye but...." He looked at me stricken and shocked. "Someone has plugged the holes. They should go all the way through and... they don't . And what's left of the louvres. They are closed."

I jumped onto what was left of the support for the wheel, a stone built wall in the water. I peered into the nearest hole. They went all the way from about six feet up to the second storey at every two feet or so. With the end of my eating knife I could, with difficulty, prise out what looked like a mud, a dense pale clay which had been pushed into the gap. I looked up at what was left of the small horizontal windows. I would check from the inside but I was certain they had been fixed shut.

Edmund began to sway. "Come, let's go to your place and sit," I said.

The man had one room for sleeping and eating at the western end which was as I said untouched by fire or blast. There were two beds. I sat Edmund down on one of them. He took off my gloves and gave them back with a weak smile. "Thank you sir, you are most kind."

I poured him some ale and made him drink.

His lips were parched and dry and no doubt as burnt as the rest of him.

"So, someone we think has filled in the air holes so that the flour built up to a dangerous level? I said at last.

"That is all I can think, sir."

"Would the millers not notice?"

Menier looked down abruptly. "Perhaps. Maybe an experienced man...."

"Hmmm. If the grindstones are touching each other surely there will be friction?" I asked. "How is this prevented?"

After a while Edmund looked up. His eyes were filled with tears again.

"Grooves in the stones sir. And the miller will set the stones just a tiny little bit apart so that they do not wear each other down."

"But they still allow for grinding of the grain?"

"Aye sir. It's an exact art. One stone is fixed and the other revolves."

"So an experienced miller will set his stones at just the right height so as not to cause friction which might allow a spark to be generated and ignite the flour in the air?"

"Yes sir."

I tapped my lips with my finger.

"Might this be tampered with, Edmund?"

He looked up abruptly again. "The stones will be set at the onset of milling and the miller will test the coarseness of the product throughout the job by rubbing the flour with his finger and thumb. He will reset as he goes along."

"I see." I blinked as a thought came to me.

"If this isn't done?"

"It's always done."

"Yes. But ... I will repeat myself, might it be tampered with?"

Tears flowed from the poor man's eyes now.

"My son was a good miller sir. He would never...."

"No, no Edmund... not your son... some outside agent?"

If the man had had eyebrows he would have raised them to the roof then.

"For if the grinding wheels were tampered with and the air holes blocked... then Edmund, your son Henry, your good miller son, and his fellow worker, were murdered," I said.

Chapter Four

I left Menier with one of his colleagues and made my way to the outside.

There in the yard, propped up on the millpond wall, was an old millstone. I hunkered down to have a look and to try to understand more fully what Edmund had been telling me.

On the surface of the granite I noticed little grooves, just as the miller had explained. This allowed the flour to escape once milled and fall into a hopper where it would be bagged.

My friend Nicholas Barbflet was an astute man. He would never allow malpractice by any of his millers, nor, as this old wheel testified, would he skimp on new equipment once the old began to become dangerous.

I stood and looked over the mill pond to the river. Two ducks lifted off and wheeled overhead as I watched.

As I squinted to follow their progress my eye was drawn to the figure of a man making his way along the riverbank, downstream on this side. Why should that have drawn my gaze in particular?

There was no doubt he was furtive, looking back towards the mill and its damaged end every so often as he walked, though I could not see a face and at this distance I would not be sure of identifying him. He was hooded. The afternoon was warm - no need for a hood. Now you will say I was making this up but, as I watched him his arm arced out over the river and he threw something into it. Thereafter his step was jaunty and... I would say rather cock of the heap.

When I had set off in the early morning it had been chilly and I had snatched up my cloak for warmth. Good job I did for it had proved useful to smother the flames in Edmund Menier's hair. Now it was too warm for a cloak or hood.

That reminded me... where was it?

I scanned the bridge which connected the mill island to the town. There lay my grey cloak, where I'd tossed it. I picked it up. Blackened but in one piece. It would need to visit the fuller who would bring it back to clean again.

I made my way up the lane and onto the High Street. I saw Bayard tearing the weeds from the base of a building further up the street and whistled. His ears pulled back, he turned his head and trotted to me.

I now debated whether I should intrude on the business at the Barbflet house, or walk away. I could not at this stage tell Nick that the damage to his mill, the death of his workers and the injuries to his legs were a result of sabotage. I would save that for when he was feeling better.

I knocked on the outer door and once more Bayard had to wait for me.

A small maid opened the door. She had been crying.

"Aye sir...." she said before I had opened my mouth, I know who you are. Come in m'lord please. The mistress said you would probably be along."

I smiled and stepped over the doorstep.

Nick was lying on his bed, his head swaddled, his knee immobilised and swathed in bandages his left leg splinted and wrapped.

He looked up when I entered and I have to say he seemed bright and pain free.

"Sir Aumary." He always used my title when in the presence of other men of rank but we were on first name terms amongst ourselves.

"Nick, how do you feel?"

"Feel?" he chuckled. "Lucky and grateful. Thank you for rescuing me."

"I was just able to be there at the right time, that's all. You must thank Master Tanner too."

Johannes stood. "Not as bad as we feared Aumary. The knee is probably cracked but none of the bony parts of it are crushed. It will mend. The leg is broken in two places but again, it will mend and the head... well, the head - that will never be right."

I laughed out loud then. Nick took a cloth lying by his side and threw it at

64

Johannes who giggled like a girl.

We grew serious. "I'm so sorry about your dead. I feel sure they will have told you. Wheeler and Menier Junior."

"Aye... thanks to you too for what you did for the old man Menier. They told me."

"Right place, right time Nick. The mill can be up and running again soon?" I asked.

Nicholas took a deep breath. "It will take time but yes, we can start to rebuild soon."

"You will be staying in your bed for a while," said Johannes pointing his finger. "No gadding about on crutches."

"No, not yet" said Nick with a smile. "I have plenty of good folk left to delegate too."

"See you do."

The doctor and I made for the door. "And take the pain liquid. No suffering now just because...."

"I will, I will Johannes. You know Felicity will make me." That was why he was so jaunty; Johannes' medicine made one jolly - I had reason to know, for I'd had it myself.

I turned in the door hole. "Nick - I know what happened. Old man Menier told me. But there's more and I will drop in another time to discuss it with you. Now isn't the time."

"Aye, dust blast. What puzzles me is...."

"Why it happened in your mill when you made provision for the air to be thin of flour dust?"

"Aye, just that."

I nodded. "We shall talk about it another time. There are two things I need to ask you though, before I go."

"Aye?"

"Who stays in the mill overnight? Just the Menier's?"

"Elder and younger, yes and Bullard. He has a room there too."

"Two old men and a youngster just out of his indenture."

"Aye... why?"

"No matter. And the other question. Who holds the fund for the bear - the one the council want to buy for the fair in August, Nick?"

"Why? How did you hear...?"

I did not answer but cocked my head for a reply.

"I was outvoted. Cordwainer, Gallipot and myself were outvoted. We don't want a bear at the fair but the others...."

"So who holds the fund... who is responsible for raising the money and buying the bear?"

Nick sighed.

"Eustache Tylor," he said with irritation.

*****

The outer door was almost closed behind me when I saw that the young maid had red rimmed eyes and was still crying. She hiccoughed and wiped her nose on her apron.

"Cheer up girl," I said, "Your master will be all right. His wounds will mend with time. There's no need for so many tears."

"No sir," but she wailed out loud then and covered her head with her apron.

I pushed the door open again. She pitched against me and I grabbed her, stopped her from falling.

"Whatever is the matter?"

I could not understand the garbled words she cried into my shoulder but I let her go on for a moment or two.

"Now then, Alyson isn't it? See, I remember your name." She nodded.

"Tell me what's the matter."

"Oh sir!" she wailed "He's dead," and she sobbed into her hands again.

"Who is...?" Then I stopped and drew her to me again in an embrace. "Yes, I understand. Awful for you. Just terrible. But let me tell you he died bravely and quickly. He felt no pain. I promise. Now he is with God."

I had all at once realised that the Barbflet housemaid had been in love with the younger miller Menier, who lived in the mill house at the end of her lane.

"We were courtin' sir. Me and Henry. We were walkin' out together."

"I am so, so sorry." I said as I handed her over to Felicity Barbflet who had come clucking and sighing from the depths of the house, alerted by the noise. I shut the outer door quietly.

*****

Her sadness kept me silently contemplative the whole journey back to Durley and thoughtful all evening. My dogs came romping over the grass outside the gate to greet me and for the first time in an hour or more I smiled and was joyful that they were happy to see me.

Father Crispin came in to eat in the hall and I told him the story of the mill and the millers. We were both quiet after that until I realised that I had not been to see the bear.

"There's no need to worry," said our priest, "Peter has taken on that job. He's an absolute natural with animals - I've watched him."

"He has a deal of patience with animals, it's true."

"He's fed her, changed her chain for a rope - much kinder; and walked her round the meadow... what... three times today. I can see from the chapel and from the upper rooms of my house. Once his forest duties were done this evening, he went back into the barn and took her out to sit on the green. I watched as did a few others. We watched him put her through her paces. How he knows what to do to make her dance and sing...."

"Sing!"

"Well, it's not really singing more a howl... but she thinks she sings."

I laughed. "That's astonishing."

"And he has taught her, though I suspect he has seen others do it and knew what to do to bring it out in this bear, yes, he has taught her to count."

"No!"

"No word of a lie."

Crispin imitated the words of young Peter.

"Now Isabella what is one and one? He nods his head twice and she paws the ground."

I laughed out loud again. "These are all things no doubt her old bearward taught her."

"Aye, no doubt."

I shook my head. "What are we to do Crispin? Peter has grown fond of the creature. It will be a wrench when we have to part with her as we must."

"Not only Peter, I fear. Hawise...."

"Oh no. Not...."

"Yes. She has been keeping him company. It was she who bathed the beast's wound on the leg and somehow bathed and got some of Lydia's salve into Isabella's eye."

I shook my head.

"Oh dear, I said. "Johannes was to come out to us after noon but sadly with the catastrophe at the mill he was not able. I suppose we shall not need him now."

"Are you not worried Aumary, that the bear will...?"

"Naturally I worry. A bear is a wild creature but this one I have to say, seems to have been so well treated that there is not an ounce of malice in her."

"I would not like to test her, Aumary, but yes, it seems you are right. I know that Lydia is worried though."

I smiled. "I'll go up and speak to her. It's time I saw my son anyway." I shook my head, "Duty takes me away far too often and for too long."

*****

After a peaceful night - well perhaps not as peaceful as I would have liked for of course, Lydia was up in the night to feed Simon - I dozed through the croonings and kissings….

What Paul? Oh no, you foolish lad, the crooning of Simon's mother. That is what mothers do with babies. They speak in sing song voices and kiss and pet their infants. Tut... it was nothing to do with me!

I saddled up Bayard again and we rode for the town. Before I left, I looked into the hay barn and with a piece of string I attempted to measure the bear for a harness. I will gloss over my foolish attempt but after a while and with some help from Peter, I did manage to get an idea of how large the creature was.

Once in Marlborough town, I stopped at the workshop of the saddler and gave him my piece of string and tried to explain what it was I wanted him to make. He looked at the knots I had tied at the measured spots and creased his brow.

"I'll do my best. I'll make it first in rope myself and then if you think it right, I'll remake it in leather."

"Thanks Judd. I will not forget this."

Then I made for the Barbflet household again. This time Felicity opened the door to me herself. "I've sent the chit away to her grannie's on Back Lane," she said of Alyson.

"She needs some time away from the place where...."

"Aye, I'm sure you are right Felicity. Is Nicholas able to speak to me, do you think?"

She tutted, then, "He has had some poppy juice - I think that is what Dr. Johannes called it sir. It's for the pain; his leg is very sore."

"I'm sure it is."

"He may not be quite the man he usually is but you are welcome to speak to him. Go on up. You know where it is."

I bounded up the stairs wondering if Nick would ever go up these stairs again two at a time as he often did.

He was dozing but stirred as I entered.

"Aumary... please sit. Might you pass me a drink of water? This damn pain stuff makes my mouth so dry."

I fed him four sips of water and he leaned back on his snowy white linen pillow.

"You know yesterday I told you that your man Menier the elder had explained to me the workings of the mill and how you were greatly affeared for that thing called dust blast. He also told me and indeed showed me, the measures you had put in place to prevent such happenings."

Nicholas lifted himself up to sit straighter and grimaced at the pain of it.

"Aye. I have spoken to millers in Devizes and Salisbury. I also wrote to one man of Oxford who had made a study of such things and he wrote back. The open air is very important. There must be as much of it passing around us as is possible. That is why we always leave the door to the mill room on the upper floor, open."

"And you drilled holes in the walls."

"Yes."

"And made... what did Menier call them?"

"Louvres."

"What if I were to tell you that those holes had been plugged from the outside? That someone had put clay into the holes and the louvres were fixed shut. There was very little air coming in yesterday, Nick."

Nicholas looked confused. "Blocked up the holes? But, why and how? How would they get into the mill. Someone would see them, a person not familiar to the mill?"

I drew my stool closer to him and carried on. "So that the air would become filled with flour dust. I also noticed that the door to the mill room was lying in the yard. Had it been open I don't think it would have been blown there."

Nick tried to grasp what I was saying and struggled with the words. "Someone had closed the door?"

"Fastened and locked it, I think."

"How did the flour ignite?"

"I have a feeling that somehow the millers were distracted and the stones were tampered with so that when they started up they would grind each other and...."

"Boom!" said Nick.

"Boom."

We sat in silence for a while.

"Who would want to do this, Aumary? Who?"

I shrugged. "I don't know. But you remember our earlier conversation - I suspect you have rivals, or that this is about revenge."

"No surely... not. They would not kill two innocent men and injure a further seven if they were just trying to get to me."

I shrugged again. "Leave this problem to me and I will ponder on it, and I'll come and tell you whatever I find out."

As I turned to go Nick grabbed my arm and half raised himself.

"If you think it's revenge... then might Felicity and the children be in danger?"

I looked down at him.

"I'll get Peter and Stephen to come up from the castle and look to you all." These were my two men at arms whom I kept at the castle in readiness for the time when I might have to go and fight for my king and country. They were usually part of the castle garrison but they were Belvoir men, heart and soul.

"You know them and they you. You will be safe with them around."

He fell back on the pillows. "Thank you, Aumary. I feel so helpless."

"Rest and mend old friend," I said. "And leave it all to me."

I had just exited the house and was drawing on my gloves when an almighty high pitched screaming began at the bottom of Crooks Lane.

71

I peered round the end of the building but could see nothing, save the people running from the gates of the cooper's yard, the wheelwrights' and the weavers' houses situated along the lane. They too had been alerted by the screaming and were crowding in their groups trying to see what was amiss.

"What now?" I said to myself as I hurried down the lane and through the crowd.

I approached the millpond with its wall and could see beyond it the hulk of the mill, partly demolished; the mill wheel left at a jaunty angle by the blast. Men had been working on it and now some came up to see what all the fuss was.

The screaming continued pierced by a few unintelligible words.

The dairymaids were in the town again for it was market day today and the people had come in from the outlying places to sell and barter, buy and beg. Rich pickings for milk sellers, as my maid Audre had said.

I followed the voice. There, at the edge of the millpond was the second dairymaid. The one who had not spoken much on Wednesday; the first time I had seen her.

The harness she wore to hold her wares was shrugged from her shoulder and lay on the ground. One of her buckets was upended and milk ran over the cobbles in rivulets and gathered in puddles.

I reached for her shoulder and she pointed out into the water.

There in the middle of the pond, floating, with her red brown dress billowing around her was Audre, the milkmaid. Her head was partly submerged and the harness which secured her buckets was wrapped around her. Her hair flowed free with no sign of her cap.

I threw down my gloves, shrugged off my cotte, dragged off my boots, hoisted myself up, stood on the edge of the wall and launched myself into the water.

The day was warm but the water was cold and for a moment it took my breath away. I spluttered to the surface and looked around for the maid.

I could see more people were now peering over the wall. Master Cowper

72

looking worried. Master Wryghte shaking his head, Master Bullard shaking all over.

I swam to the maid and took her under my arm, lifting her head from the water.

With what breath I had, I said to her, "You are all right now lass, just let my arm support you and we shall swim to the wall."

As I lifted her head I felt no resistance. It lolled at an odd angle, even with the water and my arm supporting her chin.

I swam for the wall and several hands came over the edge, Master Cowper leaning over dangerously to receive the girl.

I dragged myself up with a hand from Grist, who had come out from the mill to see what all the screaming had been about. Dripping, my hands on my knees, I got my breath back and wrung out my hair and clothes as best I could.

The maid was laid on the cobbles. I knelt beside her. I knew that it was pointless but I yelled "Fetch the doctor."

I straightened the poor girl's limbs, made her decent by pulling down her skirts and apron and wiped the weed from her face.

"And the priest," I yelled as an afterthought.

I took her head in my hands and pushed back the hair from her face. Her eyes stared at me and I closed them.

Then still dripping, I sat back on my haunches. Someone brought me a blanket and one for Audre, though she would not need it. It was thoughtful for I was beginning to shiver.

I could not resist it. As I sat by her side I leaned forward and with two hands lifted her head and moved it. It was as I suspected. Her neck was broken.

I would have to inform the coroner, for I suspected she had gone dead into the water.

Johannes came running down the lane and when he saw my face, slowed to a walk. He knew the girl was dead.

"I was just at the market when...."

"Broken neck, Johannes."

"Another one?"

I stood and let him examine her. This time the wound to the neck was higher and had completely severed the bones. Her head was floppy.

Johannes turned the girl on her front and began to push on her torso. A little water dribbled out of her mouth. He pushed harder but no more water exited.

"Dead before she got into the water. She wasn't breathing."

"That's something then. Poor girl."

Johannes draped the blanket over her head. "The same person killed the bearward as killed the maid."

"And I suspect sabotaged the watermill. Oh yes, I'll need to talk to you about that."

Johannes put his arm loosely around my shoulder. "Then let's go home and get you dry and you can tell me."

I looked around for Grist. "Can you tell the coroner please? The body must lie here until he comes. I will be at the doctor's house." The miller nodded. "And the maid there," I pointed, "is the first finder. She will need to give her statement to him."

I peered over towards the second milkmaid who was being consoled by one of the weavers - a woman in her forties who lived on the lane and had a weaving shed up in her loft.

"Mistress...?"

"Webber m'lord, Elinor Webber."

"Can you take the maid to your home please? She is the first finder and must report to the coroner when he comes."

People were becoming more familiar with the role of coroner, and the rules governing the scene of a crime.

"Yes, sir. I will," she acquiesced as she put her arm around the sobbing milkmaid.

"Thank you."

Johannes and I collected Bayard from his place by the Barbflet house door and walked him to the doctor's house.

We said not a word to each other as we walked.

*****

"Four deaths in as many days," I said to Johannes when I was dressed in one of his old tunics and some rather threadbare hose. My own clothes were drying by the fire in the kitchen.

I towelled my hair dry.

"Whatever is going on, Johannes?"

"Someone is going to great lengths to protect themselves. What did the poor milkmaid know?"

"I'll need to question the second one and I think it's best she is guarded, for what one maid saw, perhaps the second also knew about but doesn't know she knows it."

"It's possible. So you promised to tell me what was going on at the mill."

Slowly I went through my evidence - the blocking of the vents in the grinding room, the closed and fastened door and I explained the workings of dust blast and the safety procedure of the checking of the grindstones.

"They can have a similar problem at sawmills, I have heard," said Johannes. "When I was a youngster, there was such a blast and fire at the sawmill at Shotover, near Oxford. Some were killed."

I then told him about the man I'd seen.

Johannes narrowed his eyes. "Could have been anyone off home, after the excitement of the fire."

"It was his manner… it was…," I made a moue, "furtive, secretive. Then he tossed something into the river and his whole body became cocksure and confident. I lost him around about the narrowing of the river by the fuller's yards."

"You could tell at that distance but could not identify him?" mocked

75

Johannes.

I shrugged. "I know what I saw."

"Hmmm."

"I'll have to speak to the dairy maid. Then I'd like to look at the river just there... see if I can find anything."

"How... how will you do that? And how do you know what you are looking for?"

"I don't know. Sometimes the river isn't too full of water... you know how it fluctuates along its length. Maybe I can wade in and see what's been thrown in?"

At that moment there was a scratch at the door and Agnes, Johannes' housekeeper peered round the jamb and nodded to us. She made a sign of knocking on a door.

"Visitor?"

She beamed.

"Bring them in, Agnes."

Bertrand Grist came in, his cap firmly held to his chest.

"Sirs, the coroner can't be found. He's away somewhere, it's said, down county. What do you want us to do?"

I looked at Johannes. "Will you write a report on her injuries for the coroner? I'll do the same for her rescue. We can get a statement from the milkmaid and she can go home. I'll send one of the castle men with her."

Johannes nodded "We'll deal with the body, Grist, and the coroner too."

He smiled obviously relieved. "Thank you sir."

When he'd gone I stood and tested my clothes hanging by the fire. Damp still.

"We need to get the body to the church at Preshute." The village, where the lass had lived had no church and they all travelled half a mile each Sunday to the church at Marlborough. Some folk came into the town to St.Peter's. Preshute church was being built at this time.

"And we need to tell her family."

76

"I'll go and ask Simon Smith across the road if we can borrow his cart. He's usually amenable if he isn't using it."

I rose.

"No, you stay here. You look terrible. This has affected you more than you know. Stay by the fire and get dry."

And he was off, out through the kitchen door.

*****

"You two stayed together most of the time. What happened today? Audre went off on her own?" I asked the milkmaid a bit later when my clothes had dried.

She was sitting on a cushioned bench in a patch of sunlight in the widow Webber's house. Her name was Berewynne.

She simply stared at me.

"Berewynne it's important you tell me." I glanced at the scribe Bullard who I'd asked to come and put down the girl's statement for me. His pen was poised but nothing had been written.

"We shall not find her killer if you don't help."

The girl looked down at her feet.

"She were always making eyes at the men."

I squirmed on my bench. I'd had first-hand experience of this.

"So she went off with a man?"

"I was in the lane, selling to the wheelwrights and coopers. Audre went off to the mill, though there were few folk there since they had the accident."

She lifted her chin. "This one was there - he knows."

"Master Bullard?"

"Aye."

"Who else was there?"

"The one called Grist."

I waited. "There were a few men at the damaged end fiddling about as men

77

like to do with stuff," she said

I looked at Bullard and raised my eyebrows.

"Grist and Hathaway were there, sir, assessing the damage. Master Wryghte came up a bit later and helped to get the wheel off."

"Ah."

"There was more men there than that," said the maid truculently.

"Yes," said Bullard. "Helpers, not masters of their trades. Do you want a list of names sir?"

"I do."

Bullard looked to heaven. "Tom Gilchrist, apprentice wheelwright; young Hathaway, Fred's son; Peter Downy, apprentice carpenter and helping to drain the water from the mill leat was Wat Fisher."

"Write them down please, and the masters."

Bullard scribbled.

"So all these men were at the eastern end dealing with the wheel in full view of everyone else?"

Berewynne nodded.

"Anyone else?"

"I saw Audre go round the other end of the mill. She seemed… well… startled."

"She was surprised by something?"

There was another nod.

"Did you see anyone there?"

She shook her head.

"When next you saw her...?"

"She was in the pool sir." She swallowed hard, "drowndid."

"Tell me, do you know where her buckets are?"

Berewynne put her tongue out on her lips and clamped it - it was, I'd noticed, one of the things she did when she thought hard.

"No sir."

"Her harness was wrapped around her arms as if someone had pinned her with it."

She made no comment at that.

"Was Audre walking out with anyone, Berewynne, do you know?"

"Walking out!" she shouted "Pah! that's a laugh. You'd have half a dozen who thought they was walkin' out with her since none knew about the other."

"Ah. Bit free with her favours, eh?"

"You might say that yes."

"Any here in Marlborough?"

She shook her head once more. "All close to home."

"We need to find her buckets," I said to myself.

I stood. "Right, you can go home. You a Preshute girl too?"

Berewynne nodded.

"I am going to send a soldier with you to protect you for a while. Just until I find Audre's killer. You'll have to look after him and feed him. Understood?"

"Me ma will go wild."

"She'll be even more wild if you end up dead, Berewynne."

The girl gulped and nodded.

I went out into the sunshine. I looked round for an errand runner.

"Hoi! Algar!"

The young lad from the mill, whose head had been injured turned and ran up to me. The wound was now a beautiful purple bruised splodge with a graze to the centre.

"Can you run up to the castle and ask Andrew Merriman to send me a man at arms to go to Manton with the dairymaid? I want to give her some protection, tell him."

Algar's eyes grew round. "Yes sir. Do you think that... that Berewynne...?"

"I don't know Algar. And neither do you. Run now."

*****

I wandered over to the western end of the mill. The mill stood on an island accessed by a bridge from the lane. In some seasons and river conditions it was possible to ford the water on foot at this end and gain the far bank. Here the sluice gates dammed the river and allowed the filling of the mill pond. The faster flowing stream would then run under the bridge and past the wheel, turning it with speed.

I searched amongst the waterside plants and went out onto the river bank from here. Across the river the blank wall of one house stared back at me. I looked to my right. The wall of the priory loomed up and I saw the roof of the little house which housed the infirmary built out from the wall. Only one window high up in the block overlooked this spot.

I flattened myself against the wall and stepped carefully over the river bank, here only three feet wide and peppered with riverside plants.

There, one propped upside down, the other turned on its side, were the two dairymaid's buckets. No milk to be seen. Drained into the river no doubt.

I took them up and inched my way back. A few feet from them, I found Audre's coif.

Now we knew where she had been when she met her attacker.

Yes, Paul, you're quite right, they might have been seen from the road at the other side of the river if anyone was passing. But it was market day. Few folk were about. Most were in the High Street. It was still audacious, as you say.

I gave the buckets into the keeping of one of the wheelwrights asking him to keep them for me. Then I walked round the back of one of the weavers' houses and made my way along the river bank, following the route taken by my mystery man. Past the tanners yard with its foul smelling vats. On to the fulling mills downstream. Here too the smell was pungent, for urine was used in the fulling process and it was mixed with fuller's earth, some kind of clay. Woollen cloth was whitened, thickened and scoured in great vats and then laid out on hooked frames to stretch and dry in the tenteryard.

As I passed, I scanned the river, which in most places was quite clear, for anything foreign which might have been tossed in.

There were two deeper places by the fulling mills and as I heard the paddles slapping and thumping, the mill wheels powering the vertical hammers which pounded the cloth, I searched the river to see if I could see the bottom. Here I couldn't. The wheels muddied the water. By the tanning yard the water had been a sludgy brown. I passed on. The river became shallower again as I approached the back of the buildings of the ropery.

Pah! It was impossible, as Johannes had predicted, I said to myself.

I walked back to Culvermead stepping stones and stalked up the road known as Angel lane.

I needed help to dredge the river.

*****

Wat Fisher and his son Perkin lived at the westernmost end in the very last house of the town. Their little bothy backed almost onto the river where they kept a boat or two. I walked down the High, ducked down into Figgins Lane and scratched on the door of the little house. I had collected Bayard as I passed and now let him graze the grass on South Field Meadow.

Wat opened the door, a beaming smile on his face.

"M'lord Belvoir. Good to see you this fine day, sir."

Wat was always happy. It would be a sad day indeed when he sported a long face.

"I have a job for you Wat... and for Perkin if he's around."

Wat leaned out of the door and stretched his head, "PerKIN!" he roared and I put my finger in my ear to clear the passage for his voice had been stentorian.

I risked a look around the corner of the house and Perkin came shambling up, holding a net he had been mending.

81

"Yeah Da."

He saw me and bobbed his head. "M'lord Belvoir," he grinned.

"Now you two, I have a river job for you. Your biggest net please, a stick and your little boat."

We dredged the deepest pool just before the fulling mill and made our way upstream, myself standing on one bank and Wat the other and pulled the net as close to the bottom as we could. We netted a few freshwater crayfish which Perkin slung into the bottom of his boat.

The moorhens and ducks chucked and quacked as we invaded their homes and though we searched hard and long, we could find nothing which might prove useful. Half a shoe, a rusty bolt of some kind and several kinds of arrowheads all churned up the river bottom as we dredged so that we couldn't even see the water for suspended mud. The water wasn't clear here for the fullers had churned up the bottom with their wheels.

Whilst we dredged I spoke to Wat about the day's work on the water wheel. No, he'd seen no one who had not been helping with the wheel or the wheel pit.

Finally we threw the net in the very middle of the cleanest bit of water and wriggled it around more to free it of debris it than anything. It came up dripping and Perkin was just about to drag it in when he stood in his little boat and took up a stick. Gradually he carefully brought the middle of the net to him by paddling the stick into the water.

There in the bottom something heavy dragged the fine net down and Perkin pulled it close.

Upending it in the bottom of his boat, he gathered in the rest of the net and stowed it.

"What have you?" I shouted.

Perkin sat and rowed to the bank, a matter of only about ten feet.

Into my hands he put a large iron key.

I stared at it, then fished in my scrip for some coins for the two fishermen. "Well done."

"Is it what you wanted, sir?" asked Perkin, ever helpful.

"I think it might be, Perkin but I'll need to ask."

I held the key up to the light. The water sparkled on the surface. The key was black with age but not rusty. It had not been in the water long.

If I was correct in my guessing, this key was the answer to how the mill could have been tampered with.

I just needed to find out by whom.

Chapter Five

I had a long list of names of people to speak to. I would never achieve it today and so I bedded down again at Johannes' house and was up early the next morning. This time I left Bayard in the comfortable stable with his old companions, Johannes' horse Titus and his mule Mary and walked along the High.

I started with the folk still working on the mill building.

I took out the key.

"Do any of you know this key? Does it belong to the mill?"

" 'Aye, that it does," said Grist in surprise. "I've been looking for it. Not that we can lock the building with no doors an' all but I wondered where it had gone."

"Thrown into the river, Grist." I said. "To me, it explains how the mill wheels could be tampered with and the air holes blocked. So who kept this key?"

"Master Miller… Menier kept it. I think Master Nicholas has one too but he keeps his at home."

"Where was this one kept?"

"On a hook in the bagging room."

"So anyone visiting could have taken it?"

"They would have to know which door it was for - it wasn't marked or anything. Menier would lock up at night. Lock him and Henry in. Bullard has a smaller key of his own to the side door. There's a key to the gate too. I keep that and the master has one too."

"That stops anyone from coming in from the town but not from the river bank."

"No, that's true sir," said Grist.

I asked them all if they had seen anything untoward before the death of Audre.

Like Wat, none of them had seen anyone who should not have been at the mill until afternoon. They were all too busy with the damaged wheel and the crumbling building.

I worked my way up the lane, through the weavers. They of course were all up in their lofts doing what they did all day; weaving; and saw no one until the screaming started.

Next I tackled the two wheelwrights yards. From the second yard, a couple of them had been out helping to dismantle the mill wheel. The rest were busy in the yard and because it was surrounded by a fence, they too saw nothing.

It was the same story with the coopers.

I started on the other side of the lane. Here there were mostly houses but many folk had been out in the marketplace and had seen nothing until again, the screaming started.

"I stayed out of the way," said one old crone, "I din't wanna be blamed for nothing."

"Why would that be?" I asked as I watched her with her misshapen arthritic fingers, ply her distaff and talk at the same time. A marvel. I could never have done the two things at once, let alone with sore fingers.

"Aw you know how it is. Ol' woman lives alone with her cat. Must be 'er fault. She's a witch."

"None of your neighbours would say that I am sure." I said hastily.

"Maybe not to my face but who's to say what they thinks?"

"Has anyone ever accused you of being a witch, then?"

The old woman stopped her spinning. "Some'a the children are less than kind."

"That's children for you." I smiled leaning up against her bothy wall.

"Coupla the tanners aint kind neither."

"I'll have a word with their master. It will stop, I promise."

The woman raised her rheumy eyes to my face. I suspect she didn't see very well. Her spinning was all done by touch and years of practice.

86

"Who did you say you was to 'ave so much power over folks an' what they thinks?"

"Sir Aumary Belvoir. Durley, Warden in the forest."

"Geoffrey Belvoir?"

"He was my father."

"Ah...."

"Mother if you have any trouble with anyone, you should tell your neighbour, the town reeve. He will sort them for you."

"He's injured, I 'ear."

"Yes, in the blast the other day but he will be back to work soon. Meanwhile I will do what I can for you, I said.

She resumed her spinning.

"Nasty lot them fullers."

"Are they?"

"Smelly. Unkind and smelly."

I chuckled. "It's the nature of their job, just like the tanners."

"They smell too, yes. They ain't so nice neither, some o 'em." She stopped.

"I smelt one o' em yesterday when I went up to the pool to bucket some water."

"You take your water from the mill pond?" I asked.

"Aye I do. Easier on me old back than bending over the river. The milk girl... what's 'er name, Audre she gave me some 'elp."

"You saw the dead girl?"

"Oh! Is she dead?"

"You did not hear?"

"I hear all sorts, it's me seein' that ain't so good," said the old woman, cackling.

"Hmm. So Audre helped you to fill your bucket with water. When was this?"

"Early."

"Ah. And you said you smelled a nasty smell?"

"I was waiting for one o' them to give me a push or tip over me bucket like they does, but 'e din't."

"Then what did you do?"

"Came 'ome."

"And you didn't see who the milk girl was with?"

The old crone cackled then. "See? Nooo." She looked up at me again. "You see, standin' there you are jus' a blur... oh I can tell yer a bonny lad an' tall too but... I go by voices mostly."

"Did this tanner or fuller speak? Did you know his voice?"

"Nah. An' anyway when they'z callin' me names they'z a shoutin'. Hard to put a name to a shoutin' voice," she said.

"Corse, it mighta bin one of them lads from the slaughterhouse. They don't smell too sweet neither."

I rubbed my forehead.

"I will talk to them all. The calling of names and the tripping you will stop."

"Who did you say you were again? You must be a powerful strong man to take on the tanners and fullers. Not to speak of the shambles men."

"Yes mother, I am. I'll deal with them," I said, pushing off the wall.

The tanners worked in Angel Yard, on the next lane along and I made my way there by the river path coming out by the culverstones; the large sarsen stepping stones which made a bridge across the river here.

I walked into the yard straight into Master Tanner.

"I've come to thank you, Tanner, for your help the other day with Master Barbflet."

Gerard Tanner was a big man with hands the size of saddlebags. His short curly brown hair was cut sharply above his ears rather like the martial Norman cut of old, almost shaved at the back. His face was as leathery as his product and closely bearded but his voice was high pitched and squeaky as if at some point his vocal apparatus had been damaged.

He shrugged his massive shoulders and smiled.

88

"I heard the boom. Took me a while to work out where it had come from. I got the lads to stay put then came by the river... same way as you came today, M'Lord Belvoir. Then I saw the weaver's lads climbing in the gap in the wall and well... the rest you know. Nick is a good friend of mine, not to mention one of the best businessmen in the town. Honest and true." He laughed "Strange for a miller, they aren't usually so straight. We need folk like him."

"Aye, we do indeed."

I scratched my head. "Gerard, I've heard some things I don't like about some of your lads."

"Oh?" Master Tanner crossed his brawny arms over his deep chest.

"That they have been harassing the old blind crone who lives in the next house to Nick's on Crooks Lane."

"Have they now?"

"She finds life difficult enough without the added worry of being tripped up and her water buckets upended. They call her a witch. That sort of nonsense can stick, you know, and become troublesome."

Master Tanner sighed noisily through his nose. "Do we have names?"

"No, no names. Though the crone says that one of them might have been out very early yesterday, just about when little Audre was being killed."

His eyes flared.

"One of my lads was out at the mill?"

"Aye... she cannot swear - the old dame, but she has a keen nose. Forgive me but she says she could smell it was a tanner. You know how the smell lingers. Especially with those who work the vats most of the time."

"Aye, it's a hazard of our job. Course, we get used to it, but others...."

"Might you have a word with them Gerard and get them to leave her alone?"

"Aye I will. I'll not have it. Does this crone know anything about the murder then, of the milk maid?"

"No, I doubt it. She cannot see well she tells me, and she's not quite as wick as she used to be. She will forget a lot of what she hears and what's told to her

89

I'll be bound."

"Ah... we all have old age a creeping up on us eh m'lord?" he chuckled, "With its losses."

I smiled. "Do you mind if I have a word with your fellows? See if I can get one of them to be honest about where he was yesterday morning."

"Not at all."

"Doesn't mean of course that he's the murderer; just that someone might've seen something."

Gerard moved out into his yard and I stayed put. The smell was bad enough here. The further in you went the stronger the smell would be. I had no wish to be asphyxiated by the smell of old urine and dog faeces, used to take the hair from the hides.

Fifteen or so men trooped into the place by the gate and stood about whilst the master chivvied the latecomers from the back.

Ten grown men. Three apprentices and two boys just below apprentice age. One clerk and one woman. This was the tanner's wife, Magda. She stood at the back watching carefully.

"There you are, m'lord," said Tanner, "ask away. I'll know if any of them are lying."

Firstly I walked around the motley bunch trying to imagine my jaunty man with his hood up but it was impossible.

"You all know who I am and that I have been given special powers by John our King, to seek out and arrest those felons who break the law. The law was broken yesterday, at the mill yard."

The men shuffled their feet.

"God's law too. The sixth one. Thou shalt not kill."

Some of the tanners looked at each other; they all knew what had happened. The story had gone around the small town like the smoke from a bonfire.

"I am not accusing any man."

I paused and folded my arms across my chest. "The man who was in the miller's yard with the murdered girl early yesterday morning, may be completely innocent of her death. I am just trying to work out who was where and when so that I can move on with my inquiry."

Master Tanner interrupted "On your oath now, all of you. Answer the Lord Belvoir."

"Which one of you was in the miller's yard early yesterday morning?" I asked.

No one owned up.

"Did you see the girl? Was she with someone?"

Three or four men looked at their boots. A couple looked defiantly back at me. Two or three folded their arms, rather defensively, I thought, across their chests. The rest looked bemused.

"Once more... was any one standing before me here today, talking to the murdered milkmaid yesterday morning?"

No one answered me.

I turned to the Master Tanner. He shrugged.

I looked over the heads of the men at Magda's face. She too shrugged. Neither of them had detected anything which might mean guilt.

One man spoke up. "Last time I saw her, she were here at the gate, sellin' her milk, m'lord."

"When was that, Paega?" asked Master Tanner.

"Day of the large fire at the mill."

Most men then piped up that this too had been the last time they had seen the dairymaid alive. There was an assortment of denials and offerings of times of day.

I thanked them and Master Tanner and passed through the gates.

I took a deep breath as I reached the river bank. However did they stand it?

*****

The fulling mills were just along the bank from the tanners. Three mills were situated one after the other, along the river. Each belonged to the same owner but they were managed by an overseer, Master Pounder. Again I heard the rhythmic beating of the hammers on the cloth and realised why he was thus called.

I entered the yard and made for the door of the mill. The noise was deafening. The smell was no less noxious than in the previous yard.

The welcome I'd had here though, could not have been more different from that at the tanner's yard.

"What do you want?" shouted a voice over the noise.

"Master Pounder, Good day."

"Ah, M'lord Belvoir. What can I do for you?" said the man in the yellow tunic.

Godwine Pounder was a little man with pointed features which I always thought made him look like a weasel or ferret. He was about thirty five and had teeth missing at the front of his mouth. His speech was slushy and lazy as a consequence. His hair was a dirty blond and his beard just a little too long for tidiness. He worked for the wealthy Warin Fuller who also owned the mills at Elcot, a tiny place just half a mile or so from the town.

This was the fuller who had competed with Gilbert Cordwainer for the hand of Grace, his wife and who was entering the lists, we thought, to contest the title of town reeve.

"As you know I'm investigating the death of the dairymaid Audre Smythson and I have a witness who says they think a fuller might have been seen with her early yesterday morning."

"Where?"

"At the town mill where she was killed."

"None of my men."

"You know where they all were?"

"Here working."

"Do they all live on the premises then?"

92

"No. None do."

"Then how do you know where they were before they came to work?"

Pounder looked at me with a disgusted expression. "They have no need to be at the town mill."

"So you would have no objection to me asking them and you, where they were just an hour after dawn, then?"

"They are all very busy." He said puffing out his chest.

"I too can be busy - getting a warrant from the Sheriff to search your building. Though I don't need to. My warrant from the king is enough. That would not reflect well on your master's campaign for the post as town reeve, now would it?"

Pounder glared at me.

"I am not stopping the machines. You'll have to do it one by one. We are, as I said, very busy."

I nodded. "So let's start with you. Where were you?"

"Here. Preparing for the day."

"Witnesses?"

"No, I don't suppose so."

I left a little gap into which Pounder inserted an irritated sigh.

"I'll start with the tentermen. Leave your vatmen till last," I said eventually.

There were eight men who strung out the cloth on their stretching frames and who helped to take the fulled cloth every two hours or so from the vats of disgusting mixture, to be untangled and to get out the wrinkles.

None owned up to being at the corn mill.

One by one I went to each team of fullers, in three sheds, and questioned the men working the heavy striking paddles. Only one man admitted to being in the mill yard and he lived there with his family, the rest of whom were weavers. He'd come to work by the riverside path I had taken that morning, he always did. The man had witnesses for he had hailed two friends across the river and the men would vouch for him.

93

They all knew the milkmaid Audre but none had been alone with her that day, they said.

"My witness says that a man who smelled like a fuller was with Audre just before she died." I told Pounder. "If anyone remembers anything, leave a message at the town reeve's house and it will be passed on to me."

"Would that be Old Gytha?" asked Pounder. "The old witch at the top of Crook's Lane? She always had it in for us full...."

"Ah... yes. And that is another thing. If you could please tell your men that I will not, and neither will Master Barbflet nor the rest of the town council, have that harmless old lady branded a witch. No more name calling. No more accidents shall happen to her. Do I make myself clear?"

"Perfectly," grinned the toothless Pounder. "I suppose."

"Perfectly, *my Lord*," I said.

Pounder went on grinning. Then turned to walk away.

I quickly stuck out my foot and caught the man at the front of the knee and he folded onto the floor with an 'oomph'. I did not normally stand upon my rank but this man had irritated me.

Some of his men looked up from their labours. A couple smirked.

"I trust I make myself perfectly transparent, Master Pounder?"

He jumped up quickly. "Admirably," he grimaced, rubbing his knees. "M'lord."

As I left, I saw him taking a rod to the back of the two tentermen who had grinned. Pounder by name and by nature.

I spent the rest of the day questioning folk coming and going in Crook's yard and talking to Nicholas but no one had anything to add.

It was a beautiful evening and I sat with Johannes and Agnes in the yard at the back of the house, catching the last rays of the sun.

Round the gate post came the cheeky face of the young saddler, Judd.

"M'lord," he bowed. What a different approach this man had to the surly Pounder.

94

"I have a harness of sorts here. Would you like to see it?"

I put down my beaker. "Aye, I would, Judd."

He gave it into my hands.

Made of rope the harness was stiff but with some coaching from Judd I managed to get it the right way up and fastened around my imaginary bear.

The longest piece went round the bear's chest and under each foreleg. Two pieces passed over each shoulder and joined with what would be buckles at each side of the beast. There was a large metal ring threaded onto the front piece where another rope might pass and be tied. This would form the leading rope.

"There is nothing to stop the bear from chewing through the rope or leather, so I think perhaps the leading rope should still be chain in part but there will be no metal parts to chafe the skin of either bear nor handler sir," said the saddler.

"Judd, this is magnificent," I said grinning. "You are a clever man. Make this then in your leather and chain and I will require you to make others, smaller ones, for my dogs later."

"Thank you sir," said Judd bowing again, obviously pleased with himself.

"I am sure there will be other men who own animals, larger dogs in particular, who will clamour to have you make them a harness of the same kind."

"Aye, dogs off leash can be a problem in the town, especially on market days. It's hard to control a large dog with just a rope threaded round their neck," said Judd.

"Indeed it is," I said as Johannes took the contraption from me and turned it this way and that.

"Last market day, Tylor's dog got free and carried off one of Master Chike's hens."

"Yes I know...," said Johannes. "The beast ended up here in my yard, penned in. Took me all my time not to let Robert, Master Chike, beat the dog to death with his stick."

"Here?" I asked.

"Ran straight down the High Street, into the alleyway and in here, pursued by half the town."

"And the chicken?"

"Flew off unharmed up onto the stable roof."

We all laughed.

"Eustache Tylor's dog?"

"Aye, the same," said Judd, "name of Aura I think."

"A bitch?"

"Yes sir. She's always getting free. Tylor has been in dispute with a lot of folk over what that dog does. His neighbours are fed up with him. One day he'll find her dead in a ditch, I'm sure. He had to be fetched from Crook's Lane and he came and tied her up again."

"Where does he live, Judd?"

"St. Martin's sir. On the Mildenhall Road by the river Og."

"He has a brick yard there, you remember, Aumary?" prompted Johannes.

"Yes, yes I do remember. I think tomorrow I shall pay him a visit. I want to talk to him about a bear."

The following day dawned clear and bright but soon clouds banked up from the south west and the day continued dark and dismal.

I collected Bayard and rode up to the middle of Barn Street where the slaughterhouse men had their houses.

Naturally they too were warned to leave the old woman on Crook's Lane and not to tease or torment her. They swore it was not them. No, it was the tanners and fullers. Common, plaguey, pests they called them and put on their most innocent faces.

I asked them about the day that the milkmaid was murdered.

Oh no! They said, they didn't know the girl well. She never came to the slaughter pens to sell her milk. She liked the other trades better. If they wanted to buy milk they had to go to her and they were far too busy on that day - it being market day, to take time from their work to do so.

I then rode the rest of the distance up the hill and turned right at The Green into St. Martins. Down the hill I met and forded the little stream of the Og and turned into the yard belonging to Eustache Tylor.

Everywhere you looked there were tiles, large and small piled up and a few stacks of the new-fangled bricks now being made for the fancier houses of the wealthy. Bricks, I was told, were becoming the preferred construction material in areas where there was little good stone to build with. They were however, extremely expensive. The tiles were not only those for roofs but decorated tiles for floors, some of them rather beautiful, in rusts and yellows with interesting patterns.

Only four men and Tylor worked here and two of those lived in Mildenhall, the next village along the road to Ramsbury.

Eustache Tylor was a good looking man in his late twenties with corn gold hair and blue eyes. When I first saw him he was dragging a large empty wooden pallet across the yard and he threw it down to come to see me.

I entered the gates, Bayard following me tossing his head.

"All right old man," I said quietly. "Yes, there are dogs here but they won't harm you. You could get the better of them anyway."

"Tylor?"

"Aye sir?" He squinted at me. "You are the castle man, Lord de Neville's right hand."

"Aumary Belvoir, Lord of Durley and Warden of Savernake."

"What can I do for you sir? Replacing thatch with tiles, are we?" He bowed.

"No, no nothing like that. In my role as constable of the county...." I saw his eyes go up.

"Aye another of my roles. I am charged with gathering information about two deaths and the murders of the bearward Godfrey Barend and the milkmaid Audre Smythson."

Tylor gestured and I followed him to a hut at the edge of the yard. We sat.

"You alone here, Tylor?"

"Just for the moment. One is off sick and the other... well... I lost him last

97

year when the reeve imprisoned him for the attack on the Jews. Afterwards he fled. I never replaced him. My remaining men are out delivering some tiles to the new houses on the Manton Road. "

"Widow Partridge?"

"Aye. The woman had thatch on some but then...."

"Yes, I know it, your fellow councilman Giles Thatcher did the job last year."

He nodded, "Well now, the rest must be tiled" he tutted. "I can't complain - it's business - but tile on such houses. Whatever next?"

I smiled.

"She will rent them for a higher price, I suppose."

"Aye."

"So, did you know either Barend, the bearward or the maid, Audre?" I asked.

"The bear man, very little, the maid, yes, I knew her. She never came here of course, too far out, but I met her at the market once or twice. Pretty piece if a little...."

"Inconstant, I'm told?"

"Aye, flighty. A man never knew quite where he was with her, I think."

I smiled. "You know of course that her neck was broken and that she was found in the millpond?"

"No, no I didn't. I had heard she was dead. Not the manner of it. I haven't been to town this four days with such a large order for tiles."

"Hmmm. No dogs with you today Eustache?"

"Yes, sir, they are in that shed. I haven't let them out yet."

"They are mighty quiet. Mine would be baying to Heaven by now if a stranger came into the yard."

Tylor rubbed the crown of his short hair. "Only got two now."

"You had three?"

"Aye. Aura has gone missing. No doubt she'll be back. Rabbits, I warrant. The other bitch Fetch, is old and deaf and Archer is just plain daft."

"I hear your dog got into a bit of trouble in my friend's yard at last market day. Dr Johannes told me that she ended up in his yard with someone else's chicken in her mouth." My voice was friendly and I kept the smile on my face.

Tylor laughed.

"Aye she did. But no harm done."

"Ah.... this time."

His eyes narrowed.

"And if you are serious about entering for the post of town reeve, young man, then I would be very careful whom you annoy."

He stared at me for a while and nodded. "I had thought to but... er."

I heard some dogs barking and howling not too far away and raised my brows.

"Not my dogs, Sir Aumary... someone over the back somewhere towards Mildenhall has a pack of hunting dogs... they've been there since market day last," said Tylor.

"Ah yes. Market day. Wednesday. You were there with your dog."

Tylor rubbed the back of his neck. "Aye... sorry I must have been. I haven't been out the yard since, except to go home."

"And you didn't see the milkmaid?"

"No, sir."

I looked around his little hut.

"Cosy little place here. Where do you have a home?"

"St Martin's, sir, last house on the right before the river."

I lifted the lid of a black iron pot sitting on the table. "Hmm... your midday meal?"

"Me old mam makes me a pottage every day, sir."

I lifted a large leather jack of ale and sniffed. "Ho! Smells like Mistress Brewster's nectar."

"It is. Not cheap but worth the extra."

So he bought from the woman who'd brewed the ale in Cowper's unusually laden barrel.

I took a piece of thin muslin from a bowl.

"Ah, milk." I dipped in my finger. "Not yet sour. How old is this then, Tylor?"

"Uh... I can't remember."

I smiled again.

"I shall leave you now and I hope that when I next come to ask you questions, or perhaps you will come to me, that you will not lie to me and that you will remember a little more accurately what you have been doing and when."

I made for the door. "Oh yes. I nearly forgot. The bearward. You say you knew him?"

"A little."

"How?"

"He came past the yard on his way into town. I saw him then and we spoke. He was wanting to perform at the market but I dissuaded him. I told him we didn't like that sort of thing in our town and that he had better pass on."

"Did you indeed?" I scratched my chin.

"And yet Nicholas the town reeve tells me that it is a Eustache Tylor who is responsible for collecting the money for a bear to be purchased for the fair in August. Are there two Eustache Tylors, then?"

The man's fair skin flushed to the roots of his hair. "Ah...."

"Good day Master Tylor. I will see you again." I mounted Bayard and clattered off up the stony road to The Green.

The man was a very poor liar.

Chapter Six

I took my leather harness home later that day when Judd brought it to the doctor's house.

Peter was out with the bear on the village green like he was every evening that it didn't rain. He had all the village children sat in front of him as an audience and Isabella was going through her paces.

Hawise looked up from her place on the front row, where she sat cross-legged and giggled her way through Isabella's act.

"And so, Isabella," said Peter finally, "do you think your handler is a fine fellow? Do you think him handsome?"

The bear lurched from side to side and to a child it might have looked as if the animal was shaking its head.

There was a lot of high pitched laughter and one or two lower guffaws from some of the parents standing at the back watching carefully, ready to jump should things go wrong.

I saw John fold his arms over his chest and shake his head.

Once the show was over which I was told, had lasted no longer than the time it took to say a few Paternosters, Peter came up with Isabella on her rope. The gyves were now attached to a different leg and the chafed ankle was healing.

"Try this Bearward Brenthall." I said. "It's a special harness courtesy of Judd Saddler. It will give just the same amount of control over Isabella, better I think, provided she doesn't tug and pull away and out of your hands, but it will be kinder both on her body and your hands."

Peter took it and turned it in his fingers.

"How...?"

"Come, let's try."

John came up. "Here, give me the rope."

The bear reared up when we tried to put the main loop over her head but with a little coaxing and sippets dipped in milk, we managed to fix it. Then it was a matter of pulling the main piece around her middle and settling the ring where we attached another chain. This had a leather handle with a loop.

"'C'mon old girl... let's go for a walk to test it out," smiled Peter.

John came up to me a little later when we had both watched Peter and the bear out of sight across the green and towards the church. We followed at a distance.

"Any nearer a solution to the bearward's murder sir?" he asked.

"Just that it has been followed by a blast at the mill...."

"Aye, Agnes came back from the town market with Richard and Mary in the cart, with that news. Nick Barbflet injured and two dead?"

"Aye. And the little dairymaid who used to come by the artisans' yards, dead with a broken neck. Johannes thinks it's the same murder weapon as the bearman."

"No, that we hadn't heard." John stopped and looked into the distance, over towards the forest trees, slowly sinking into the grey of the evening. "What's going on sir? Have you any idea?"

"I have theories but no evidence... well, not much yet. I have, I'm sure several folk lying through their teeth and a lot of tangled lines but no doubt with more prodding and poking...."

"You'll get to the bottom of it."

"I must John."

I yawned. How has the forest been in my absence?"

John smothered a laugh, "Green, sir, and growing."

I laughed with him. "Good." I turned to face him "I don't know what I'd do without you John. I could not possibly manage without you and all the men under you. I may be the warden but, you and the rest are the ones who really run the place now. You, all of you, have my heartfelt thanks."

John squirmed. He wasn't good at praise.

"But you sir, you are really excellent at finding hidden murder. You have the brain for it. None of us could do that. None of us. It's best you do what you are good at and leave us to do what we do, for you."

"I...." I got no further for a thought had come into my mind at John's words. We all of us had our allotted tasks and we all did them to the best of our ability. Just as the town council of Marlborough had their allotted work. They were not paid for the jobs they did. They did them for the love of the town. Or so it was said.

I wanted to find out what each of the councillors was responsible for, if anything in particular. Men were entering the competition for town reeve and they had their specialities. I felt I needed to know what they were.

I knew, for Nicholas had told me so, that Tylor was responsible for raising the money for the town bear.

I knew that my friend Gilbert was responsible for the churches and their business, along with the church reeves and the priest of each church. He had told me as such.

Nick had taken charge of the lockup in the town; a small round building up by the high cross, and the stocks on Southfield. Amongst other things, his was the job of doling out justice for petty misdemeanours to the townsfolk.

What did the others do?

Before I went to find my poor neglected wife and children and spend an evening with them, I entered my study, sat at my table, pulled a piece of parchment to me and wrote the names of all the elected councillors of Marlborough town.

Master Gabriel Gallipot, apothecary.

Master Gilbert Cordwainer, shoemaker.

Master Warin Fuller, cloth preparer.

Master Adam Fletschier, arrowsmith.

Master Jos Glover, glove maker.

Master Thomas Metier, goldsmith.

Master Timothy Roper, rope maker.

Master Gerard Tanner, tanner of hides.

Master Giles Thatcher, thatcher of roofs.

and Master Eustache Tyler, brick maker.

Above them all was Master Nicholas Barbflet, master miller. Eleven in all.

Who was to take on Nick's job I wondered, now he was incapacitated? I know he would rule from his bed but he would need to have eyes and legs out on the streets.

That was something I would ask him tomorrow.

*****

It rained from dawn. The road was running with water and I clopped down the hill to the town.

I made straight for the Barbflet house and was ushered in and my good waterproof cloak taken off into the house to be dried.

I took the stairs two at a time again and found myself in Nicholas' room. He sat straighter today and his eyes were less glazed than heretofore.

I brought him up to date with my inquiry so far.

"I found the key to the mill door, which belonged in the bagging room at the bottom of the river. Thrown there by some malefactor, Nick. I watched him do it. I'm sure it was he who tampered with the louvres and the air holes, not to mention the grindstones."

Nick's face took on a pale waxy hue. "No! I can't believe anyone would do it. You still think it an act of revenge or one of my fellow councillors out to remove me?"

"I can't think what else."

"But they are all good men, tried and tested."

"All?" I asked "For example, how did Tylor get to be on the council Nick? It's plain he's a shifty character. He lied to me with a straight face three times

104

yesterday. Gilbert warned me he was no good for the town."

"Ah, yes. We were short one man. No one else came forward. And then, we thought he would be like his father. I had thought to ask Johannes to join us, but...."

"He will not do it. You know that."

"Aye, I suppose I'd hoped."

Nick sighed. "Tylor's father was on the council until he died and I suspect the younger Tylor thought his place assured."

"Places are not hereditary."

"No, indeed. We keep an eye on him and give him the less important jobs. He will not get on the committee this year, I think."

"I want to know, Nick. Does each man have a task allotted to him? Are there...?

Nick answered me straight away, "Each man is responsible for the part of town in which he lives or is close to at work."

"So Tim Roper would be the Marsh and the ropery and wagon yard?"

"Aye."

"Fletchier?"

"The middle of the High from Ironmongers to Neates Yard."

"Giles?"

He takes up where Tim leaves off. The top end of the Marsh and Oxford Street, on up Herd Street."

"And so it goes on. It's a good system." I said.

"It's worked well so far."

"Do they have special roles? I know what Gilbert does for example, and Tylor and you."

"Well, when something special needs doing we put it to the council and we get volunteers."

"What might be special... like this bear for the fair?"

"Aye, that.... The booths for the fair in August - repairs and additions for

105

example. And the repair of the High Cross."

"I thought it needed repair last time I looked."

"Erm.... Drains and ditches to stop flooding."

"I know that Gilbert was concerned about that, some years ago."

"But it's Master Glover's area, that one. A new Bible for St. Peter's. The old one is falling apart. It's a cast off from the chapel in the castle and was de Neville's gift."

"Whose job is that?"

To raise the money? Master Tanner." Nicholas waved his hand in the air, "Mind you... where money is concerned we always have two men involved. Master Tanner has Master Fuller helping."

"Ah."

"And who is your deputy at the moment? Who looks to things whilst you cannot be out there keeping an eye on the streets?

"Gabriel, the Apothecary, Gallipot. No better man."

"No, I can imagine."

*****

I went down to look at the progress being made at the mill.

Much of the damaged timber had been removed and the rest shored up. I wandered into Nick's office. All the documents which had been there last time I had been in the room had been removed and taken to the house.

I walked around the eastern end. A set of planks had been nailed over the gaping hole made by the blast. The grinding room and the bagging room below were now secure from the elements and from unwarranted intrusions. The wheel had gone. No doubt another one was being made at the wheelwrights, as I stood and pondered.

I saw Bullard at his table and waved. In the next room Grist was sweeping up rubbish from the flagstoned floor. The main door had been repaired and reinstated and the mill could at last be made secure. Grist now kept the key, for the old man Menier had, he said, withdrawn into himself and could not be prevailed to stay at the mill any longer. He had gone to be looked after and to live with, his sister in the town.

I ambled over to the mill pond. The water level had dropped enormously. I looked back. The sluice had been pulled across and the river flowed on its own bed without any diversion.

I glanced back again at the mill pond, then once more to the river. When the sluices were in operation, the river dropped alarmingly.

I went back into the mill and tapped Grist on the shoulder. "Bertrand...," he stopped and leaned on his broom.

"Yes, m'lord."

"How often do you use the sluices to fill the mill pond? I don't remember it being quite so full as it was the day of the blast nor the morning I took the poor milkmaid out of the water."

"No sir, we rarely need it so full but when we have a deal of milling to do, we have to fill it so we have enough to complete the job and to have the pressure for the wheel."

"The mill at the castle... do they fill up a huge pond in the same way? I can't remember one."

"No sir, they aren't so busy. They supply the castle and a few others up Granham way. Here we supply the whole town and others."

How many mills are there on the Kennet, that you know about, Bertrand?"

Grist leaned his besom against the mill wall.

"The first I know about is at Clatford, upriver sir. Then there's the one at Manton... not a big one, that mill. The castle mill is the one you know about, then us. Further down there's the town fullers, three mills. They don't need any special pools for they just need the river to power their paddles. Elcot's three fulling mills and Werg and Dunford are the last I know about, m'lord Belvoir."

"Quite a few mills in a short span on one small river."

"Aye, I s'pose so."

"Hmmm." An idea was forming in my head.

"Thank you. Will you now take on the master miller job yourself, if Menier doesn't return?"

"If Master Nicholas asks me, yes I will," he said jauntily. "But I shan't take it over the head of Master Menier should he wish to take up his old job again."

"He's an old man, he might wish to give up now he has lost his son."

"Aye... it's been a terrible blow to him. To us all. He was a fine man, was Henry." He crossed himself.

I smiled. "I had no idea that milling was such a complex and dangerous occupation, Bertrand. I shall eat my bread with much greater relish from now on."

*****

Afternoon saw me back down at the fulling mills with my burned grey cloak tucked under my arm. I bypassed the irascible Master Pounder and made for a tenter who was crossing the yard.

He took my cloak and shook it out. "Aye, we might be able to get out the black and the smell of smoke, but, I don't think we shall be able to do anything about the holes, m'lord."

"Holes? Ah... yes, I see."

The tenter held it up to the light and there in the middle, was a series of tiny pinprick holes where the cinders had scorched the wool and burnt through.

"I hadn't noticed them."

"A darning job sir. Take it to Mistress Wyndecraft on Angel Yard. She'll see you right."

"It's a job for my wife, I think." I said quietly and then fell in with him as he continued on his way.

"Thank you... erm...."

"Sharp, Sir."

I walked on to the gate. "Sharp, tell me. Your hammers which flatten the cloth? How do you manage when the corn mill upstream dams the river and there isn't so much water in it?"

He looked puzzled. "Manage, sir?"

"Do you still have enough to turn the wheel in the river or does it come to a halt?"

"Oh no sir. That's when we must do it by hand. Or rather feet."

"A hard job, eh?"

"Glad I'm a tenterman sir," he smiled.

"Indeed." I answered as we reached the road.

I looked up at the sky. The grey clouds scudded past and though it was not raining, the air was damp with stray droplets.

A raucous jackdaw on a roof pulled my vision down as he flew away and I saw Master Tanner hurrying along the High towards Nick's house. I joined him.

"Good day, Gerard," I said.

"No, my lord, it's not a good day."

"Oh? Is rain not good for the tanning profession Gerard, for I think we shall have some soon?"

"Rain or shine sir, it makes no difference to us." He looked worried. "Come sir, come in to Nick's and hear what I have to tell him. He is not going to like it and... frankly, neither will the rest of the council when they hear."

The big man, shrugging inside his warm brown cloak, banged on the door of the Barbflet House. He threw off the cloak and was up the stairs before I could utter a good day to Felicity.

"Oh dear... something has bitten Gerard" she said, picking up his cloak from the floor.

"I'm sure he didn't mean to be rude, Mistress Barbflet. He's worried about something. I'll find out what it is."

When I entered the room, Tanner was well into his story and it took me a while to catch up.

"In the large coffer - the one we keep in the locked room in the crypt?"

"Yes, Nick."

Nick's brow furrowed in bewilderment.

"But two of you have the key and I can't think...."

"*No!* Neither of us would take it!"

"Master Tanner... what's happened?"

Gerard rubbed his fingers over a worried brow,

"The money which Warin Fuller and I have collected from the town for the buying of a bible for St. Peter's. It's missing."

"And you keep it in the chest in the crypt of St. Mary's?"

"In a locked room. Yes."

"When did you last count it?"

"I went last Friday week to add some more. The pilgrims staying at the priory had given a small amount to us as a thank you to the town. I added that to the amount. It was all there then."

"And now on Saturday, a week later, it's missing?"

"Aye."

"No sign of a forced entry to the chest?"

"No m'lord. A key was used."

"How many keys are there?"

"Three, Sir Aumary." said Nicholas, "Mine - Gallipot has it now. Gerard's and Master Fuller's. When anyone wishes to store or take out money, they come to one of us for the key. And the priest holds the key to the crypt's little store room. He's there too when we store the money."

"Father Torold - aye. You say Gallipot doesn't know yet Gerard?"

Master Fuller rubbed his forehead again. "No. I am on my way to tell him."

"Then I will accompany you and drop into the church to speak with the priest. You alert Master apothecary."

Gerard nodded and bustled out.

Nick closed his eyes and sighed. "Oh how I wish I could..."

"Consider me your eyes and ears, Nick." I said. "I'll see what I can find out."

*****

Father Torold was a rotund man with a ring of curling red-brown hair around a rather ragged tonsure and bright, twinkling green eyes which I think betrayed an Irish ancestry. The door to his house, a small cottage at the side of the alleyway leading to Johannes' house, was open and I looked in. Everything was tidily stored away. His cup, plate and jug lay on the table in readiness for his next meal. The central fire was covered with a turf. His bed was neatly made. His cloak was missing from its peg behind the door. I walked around the end of the church and found the deep voiced priest in prayer over a recent grave.

I waited for a gap in his recitation.

"Father Torold."

He looked up and his face crinkled into a smile. "Sir Aumary. God's blessing on you m'lord."

"And on you my friend. Please go on with your prayer. I can wait."

"No, no. 'Tis no matter. I am done."

The grave by which he stood was a new one, not yet sunken.

"The bearward?"

"Aye... now I have a name for him; your peddler came to tell me, so I am repeating my burial rite."

"That's kind," I licked my lips. "Father, I am here at the behest of the town council... or more properly at Nick and Gerard's asking. It's about the money in the crypt."

"Come. Let's get out of the spitting rain," said the priest.

The rain had begun to be more incessant now and we ducked under his dripping doorhood and shut the plank door.

"Friday last week, Master Fuller came to add some money?"

111

"That is correct."

"Today, the following week, Saturday, it's gone?"

"All of it, yes. Never as much as a few halfpennies left at the bottom. He was very angry."

"Is it stored in bags?"

"Aye it is. All labelled."

Do you keep other monies for the council?"

"I do. But after this I think I shall ask them to store their silver elsewhere. I can't have theft from the church sir. We must be above suspicion."

"I am sure you are, Torold. Listen. Who else do you store monies for? Which other funds?"

Torold sat on his oak bench.

"All of them. The chest is divided, you see, into compartments. Each bag is labelled, as I say."

"Take me through the procedure when someone, one of the council, comes to deposit...."

"Or take out to use for the thing which is saved for."

"That too. How do you organise it?"

Torold scratched his nose. "The councillors come to me and ask me to open the room in the crypt. I take the key...."

"Which is kept where?"

Torold stretched backwards and fiddled behind a spare cloak hanging from a peg knocked into the daub wall.

A large key, suspended from hairy string, was hidden on a separate hook behind the cloak.

"Here."

"And then...?"

"We go to the crypt, I unlock the room. They then unlock the chest. I stay out of the room; they count or add or take away money, relock the chest and I relock the room."

"Who keeps the records?"

"Each pair of councillors have their own tallies but I believe it's all entered into a large book for all to see - those who can read that is - by Master Bullard at the mill."

"The town mill you say?"

"Yes, sir."

"Who has been here this week? Can you remember?" I asked.

"Between Friday week and Saturday - today?" Torold scratched his razored tonsure.

"Master Gallipot. Master Barbflet, before his accident. Erm, I think in addition to the Masters Tanner and Fuller, Master Tylor and Master Fuller again."

"Hmmm. All depositing money for their allotted funds for town works?"

"Yes, though I cannot be sure if some did not take out the funds. I try not to look."

I smiled. "If they did, it will be entered in the book."

"Indeed it will, sir."

"Thank you Father. You have been most helpful."

*****

Next I paid a visit to the mill and to Master Bullard the bookkeeper. He took out his large ledger and the tally sticks associated with it.

"Master Tanner, along with Master Fuller, went to the crypt and deposited some money. It's recorded here on this stick."

I leaned over his shoulder. "I see it. And this is the total in the bag kept in the chest? The one for the Bible fund? Expensive things, aren't they?" I said as I registered how much was originally in the bag.

"Even those with no embellishments, sir."

"Hmm. Father Torold said that Masters Gallipot and Barbflet visited to check their own fund. That one is?"

113

Bullard turned a page. "The fair in August sir, St.Peter's Fair, money for the new booths and repairs. The fair has grown quite a bit since its first year, two years ago. This has been raised by a town tax. A twentieth of all moveables."

This meant that the town council had asked each occupant who owned land or property or who were worth a certain amount of money for a twentieth of the value of all goods which they owned.

"They deposited money?"

"Took it and paid it to the town carpenters so that they might buy the materials, sir. August will be fast upon us. They must start work soon."

"Ah. And Masters Tylor and Fuller again? Why him twice?"

"It should have been Master Barbflet but he was, as you know sir… indisposed, so Master Fuller accompanied the brickmaker with his contribution to his fund for the town bear."

"Depositing?"

"Yes, sir."

He took out the tally stick and showed me.

"Tell me Bullard, how much does a bear cost and where do you get such things?"

Bullard looked up at me, his face aghast. "You think I would know, sir?

I slapped him on the back.

"Not at all Henry." I said, "No, not at all."

But I had an idea who might.

Chapter Seven

I retraced my steps to Nick Barbflet's house.

The rain was coming down steadily now.

I asked Nicholas if might use a room in the mill for a while. I wanted to talk to some people and frankly, I was fed up of traipsing about the town. Let them come to me.

"They have stretched a tarred cloth over the hole in the roof of my office, Aumary. It should be dry in there. I'll get Tylor to come and tile the gap and then it will be usable. Luc Mason's apprentice, Gerald, has rebuilt the wall and daubed it. Just needs a lime wash. Can't do that in the rain though."

"And Eustache Tylor is the first person I want to talk to. That should work out well."

Indeed it did, for two days later Tylor walked down from St. Martin's at the summons of the town reeve's deputy. His jaunty figure approached the mill thinking this was simply a job of measuring and estimating.

Indeed it was.

He was walking away again, when I called him.

"Tylor... I need a word with you."

He turned slowly and his face fell. "Aye m'lord?"

"In here, please."

The man took off his coif and slapped it against his leg to free it of rain, for it had continued to drizzle and entered the mill. I took him up the stairs and into the small back room.

I sat behind Nick's table and Tylor stood nervously before me fiddling with his coif.

"Have you had any further thoughts about the questions I asked you earlier last week?"

"What questions were those m'lord?"

I leaned back and frowned at him. "Did you see Audre the milkmaid? Yes, you did, for the milk you had was fresh. The weather has been warm and so it must have been bought from her or her friend on the day Audre died.

"You did go into town for you were seen with your dog. Have you found her, by the way?"

"No sir."

"And what was all that nonsense about the bearward? You said you'd seen him, on the road from Ramsbury when everyone else says he did not come into town and if he did touch the edge it was from the west."

Tylor was silent.

"And all that rubbish about the town not being the kind of place where a performing bear is welcome?"

Tylor shuffled his feet. "I didn't think it would be."

"And yet you volunteered to spend time, your own free time, going about the town, collecting money from the folk, in order to buy or hire a bear for the August fair."

Tylor looked down at the floor.

"If you are going to lie man, at least make it convincing and try to remember what lies you have told. I am not entirely stupid."

Tylor breathed in as if he was going to speak and then lapsed into silence again.

"Tell me. How have you managed to collect so much money from the good folk of Marlborough? I saw the tally stick recording the sum you had collected. It's a fair amount."

"People have been very generous, sir."

"How do you get the promises of money from people? It's more than the two gentlemen who are collecting for the church Bible have achieved."

Eustache Tylor shrugged, "I simply go about town and ask. I explain what fun it will be. Bibles aren't fun m'lord. Folk would rather spend an hour watching a bear, than an hour in church listening to someone tell them dry old stories from a Bible."

Well, that was the truth at any rate, as I saw it.

"Hmm. When you have your money, from where will you get the bear and a handler to come with it?"

Tylor's face picked up and his expression changed. "Bristol sir," he smiled.

"That's a long way for a bear to travel."

"My cousin, he has links with the traders who come from the north. They have already come a thousand miles sir, from the frozen wastes of far off lands. A few more miles is nothing."

"People import these creatures and they come into Bristol?"

"Yes sir, and some come in the eastern ports, though my cousin lives in Bristol so that is where we shall have our bear from."

I nodded.

"So what is in it for you Tylor?"

"Me sir?" His jaw clamped shut and he looked scared suddenly.

"Yes. You don't imagine that I believe that this is all being done simply for the pleasure of the Malburian crowd, Tylor. There must be something in it for you."

"Oh no, sir. I offered to do the job because I have the contacts and if you want to know, I told the dead bearward to take his mangy creature elsewhere because I knew I could get a much better creature from my cousin. That pathetic apology for a bear wouldn't excite anyone."

"Not a lot of money to be made from it, you mean."

Again, Tylor clamped his mouth shut.

"Why did you lie about not being in town the day Audre died?"

"Dunno sir, I s'pose I just forgot."

"Oh spare me Tylor!" I raised my voice. "You knew Audre well. You were much more familiar with her than just buying her milk and passing the time of day. How else would you know - and these are your own words - how flighty

117

she was?"

"She knew a lot of lads in the town," said Tylor, licking his lips. "Not just me."

"I'm sure but I'm asking you."

Tylor took a deep breath.

"Once upon a time, I thought that she and I might... you know, get together, but it turns out I wasn't the only one thinking it and so I dropped her."

"Dropped her in the mill pond eh?"

"No sir... never!"

"Oh, get out of my sight." I said, rubbing my hand over my forehead where I had the beginnings of a headache. Two years ago, I had been walloped on the head and ever since I had suffered with these pains in times of stress.

"And make sure that you give the town reeve the best price you can for your tiles. I will know about it. Now get out."

He fled as if the hounds of hell were after him. I saw him bump into Master Fuller as he left and they exchanged a few words.

This was the next person I had asked to see.

Master Warin Fuller was a tall man in his middle forties, with a long face and thinning mousey brown hair wiped over his balding pate. Today he wore a scarlet tunic to his ankles covered with a sleeveless surcoat of dark blue. A red hat, a round embroidered crown of a thing, sat perched on his head and a belt of red leather dangled down almost to his ankles. The cloak he now shook off was the darkest blue I had ever seen, so much so it was almost black. His ankle boots were fine supple red leather; all his clothing screamed his wealth and status.

"Thank you for coming Master Fuller on such an inclement day."

He smiled and looked around for somewhere to sit. "Not at all my Lord Belvoir. I am happy to be of help."

He hooked out a stool from under the table and arranged himself on it.

I leaned forward and found him gazing around at the damaged mill.

"Oh dear... what a mess. This will take some time to repair and have working properly again."

"The wheel, I'm told, is already in hand. The holes in the fabric are being repaired by the mason's lad; the carpentering by Master John Wood and his gang. It will be working before you know it."

"Good!"

"Did you ride?"

"I did. I have however left my mount at my mill. I apologise for the wetness m'lord," he said, smiling and lifting his arms to show me the rain droplets sparkling on his finely fulled and dyed garments.

"Think nothing of it."

"Of course, when I am resident in the town, I shall be able to walk everywhere and know all that goes on here."

"You are planning on moving to Marlborough from Elcot?"

"No, I am taking possession of the house on Neates Yard. The house on the corner will be my town dwelling. I shall keep Elcot Mill. My wife will not move, alas."

"That is the house which used to be lived in by the Chandlers, Master Fuller?"

"Aye, it's been empty these five or six months but I am engaging Master Mason to overhaul it for me. I will then be eligible to stand for town reeve."

I nodded. "Then being resident in the town."

"Just so."

"I am sure the council will be happy to have you nearer," I said.

"Talking of town council business... I heard you wished to talk to me about the money which has gone missing from the funds at the church."

"Yes. I saw Master Tanner shortly after you and he discovered the shortfall. Can you tell me in what happened when you went to the crypt?"

"I cannot tell you where the money has gone, Sir Aumary, only that when Gerard and I came to add to it, the existing sum we had collected through the tenth town tax had gone."

"You were both responsible for opening the chest?"

"We were, and neither of us had the opportunity to take the money without the other being present and seeing us do so."

"You also went with Master Tylor to add monies to his fund?"

"I did, in place of Nick."

"Why do you think that the chest was not completely raided? Why only your fund? The money for the fair and for the bear and the disposal of rainwater in the town, the town High Cross fund - all these monies remain in the chest."

"I cannot explain it, my Lord Belvoir."

"It seems our thief does not want the town to benefit from a new Bible," I chuckled, but he did not smile.

"It is most perplexing."

"I'll continue to question all who have access to the chest...."

"All the town councillors? Surely they are above suspicion. Have you asked the priest of St. Mary's? Does he have anything to say."

"He has no key to the chest."

"No, I suppose he does not." He said, looking down at his fine red boots.

"So you were in town when the dairymaid was murdered, Master Fuller?"

"I think you will find that I arrived shortly afterwards. I am not early in the town on market day."

"Ah. Can anyone vouch for you?"

"Vouch sir? I need someone to vouch for me?"

"I am asking everyone who knew her. Everyone must have a shield to protect them, sir." I said.

"Hmm... then I suppose half a dozen tenters and vatmen and my man Pounder will tell you I was in my office."

I scrutinised his face. He was completely blank.

"Very well, I shall ask. You did know her did you not?"

"Not well, no. To say I knew her would be an exaggeration. I saw her about the road opposite the yard selling her milk, but that's all. I have no need to... mix with such people my lord."

"And the bearman?"

"No sir, I had never set eyes on him. I do not approve of such frivolities and had no opportunity to see him."

"And yet you helped Tylor with the bear fund and I don't think that Gilbert Cordwainer said that you were amongst those who voted against getting a bear for the fair."

"A favour for Nick... and...," Fuller shifted his rear end on the seat of the stool, "I voted for the bear because that is what the town wished... not myself. I put my own wishes aside, sir."

"Commendable, Fuller." I said with a slight sarcastic tone which he missed.

He acknowledged my words with a small bow of his head.

"Thank you Master Fuller." He rose and made for the door.

"Oh. There is one more thing. Do tell me, when the miller here fills up the large pool by damming the river and diverting it, how do you manage at the fulling mills with the reduced flow?"

I saw his nostrils flare and his smooth shaven face became a blank mask once more.

He pulled the hat from his belt, teased it into shape and jammed it on his head, pulling the brim down over his forehead.

"We have enough water to make our hammers work."

"But surely the lessening of the flow makes them much slower?"

Fuller pulled his cloak around him. "Not noticeably. If we do need extra power, the men will pound the cloth themselves."

"I can imagine that is a really popular job, Fuller," I scoffed.

Fuller turned back to look at me and his contempt was palpable. "The men do as they are told, my lord. Or they do not have a job. At all."

He opened the door.

"Good day."

Why did I feel I had just been spat upon?

I sighed and made notes on a small piece of birch bark paper I always carried with me when taking charge of an investigation like this. I would make proper notes later when I returned home, on parchment.

Return home I did. I was rather fed up of sleeping on Johannes' parlour floor, even if the mattress was comfortable. I wanted to be with my wife, Lydia and my children.

Little did I know that in less than a week I would be back in Marlborough at the request of the town reeve for there had been another murder.

*****

"I turn my back for one moment!"

"One week, Aumary," said Nick, who could now, for short periods of time get out of bed and sit in a chair.

"Well… a short time then."

Nicholas smiled but it was not a full smile, for the situation did not warrant it.

"April has been a bad month for the corn mill, Aumary. No income from it for days and days and five deaths in its vicinity. I'm thinking of becoming a shoemaker aren't I, Gil?"

Gilbert Cordwainer also smiled. "Aw c'mon Nick. It's not as bad as all that. That court case didn't lay you so low surely. Besides, I'm full up with apprentices. Can't take you on."

I chuckled. "So what do we have that I must come hot-trod from Durley on a miserable spring day? What important things have removed me from my paperwork?"

The two councillors looked at each other.

"The old dame," said Nick, "the one who lives next door to me. She's dead."

"Oh, no." I put my hand to my forehead. "I spoke to her only last week."

"She was found this morning in her home."

"How did she die?"

122

"Beaten to death with a stick," said Nick, "by all accounts."

"Have you asked Johannes to come and look?"

"Yes. He will be here soon."

"Who was the first finder?"

"I was" said Gilbert shakily.

*****

Johannes, Gilbert and I made our way down the lane and into the small home of the woman who had complained about the fullers and tanners.

Two of Nick's men stood guard on the door and moved aside as we entered.

"Why were you here, Gilbert?" I asked looking down at the bloodied corpse of the tiny woman who still clutched her distaff in her right hand.

"She had lamented about it to Nick. She explained to us that Geoffrey Belvoir had told her to make a complaint about the tanners and the fullers. I was here to get the truth from her because I look to this part of town. But before I could, someone silenced her."

"Yes, she meant me. She thought I was my father." I grimaced as I saw the damage done by this frenzied attack.

"I cannot think this is about silencing an old lady for telling tales about name calling, can you?"

Gilbert shook his head slowly.

Johannes hunkered down by the body.

"Beaten repeatedly with a stick of some kind. Poor old soul. Her little body would not take such treatment. I would not be taken aback if the beating didn't cause her heart to fail her. The shock of it might make it stop. There are a few bones broken, I think."

He lifted her chin and blood trickled from her mouth.

"And it wouldn't surprise me at all if a rib wasn't broken and pierced her lung. That would bring about death fairly quickly in one so old."

123

"How old was she Gil?"

"I have known her all my life and she has always been old. She might even have been ninety."

Gil and I stood looking down at the poor woman with great respect.

Johannes removed the distaff and gave it into my hand.

There was a gathering of wool at the top and the thread she had spun was collected on a loose spindle. This seemed a newly carded dressing for she had had little time to fill it.

"Ah. What's this?" I asked him.

The doctor stood and took the implement from me again.

"Looks like she managed to injure her attacker."

"This is not her blood?" I asked.

"On the very point of the distaff? She scratched someone with it. The point is quite lethal."

"Pity she didn't stick him with it" said Gilbert moodily.

"No sign of the weapon?"

"No."

Johannes screwed up his eyes. "Do you see what I see?" We crowded round. "Blood, yes but also hair and what looks to me like a scrape of skin."

Gilbert took the tiny fragment of hair from the tip of the distaff, laying it on the waxed tablet he took from his cotte.

"Fair hair. Or maybe silver grey. Hard to tell with such a small amount," he said.

"So we look for a man with fair or grey hair, who has a bloody scratch to the hairline?"

"How many men do we have in this investigation, who are blond, grey or white?"

"Well, that rules me out," said Gilbert jauntily.

"Aw c'mon, old friend," I said, "It's a known fact the first finder did it. Always does."

Gilbert smirked. "Not this time, Sir Aumary," he chuckled. Then he grew serious.

"I cannot think right now but I will apply my brain to a list as soon as I get home and send it down to you."

"I'll do the same. And Gil?"

"Yessir?"

"We need to tell the coroner."

"Oh, must we inform that pompous old windbag?"

"Gilbert Cordwainer!" I chuckled "Sir Hugo Ramsbury is a fine fellow. He is related, loosely you understand, to our Durley priest, Crispin."

"That doesn't make him less of a pompous old...."

"Old he is not, pompous he may be, windbag he most certainly is. But sadly he's all we have to work with."

Gilbert sighed. "He's off somewhere else on business. I don't think he's returned yet."

"Then we shall add this information to the previous depositions we made and he can sort them on his return. Meanwhile we need to keep the hair and the distaff."

"Leave that to me, sir," said Gilbert.

Gilbert told me the priest of St. Mary's had been quickly on the scene and her soul had been saved from the devils which, they tell us, clamour to drag it down to hell with them, soon after death.

I knelt by the body of the old crone who, it was said, was a witch.

"I am so sorry old woman," I said, "if this has happened because you were seen talking to me, I shall never forgive myself." I made the sign of the cross over her and then for good measure over myself.

I got up and looked around the cottage.

This was no robbery for there were a few pennies, not many but some, tucked under the mattress of her bed, kept in a twist of cloth. The place was tidy save from where she had struggled and fallen.

125

She had food in a crock on the table. There was very little a thief might want here, but people had been killed for a loaf of bread or the cloak that covered their body. Hers was still on a peg behind the door. A serviceable, but old, rusty brown blanket like garment with two black patches.

I took it down and laid it reverently over her.

"Go in peace. I make you a promise. Your killer will hang. He will," I said.

I spoke to the two millermen outside. "The body can be released now. Is there any family, do you know?"

One shook his head. "Outlived them all, did old Gytha. Husbands, two of them, four children and four grandchildren and a few great grandchildren."

"No wait!" said the miller who I'd met the day of the fire. I think he was called Alfred Hathaway.

"Isn't there a great grandson still?"

There was a lot of shrugging and idle speculation and we got no further. "Well, if there is he never comes to see her," said the other man.

I was glad that I could put a name to the old woman.

Now I questioned her neighbours. Had anyone seen anything suspicious?

"We are all a bit jittery down here, m'lord, since we've had so many deaths on our door step. We keep indoors unless we have to go out and then when we do, we look over our shoulders first," said the woman Mistress Webber, who had looked after the remaining dairymaid.

"You heard no screams? None of you? Surely she would have cried out as she was being beaten to a mess?"

They all shook their heads.

"Does anyone know of a man who has a wound to his head... a deep scratch? Perhaps on the brow line."

"Aye" said one weaver, "I saw Grist this morning. He's a nice scratch and a shiner too."

I thanked them and passed on down the lane.

"Ho ho, Grist! Whatever happened to you?

The miller turned in the action of folding some sacks. He did indeed sport a long scratch to his hairline and a black eye. He was brown haired but in amongst those hairs there were some fine silver threads, especially at the temple where the wound was situated.

"Ah m'lord Belvoir. Yes…," he chuckled. "Teach me to walk into a dark room without a candle."

"Where was this?"

"Here sir, in the mill."

"When?"

"As I was locking up last night. Thought I'd enough light to see by… nights are getting lighter. Pah! Turned straight into one of the shattered ends of the roof beams. Lucky not to lose an eye…."

I looked carefully at his wound. "Aye, it was mighty close. You should get it seen to."

"Nah, it'll be fine in a few days, sir."

"You know of course that the old lady at the top of the lane has been murdered?"

Grist crossed himself. "Aye, poor old Gytha. Who would want to do a thing like that? Stealing from her I suppose and she surprised them."

"No, it was not a robbery gone wrong." I leaned on the mill wall. "Did anyone report any noise here last night before you locked up and went home? She must have cried out and I can't find anyone who heard anything so I don't have much idea when it happened."

"I saw her sir, outside her cott, oh, must have been as I was shutting the mill gates. Yes, that's right. I'd locked up the mill and was holding on to me head, 'cos I'd just done the damage and she was at the top of the lane talking to someone."

"Who?"

"Tsk" he shook his head "I was a bit dazed and could think of nothing else but getting back to my missus and getting me hurt fixed."

"You didn't see who it was?"

"Had his hood up and his back to me."

"As far as you could tell, was the conversation amicable?"

Grist pursed his lips. "Couldn't tell. When I turned back to go up the lane, they'd both gone. She into her house I suppose and him into the High."

"Or into her house?"

"Well yes, I suppose he could have followed her in."

"This was as it was going dark…Vespers?"

"Yes, sir."

"Thanks Grist."

I was a few feet from him when he threw down the sack he had been folding onto the pile and called me back. "Sir. I'll tell you who I think it looked like though."

"Oh?"

"That man Tylor. He'd been here all day fixing the roof. I gotta good look at him."

Grist folded his arms over his chest "Yeah. Mucky yellow tunic, mucky green capuchon, brown cross gartered hose. It looked like him."

I nodded. "Thanks."

*****

The day grew older. I sat in Nick's office and wrote down everything I knew about all the murders. I sat looking at the papers for so long I started to nod and decided to walk about town, get out into the air and ask a few more questions.

I stood at the top of Crook's Lane and looked left and right down the High Street. People were hurrying home now. The sky looked threatening so I backtracked for my cloak which I'd left in the office.

Grist came to ask if he might lock up the mill and secure the gates to the yard.

"Aye, I'm off now. I shall be at the doctor's house overnight. But I am going into Angel Yard via the river first."

As I passed the eastern end of the mill on my way to the river path I saw, in the gloom, the scribe Bullard staring up at the ravaged building.

He stared through me until something; a dog barking, a man laughing, a baby crying, brought him back to the here and now. His eyes focussed on me.

"Oh, my Lord Belvoir. It's you. I was just looking at the mill and wondering...."

"How much all this will cost to mend?"

He shrugged. "Master Barbflet is a wealthy man but...."

"Things progress though, don't they Bullard? The roof is now retiled."

"Aye. Tylor spent nearly all day here."

"Master Bullard, might I have a look at your book and your tally sticks again?"

The bookkeeper lifted the lid of the chest where the books and sticks were kept.

"Which fund do you want to examine sir?" he asked

"The bear and the Bible please."

He chortled, "Sounds as if it should be the title of a story sir. The Bear and the Bible."

"If I'm correct Master Bullard, it will make a good Marlborough story - one that might be handed down and recited for many years, over countless suppers."

Bullard creased his brow.

"And become a Marlborough legend, sir?"

"Perhaps." Bullard turned the book round to face me.

I scanned the page and took in the last amount deposited by Master Tylor, helped by the master of the fabric mills, Warin Fuller.

Then I turned a page or two and ran my finger down the columns of monies deposited by Master Tanner, with Master Fuller looking on.

"Thank you Henry," I said, "that has been most informative."

As he put the book back into its chest, I chewed the edge of my finger.

"What now?" I said to myself.

*****

The river path was boggy and I squelched my way to the lane which led to the fulling mills.

The same tenterman, Sharp, whom I'd met earlier told me that yes, Master Fuller was still here but that, as the light was fading they would be shutting up soon.

He ushered me into the largest building and scratched on an inner door, disappearing through a small gap so that I might not see into the room.

Out came Master Fuller, a little flushed. He too squeezed through the door.

"What can I do for you again, my lord?" I felt he was defensive and nervous; this man who was normally so self-possessed.

"My office?"

So the room he had been in was not his own office.

I was settled with a beaker of fine wine on a chair, the seat of which was covered with leather. I had never seen the like, except, of course, my own monk's chair at Durley. Mine was a special shape with a hood which towered over the occupant and with wings which extended around the side keeping one from draughts. Often called porter's chairs, my chair too had been made with hides tanned by Master Gerard Tanner. I had caught the idea from the king's own version of this chair kept at Rouen Castle, in Normandy.

Yes, that's right Paul. It's the one I am sitting in now.

"I'll come straight to the point sir."

"I am a straight man m'lord. I would hope you can be so with me."

"The stolen money."

"The Bible fund?"

"Yes. It isn't stolen at all is it?"

130

"I beg your pardon sir. I do not follow you."

"It is still in the chest."

"Oh no sir. There you are mistaken. Not even a halfpenny remains in the bag. It has gone. I doubt we shall ever recover it."

"I can recover it, Master Fuller, every penny."

Warin Fuller felt his way across his desk and sat in his own chair, a shocked expression on his face.

"How sir?"

"It's simple. The money was taken from the Bible fund bag, and then deposited in the bear fund bag and replaced in the chest."

Warin Fuller blinked.

"The amount taken and the amount deposited are the same to the penny, Fuller."

"That must, with all due respect Sir Aumary, to your powers of deduction, simply be a coincidence."

"I do not think so."

"Then how?"

I sipped my wine and peered at his face over the rim of my cup.

"I think the term is called 'turning a blind eye.' " I said slowly.

Fuller stood up and shouted "No sir. Indeed not."

I put down the cup and raised myself, my knuckles on his table top.

"I will leave you with my," I stopped and stared at him, "...theory."

I took the door's edge in my hands and opened it.

"If you think of anything you might like to tell me, Fuller, I shall be at the doctor's house tonight. Good day."

*****

The day was fading now. Few people were about. I made my way up Angel Lane to the High Street.

I stopped to look at the High Cross which reared above me on its three stone steps. This cross had been in this position all my life; I could not remember a time when it had not been there. I saw the wear on the steps, the crumbling masonry of the plinth. I ran my hand down the stone of the supporting column. Made of sandstone, it had not fared well in the weather.

Yes, it needed work.

Ten more steps and I would be in the alleyway between Johannes' house and the next dwelling, which if I remembered rightly, belonged to a Marlborough businessman and which was let out to a widow and her two daughters, all spinsters - spinners of wool thread.

The gap was black and the covered alley was about eighteen paces long. Five paces in, I heard a swooshing sound and was hit over the head with something hard. I remember thinking, 'oh no, not my head again.'

The rest was darkness.

Chapter Eight

I came to, to a yelling and shouting. I tried to rise but my legs were like water.

"What?"

A voice close to me said, "Smith, my lord, Simon Smith. I saw the man following you. I didn't like the look of it."

Another voice. This person who was now trying to lift me so that I might stand against the wall, said, "It's Andrew, Aumary."

Ah, my friend from the castle guard. Sir Andrew Merriman.

I lifted a hand to the back of my head. There was blood there, of that I had no doubt.

Johannes, alerted by the yelling, came round the corner with a candle and together Andrew and he got me walking and dragging into the kitchen.

They staggered with me to the nearest bench and Agnes, a look of horror on her face, turned to the kitchen fire to begin to warm some water to bathe my wound.

I do not remember much of that evening for I was in and out of consciousness but I do remember the conversation between Andrew and Smith about the man who hit me and I heard them mention that Andrew's companion, one of the soldiers from the garrison, and the father of one of Gilbert's apprentices, Castleman, had given chase.

He came back in one of my lucid moments and shook his head. "Too dark. Lost him in The Marsh."

Andrew, Smith and Castleman had been at Smith's house in the late afternoon. Castleman and Smith were cousins it seemed and Andrew had tagged along, for Smith and he shared a name day.

They had been celebrating over a jar or two and the two soldiers had been making their way back to the castle, before the curfew, when Smith saw my attacker.

From the front of his smithy Simon had seen my assailant creeping up behind me and had run across the road, closely followed by the other two.

I have a feeling that had they not been there, I too like Gytha, would have been beaten to a bloody mess.

As it was, only one blow was landed.

Johannes looked at my wound and pronounced it sore but not life threatening.

"Enough to fell you in the darkness and to strike again at the rest of you when you were down, I think."

I was feeling very drowsy, but I managed to give my thanks to my rescuers.

"Aye, if Simon had not been so vigilant, we should have been looking for a new constable tomorrow," said Andrew.

"Whom have you annoyed then, Aumary?" asked Johannes, as he applied a salve to the back of my head and strapped a pad to it.

"Would you like a list?"

"Oh dear."

"Like us to go and take a few into our cells sir, pending you asking them a few questions?" asked Castleman.

I laughed and it hurt. I had obviously bashed a rib on the way down and had a terrible pain in my right knee. Where I'd landed I suppose.

"No, leave them to stew. Usually when that happens they make a mistake and we can catch them." I closed my eyes.

"Happy nameday, Andrew and you too, Simon."

Then I fell asleep.

*****

Johannes looked at my wound the following day and told me I had a hard head.

I told him he was a hard man. He did not argue.

The pain only returned if I moved, but move I must, so after a meagre breakfast of small ale and white bread, I managed to shrug into my clothes, (Agnes had thoughtfully cleansed them of the blood) and I carefully walked outside to the yard, holding onto the wall as I went.

I sat on the bench outside the kitchen door and waited for the world to stop lurching.

Once the ale and bread had settled my stomach, Johannes came out with one of his willow bark preparations and after the bells had rung for terce I was feeling much better.

I ambled down the High Street and reached Crook's Lane just as Gilbert was beetling up with his youngest daughter, Cassie.

"Ah, Sir Aumary, the list... men with blond or silver hair." He gave me a slip of bark paper.

"Aw, you don't look too good. Andrew told me what happened last night. Bad business. Do you know who it was?"

"No. Castleman chased him into the Marsh."

"Dark down there, sir. And talking of dark... Cassie here has something to say to you."

Cassie ducked behind her father's legs.

"Aw c'mon lass, Sir Aumary won't eat you. It's about when it was going dark last night."

Cassie looked up at her father as if he was an idiot. "I can tell him," she said, but did not move, implying it would be in her own time.

"She was here at the Barbflet house playing with Adelind till late yesterday evening." Adelind was Nick's daughter.

Young Cassie jumped up and down and flapping her hands said, "I can tell it... I can tell it!"

Gilbert's eyes rose to Heaven and his lips moved silently. I chuckled.

"Right Cass, tell me your news."

"There were two men."

"Two men?"

"Yes, and they were pushing and shoving each other. Fighting."

"Where was this?"

"I saw it," she said, "out of the back window." She took my hand and dragged me back into the lane and round the corner. "The high one up there."

Right up at the back of Nicholas Barbflet's house was a small window which looked down onto the lane and the little house of the woman Gytha.

"They were standing here."

Here was a spot hidden from the main road and the lane. The projection of the old woman's cott from the wall of the Barbflet house would have screened the men well.

"This was late, yes?"

"I came to fetch her just before vespers, sir," said Gilbert.

"They were being nasty to each other but they were quite quiet when they shouted."

"Oh - as if they did not want to be seen or heard?"

"And one had a knife." Her eyes glistened. "They got hold of each other and one said. 'You will not!' just like that. 'You will not.'" Her imitation was in what passed for her bass voice.

I smiled.

"And then one struck the other and he fell over and then the other one ran away up the road."

"All very exciting, Cass," I said. She nodded six or seven times.

"No body, Gil?"

"No sir. Nothing, not here. No blood either."

"Did you know either man, Cassandra?"

She shook her head.

"Well, thank you for telling me. It might be just the information we need to help solve our mystery. I know it was going dark but, the two men, what did they look like?

"One was small and the other one was smaller and one had a dirty yellow tunic."

"What colour was his hair, Cass?" I asked. I looked pointedly at Gilbert.

"The same colour as his clothes. Yellow" she said.

*****

Did I think that I could go up to the Tylor's yard today with my sore head?

I sent Algar, the miller's lad, running up the hill to St. Martin's with a summons. Tylor must come to me in Nick's office at the mill.

He took his time.

He ambled in around dinner time and stood in front of me looking vacant.

Today his tunic was blue but it still sported the marks of his trade, the splodges of clay used to make the tiles and bricks he sold.

I nodded to his attire.

"You could do with an apron, Tylor."

"I have one, sir, I forget to put it on."

"Foolish of you."

"I wear it when I'm firing. Couldn't do without it then."

"Yesterday you were just as dirty with a yellow tunic. Am I right?"

"I get through a tunic a day I suppose, unless I run out of them. If I had that many, that is."

I sat behind the table.

"Tylor, I have a witness who says that you were with the old lady Gytha at the top of Crook's Lane two evenings ago. About the time she was murdered."

"Aye, I was. And had I stayed a while, she might be alive still."

I furrowed my brow. This wasn't the answer I had expected.

"What were you doing there?"

"Talking… you know… just talking."

I massaged my temples and closed my eyes.

"And what did you talk about?"

"Oh a bit of this and a dot of that. You know, as you do sir."

"No Tylor, I don't know - explain," I said firmly.

"She was berating me for not doing better at my job for a start."

"How would she know? She doesn't have tiles on her house."

"That's just what I told her, sir," he said.

"She told me that she was hoping for better things from me and that I ought still to try for the position of town reeve. I told her I didn't think I was old enough really."

"Hmm. I would agree with that," I said.

"She kept going on about me getting married. She says I was old enough for that."

"What was it to her, that you remain unmarried, Tylor?"

"Oh you know what it's like, sir, they always go on at you, the old women."

A thought struck me. I licked my lips.

"What was Gytha to you, Tylor?"

"Why, my old grannie sir. Or rather grand grannie. She's my grannie's mother. Last one left."

"Family then?"

"Yeah sir, my mother's mother's mother."

"Ah. I see."

I looked into his face "I am so sorry for your loss."

He shrugged. "Like I say, she was the last one left - nearly ninety and a bit touched if you know what I mean. But she didn't deserve to be reduced to pulp though, sir, did she?"

"No. I spoke to her a week before she died. Did she say anything to you which might suggest that she was frightened or thought that she was in danger?"

The tiler shook his blond head. "No sir. It was mostly about me. That day she was being bossy. As she often was."

"Have you any idea who might have killed her?"

A strange look passed over the tiler's face. "No sir. None."

I sighed and sat back.

"So who did you argue with last night, near your grandam's cottage?"

"When sir?"

"Going dark... not quite completely black. You were seen again. Whom did you fight with? I see you have a nice scratch to your head. That wasn't done in your tile making I'll be bound."

"No sir, I was scratched by one of my dogs. Got scratches to my legs too." He pulled up his brown hose and sure enough there were some claw marks on his knee

"He jumps up does Archer. Caught me a blow with his claw. Hurts it does."

"I'd go to the apothecary with it. Things like that can turn very nasty."

"Me old mam will see to it no doubt."

"Wait a moment, Tylor. You tell me that your grandam's mother was the last one. Who suddenly is this 'mam'?"

Tylor sighed. "She lives with me. Me old mam... my father's wife."

"Ah… a second marriage?"

"Right sir."

People's families were so convoluted.

"So you deny fighting with anyone on the lane that night?"

"I do sir."

I sighed.

"Now about the funds for the bear?"

Tylor shifted sideways and shook his head, lifting his shoulder. "Aw sir, we've been over all this."

"Yes, we have and I am not satisfied."

"Oh?"

"You know what is going on, Tylor, and I think I do too. Though why, I don't know, except...."

I was getting convoluted myself now.

"The money missing from the Bible fund matches exactly that which you deposited in the bear fund."

"No! It never does? Well," he laughed. "What a coincidence."

"It's no coincidence, Tylor. You took it and put it there."

Once more the young man blushed to the roots of his hair.

"Ooh no, m'lord. I couldn't do that see, because...."

"Master Fuller was watching?"

"Yessir. That's the truth of it."

"Hmm. What was in it for him, Tylor?"

"Oh no sir. You can't say that. An upright man like Master Fuller, a major man in the town, has been stealing money. No sir. He has enough money of his own. Why should he need to have money from the bear fund? He would have lawyers and such at the end of his fingertips if you accused him of that."

"I already have."

"Oh!" Tylor looked worried now. "Well, begging your pardon sir, but I think you'd better look to yourself. Master Fuller is mighty powerful in the town. He'll have the lawyers on you soon as spit, sir."

"He may do as he wishes, Tylor. I have a writ from the king which is more powerful than anything a fuller can come up with."

Tylor was silent and his face drained and pale.

"Put it back Tylor, and we shall say no more. I have it on good authority that you will not be considered for election to the council next year. Forget about the town reeve post. You are wasting your time."

For the first time Tylor's face took on an angry and thwarted look.

"Maybe I won't, m'lord. But Master Fuller is mighty powerful. If he's the next town reeve, and I think he will be, I would be careful if I were you."

I chuckled and shook my head, which hurt.

"I am quaking in my boots, man."

I stood to open the door.

"Found that dog yet?"

"No sir," said the man sullenly, narrowing his eyes at my apparent insouciance.

When he was gone, I rubbed the back of my head. I wasn't quite as unperturbed as I sounded.

*****

I slept the rest of the day in Johannes' parlour. The sounds of the street faded away and I fell into a sleep so deep I did not even dream.

Johannes said he came in once or twice to check on me and make sure I was still alive. I did not even hear the squeak of the door as it pitched on the flag stoned floor, which it did in damp weather.

At last refreshed, I awoke and poked my head around the kitchen door.

"I could murder a cup of ale, Agnes."

She chuckled silently and fetched me one from the barrel kept in the little lean-to by the back door.

"No heads in this one I hope?" She laughed her silent laugh and shook her brown curls.

I realised as I said it that I was still no further on with the murder of the bearward; the death which had set all this off.

I sat with the piece of bark paper which the cordwainer had slipped into my hand after I had been hit on the head.

He had scribbled a series of names onto it. Those involved in this inquiry who all sported silver grey or blond hair.

The favourite of my suspects was first on the list - Eustache Tylor.

Gabriel Gallipot was silver haired too, as was Giles Thatcher. He was most definitely white haired.

I noticed Warin Fuller on the list and tried to picture his hair under his fancy bonnet. He was greying at the temples. So was Master Tanner.

Grist had some grey hairs, yes. Master Bullard was brindled like a wolfhound and young Milward owned a fine head of blond hair.

Then came Godwine Pounder, the fuller's man.

I stared at the list and tried to apply my usual logic to it. A long time ago my brother's tutor a Master Quimper, had debated with me about the Roman philosophers of old. He was a very learned man and he told me about a lawyer called Cicero who, when defending a man in court, had come up with the phrase, 'cui bono' - who benefits.

This meant finding out who had a motive for a crime. It was a phrase that was used either to suggest a hidden motive or to indicate that the party responsible for something might not be who it appears to be at first.

Who, in my bunch of blond men, had a motive to firstly, kill the bearward, let alone put his head in the barrel? Then to murder two millers by blowing up the mill, then a dairymaid and finally a daft old woman?

Search as I might I could see no connection. That exercise sent me back to my bed early that evening with a headache.

This time I did dream. Everyone I knew here in Marlborough and associated with these murders were, in this creation, coming and going and they all of them had blond hair, regardless of their colour in real life. They all had scratches to their heads.

Every one of them plunged their hands into the millpond where the water was perilously high and in danger of spilling over the wall. Their hands came out red with blood.

"Cui bono?" I kept asking them, but they all shook their heads and smiled sweetly.

Finally the chest in the crypt loomed into view and I saw the bear Isabella, dipping her paws into the money within and growling fiercely. Up trotted Tylor's white dog Aura, (well I assumed it was her for I'd never seen her), with a Bible in her mouth and a fight ensued. I woke trembling and realised the noise I'd heard was not the snarling of the dog and the growling of the bear but two jackdaws on a roof nearby, squawking at each other. Above this, the beautiful melody of a blackbird singing on Johannes' roof above me brought some quiet to the world and I threw my legs out of bed, sat and ran my hands through my hair.

"Ouch." I had forgotten about my wound.

Today I would examine again all those people who were out and about the evening of the old woman's murder and all those who had fingers in the pie of the money chest. Even the most esteemed council member would not evade me.

I wandered down to the mill and watched the carpenters on the lower floor fitting out the interior again.

The beam on which Grist had, he'd said, knocked his head, was sawn off; the pegs were knocked out, the beam removed and another fitted in.

As it came out, I asked to look at it. There was a sliver of skin and a globule of brown blood on the jagged end.

No doubt. Someone *had* hurt themselves on this.

Grist had been hurt here at the mill. Tylor had said it was his dog who damaged his head. So whose blood was on the end of the distaff belonging to the old woman Gytha? I resolved also to walk about today and look at the men involved in this puzzle and find those with wounds to the head.

I started at the mill.

The first person I saw was the blond haired Milward.

"How are you now, young man?" I asked, " Recovered from your ordeal?"

Milward bobbed his head and took off his coif. His head was whole, there was no recent scratch or bruise. Just the scar of the old one sustained when the mill had been blasted. His hands were healing too.

"Thank you m'lord. I have but... but it's hard...."

"Aye, the memory will ever be with you, I know. However, it will fade with time." And I touched him gently on his back.

"Who else is about?"

"Master Bullard should be up, sir, and Master Grist. Hathaway and Wryghte are looking to finish the wheel today, though it won't be installed until the workings are made right."

"Of course."

"I think Waterman is about but he will be waiting on the word of the millwrights."

I had forgotten about that young man, but his hair was a light auburn, the colour of autumn bracken.

"He is responsible for the wheel mostly, see and the sluices."

"Where's Bullard, Thomas?"

"In his office, sir, I expect."

I wandered off in that direction, scratched on the door and opened it.

As I passed through the door, and turned to look at the table, I stepped back in shock for there was Bullard lying, his head turned sideways on his table, red blood seeping from the side of it. My heart lurched.

"No!" I cried.

The man awoke suddenly and snorted.

"Henry... Henry." I leapt up to the table and took him by the shoulder.

His groggy eyes fixed on me slowly.

"Oh my! M'lord Belvoir."

"Are you all right man?"

"Aye...," he grimaced. "I must have fallen asleep. Goodness! Is it morning?"

"Aye, probably the third hour."

"Oh... now look what a mess I've made."

Red ink had spilled everywhere from an upturned inkwell on the top of his table, close by his head. Luckily there was no damage to any document and no ink stained Bullard's hair.

"I thought... oh well, never mind" I said.

I went over to his stored and covered jug of ale and poured for him. "Here, drink this.

What do you use red ink for, Henry?" I asked.

He sipped. "Oh for cancelling or highlighting or adding notes. Not often used but... I have it on my desk. It's fearfully expensive" and he tutted, ever mindful of the money he might have caused his employer to lose.

"Had you cause to cancel anything yesterday, as it was close at hand so you tipped it over when you fell asleep last night?"

"Aye," said Henry Bullard, rubbing his sore neck and stretching his upper back, "I have been here all night. Erm yes, I think I cancelled a transaction yesterday, drew a red line through it."

"The bear fund?"

Bullard looked surprised. "No, m'lord. It was a mill matter. Master Nicholas' business."

"Ah."

Bullard ran his gnarled hands through his hair. His head too was whole. No marks.

"Well, off to your ablutions Henry," I said. "You did give me a fright seeing you there with what looked like blood pouring from your head."

"Sorry, sir, I'm getting old and I work late. I get tired. I should be more careful."

"I'm just glad you are alive, Henry. Oh before you go... no one has been to you recently to record anything from the council money chest?"

"No sir. Not in the last few days."

"Thanks Henry," I said and watched him shuffle to his room.

So young Tylor had not yet been to record the money. Would he bother?

*****

Master Tanner was supervising the rolling of a hide which he told me was destined for Master Cordwainer up the High Street.

"Business is good then, Gerard?"

"Aye, it's good. But you didn't just come here to ask me about the sale of my hides to dear ol' Gilbert, now did you, sir?'

"No." I chuckled "Any men in your yard with a wound to the head yesterday, Gerard?"

The tanner pursed his lips. "Is this about poor old Gytha? The old crone you talked about last time?"

"Yes. She wounded her attacker on the head. Any blond or silver haired men here, Master Tanner? Or men going grey?"

"Well, there's me," he laughed, taking off his coif and ruffling his hair. "But no wound to the head. The last one the wife gave me has healed."

I chuckled. "Mistress Tanner wouldn't hit you thus and I know it."

"Aye. She takes much from me and never complains." He jammed on his coif again. "Have I any grey'uns?" He scratched his chin. "Peter Reading... his hair is prematurely grey, though he's only a young lad."

He looked around. "There he is now." He beckoned the young man over but it was not him.

"And there's Philbert Goodfellow... but he was out at Ramsbury to the Durnsford estate all the days you are inquiring about. I sent him with some hides."

"Thank you. Oh, by the way, I think I have discovered how the money from the Bible fund went missing."

I told him of my idea. "But keep it to yourself for now."

He shook his head. "I can't believe it of Fuller - Tylor yes... but Fuller? We have had our differences it's true but...."

"No other explanation. Unless it is pure coincidence and I don't believe in those. There might of course be a spare key, but again, there has been no opportunity to make one, has there?"

"Why would Warin want, as you say, to turn a blind eye?"

I shrugged. "Somehow there must be money to be made."

"Aye well, Warin is as fond of money as the rest of us, but break the law for it? It's inconceivable," said the tanner.

"People may have been murdered for it, Gerard."

"Do you think we'll get our Bible fund back, m'lord?"

"I hope so, my friend," I said.

Next I found myself at the fulling yard.

Master Fuller was not there and I was directed to the room from which he had emerged yesterday. It transpired it was the office of his overseer, Godwine Pounder.

Today, the man was all sweetness.

"What can I do for you my Lord Belvoir?" He grimaced, rather than smiled.

"I'm looking for a man who may have been at the top of Crook's Lane late the night before last. One who has fair hair and who might have a graze to his hairline."

Pounder clenched his teeth. "So you want to see how many men we have who answer your description. Is that it, m'lord?"

"Yes." Try as I might I could not see Pounder's hair for his coif was pulled down on his forehead and he wore a small hood.

"Then let's go and look."

A wind had blown up since I had been indoors and it ruffled the leaves of the few trees around the yard.

As we walked he listed the men who were blond or silver haired.

"There's Waulker and Tucker, one fair, one grey. And one tenterman, name of Sharp, he's fair."

"Yes, I met him the other day."

Pounder turned to look at me, his thin cheeks sucked in.

"Did you?"

He walked on. "And what did he have to say, sir?"

I chuckled.

"He told me that I'd need to get my cloak mended, as though you might clean it, you can't mend holes."

"Ahh." I am sure the man relaxed at that.

Pounder yelled "Waulker! ... here!"

147

The man came running over from his task of handing a wet length of material to a tenterman.

"Take off your hood when in the presence of the King's man."

The man pulled down his green hood and bowed. "Sir."

"Visited the top of Crook's Yard recently have we, Waulker?" asked Pounder.

"No sir. Not at all."

"Walked past it?" I asked. "Late two nights ago?"

"No sir my home lies the other way in The Marsh."

"Right, get back to work."

The man's head was whole and his receding hairline shiny.

We passed the edge of the tenterground.

Two men were lifting a piece of cloth onto the hooks. One was Sharp. He wore a dirty yellow tunic with brown leggings and his sleeves were pushed up to his elbows.

"Sharp," said Pounder.

The man turned and beamed. "Hello again sir. Come to fetch your cloak have you?"

"No, he's come to talk to you."

"Me?"

The wind buffeted the cloth and nearly took it from the man's hands. His hair was drawn back from his forehead by the gust. There to the hairline was a livid scratch.

Pounder looked at me and smirked.

"Where were you two nights ago on vespers, Sharp?" I asked.

"Going dark sir…?"

"Yes."

"In the Green Man, sir."

"Anyone see you there?"

"Everyone, sir."

"Why would everyone see you?" I said, folding my arms over my chest and

148

tipping my head sideways in a gesture of disbelief.

"On account of the noise he was making, m'lord" said the other tenterman.

The cloth flapped again and Pounder said irritably "Get that fixed, then we'll talk."

The two tentermen between them stretched the cloth on a wooden frame, from one set of hooks to the other and pulled. They repeated this with the other two sides. This seemed quite an easy task but I was told by Pounder that just the right amount of pressure must be applied for the cloth not to shrink and not to be too much thinned by the process.

Once finished Sharp came back to me.

The other dark haired tenterman was sent on his way.

"Noise, Sharp?" I asked

"Aye sir... drunk I was."

"So early in the afternoon?"

"It was raining. We were let off early."

"And so there you are drunk in the Green Man, in full view of all your friends, when someone was being done to death at the top of Crook's Yard by an unknown assailant. An assailant who was wearing a dirty yellow tunic and brown hose."

Sharp went very still. "No, not me, sir."

"How did you get that wound, Sharp?"

His hand went up to his forehead.

"Ah... I erm...."

"Fighting I expect, eh Sharp?" asked Pounder. He too had folded his arms over his chest.

"He isn't just called Sharp because he works with sharp pins. Has a temper don't you Sharp?"

"He called me a bastard."

"Well, you are!" replied Pounder leaning forward. "No word of a lie. Yer mother was not married to yer father."

"Aye, well."

"Who hit you, Sharp? And who saw them do it?"

Sharp looked at his feet. "They all saw. It was Glanville Lovell."

"Ah yes. I know the man well," I said.

"That one's trouble," said Pounder.

"I know it. All the way from the manor of Oare. Had him in my gaol once."

I told Sharp he could get back to his work and walked with Pounder to the next man.

Tucker was a small man who worked the paddles of the fulling vats. The noise here made conversation difficult but one look at the man's head told me it was not him.

I was accompanied to the gate by Master Pounder.

"Can you please let me know when Master Fuller returns to the mill? I need a further word with him," I said.

"Yes, sir."

Another gust of wind stronger than the rest lifted Pounder's hood from his head and his coif went bowling across the muddy grass of the tenting ground.

There on his temple was a nasty tear and a snatch of hair was missing.

He followed his hood and caught it, jamming it back on his head before he reached me.

I said nothing and pretended I hadn't seen it, but he knew I had and his eyes were wary.

I wished him well and left.

As I walked up Angel Lane, I could feel his eyes on the back of my head. I turned at the top and acknowledged him.

He did not wave back.

Chapter Nine

So, Godwine Pounder too had a wound to the head. One he was not volunteering to explain.

I would deal with him later.

Meanwhile, I needed to speak to the priest of St. Mary's just to see if the fund had been replaced and whether Tylor had reported it to Master Bullard.

I found the priest this time in the church, on his knees before the altar. I waited a while, saying a few prayers of my own for my dead first wife and for my little Geoffrey, dead these many years and buried, not in this churchyard but in my own at Durley.

Father Torold got up from his knees unsteadily and arranged his robe around him. He saw me then and beamed.

"My Lord Belvoir. I am honoured. Twice in a few days. We shall not see you again for a year now, I expect."

I laughed and my laughter rang around the rafters of St. Mary's.

"Sadly not a private visit, Father Torold."

"Aye, I know. You are a very busy man. I now have four bodies buried or to bury in my churchyard as a result of …."

He looked up quickly. "I hear from Master Johannes that you were attacked last evening?"

"Yes, here in the church alley. Friends rescued me."

"Do you think it was connected to the business of the murders?"

"I can only think someone wants me to stop my inquiries," I said.

"You must be getting close…." The man rubbed his forehead distractedly. "What can I do for you now?"

"Has anyone been to you to open the chest these past two days?"

"No one, sir."

"Might I take a look at the place where the chest is kept? I don't know if it will help me, but it might."

"Certainly... let's go for the key."

We searched his small home but the key was not on its hook.

"No one ever takes it without me being present, sir" said the priest, almost in tears. "It's unheard of."

"Maybe they came and you weren't here."

"They always come and find me. Always." It's not often I am very far away and this isn't a big town even if I am. Someone always knows where I am to be found."

I furrowed my brow. "All the councillors know where the key is kept. Does anyone else?"

"No one else has any cause to go into the crypt room, Sir Aumary."

"Hmm" I nodded.

"Let us go and see if it's unlocked or if someone is there now."

Someone was there. He was stretched over the chest on his back. His eyes stared into the blackness of the barrelled roof.

Torold crossed himself and leapt into action, mumbling the rites for the dead and making the sign of the cross over Eustache Tylor.

A small candle was still burning in the dark space. I touched the tiler's hand. He was not quite cold.

When Father Torold had finished I asked him how long he had been in the church.

"Enough to say a couple of prayers perhaps. I stayed after sext."

"And before that?"

"I was out in the community from dawn, sir."

"Do you ever lock your door, sir priest?"

"Jesus never locked his door against the needy, Sir Aumary," he said, "and neither do I." I did not like to point out that nowhere in the Bible, did it say, that our Lord owned a property with a door to lock.

"So Tylor might have come fairly early, to get the key when you were out and might have been here a while for a new candle to burn down so far?"

I was rapidly running through my suspects now my chief one had been done to death.

"I must ask Johannes how long he thinks Tylor has been dead. This will help me find answers to where everyone was located when he was killed."

"I see your meaning, sir." He passed his hands over his face; that gentle, kind man and when he looked up at me there were tears in his eyes.

"Please, my Lord Belvoir, find out who is doing this. I am used to death. But this." He shook his head.

He looked up at me quickly.

"The devil is busy in Marlborough, sir; so many souls."

I grasped his shoulder with my right hand and gave it a little shake.

"You have saved them all sir priest. Every one."

*****

Johannes got up from his knees.

"Dead a couple of hours only I would say, though it's colder down here. As I have said before, cold delays the onset of the rigor, though I do not know why."

"The manner of death, the same as the bearward and dairy maid?"

"Yes, a blow with a knife to the spine. I suspect he was not anticipating the blow and had his back to his murderer. Then he was tipped over."

"It's a very exact way of killing, Johannes."

"Aye it would take practice."

"Immediate death?"

"Yes, I think so. High to the neck. Severs the bones and the line in them."

"What did the Tyler know? Why had he to be silenced?"

"Six people dead for a bear fund? I think not," said Johannes.

"I must report to Nick and to Master Gallipot and then I am going into the

153

Green Man to see what Glanville Lovell was doing there the other afternoon."

"Not him again," he said, then added, "would you like me to go up the hill to Gallipot? I have business with him this afternoon?"

"Would save my legs Johannes."

"I will tell him then."

"I'm for Nick's. I'll see you later. Father Torold will take care of the body. The coroner has still not returned. He will have a whole room full of corpses to contend with when he comes home."

"Serve him right for going down county."

Gilbert was with Nicholas Barbflet when I arrived and the two of them were apprised of the death of the youngest town councillor.

Gil sat down heavily on a carved chest in Nicholas' room and stared at the floor.

"My God, Aumary," said Nick. "We had him down as the villain, did we not?"

"Not a murderer, but yes, a thief."

"But the yellow tunic, the scratch to the face?" said Gilbert.

"Not the only one with yellow costume or scratches," I replied.

"What is happening to our nice little town?"

"It's growing. It's expanding. It's becoming more organised. There will always be an element who...."

"Ruin it for the rest," said Gilbert.

I shrugged. "I am off to the Green Man to check a story. I'll keep you informed."

I turned for the door.

"Aumary," said Nick and Gil together,

"Yes?" I said. They locked eyes.

"Take care."

*****

The Green Man was a drinking house three quarters of the way up the High Street from the castle opposite the shambles and by the entrance to Angel Lane.

It had been only two years since the man who owned the building had decided to open it as a place where ale could be had all day. He brewed it on the premises and unlike the alewives who brewed occasionally and let the town know by setting a green branch at their eaves when their ale was ready, this place brewed every day. Other brewers sold to folk taking the ale home only and had no facilities for drinking in their building. The place was named for the owner, Master Green.

The ale was not of the best, I'd heard. In fact I'd sampled their small beer a while ago when my men and I had visited prior to a horse race up on the downs.

This time I ordered a pint of the strong ale and sat in a corner to see who might be in the place.

A few faces I knew stared back at me as if I should not be there at all, spying on them.

I smiled at them all and sipped my ale.

I looked into the furthest corner. There was Grist. He held up a hand.

I took up my mug and threaded through the wooden tables and stools to sit beside him, my back to the wall.

He stood up. "Good day, my lord."

"And to you, Grist. I didn't have you down as a drinking man in a place like this."

Grist chuckled "No sir. Nor I you" he added, "A rest from my labours and I'm here to keep an eye on my brother in law."

I looked at him under lowered brows. "Your brother in law?"

"Hmm. Sister's husband. He comes in here and spends too much time and money. I pitch him out when I think he's had enough."

"Is he here?"

"Not yet."

155

"What does he do this brother in law of yours?"

Grist smacked his lips and put down his ale. "Fuller, sir."

"Ah... at Master Warin Fuller's mill?"

"Yessir."

Grist shifted to make a little more room between us as if he might not be allowed to sit too close to one of the 'quality'.

"Why are you here, sir?"

"No, you're right Grist, it's not for the ale."

"Pretty dire stuff, m'lord."

"No, I am here to make inquiries about a fight between a fuller called Sharp and a man called Glanville Lovell, a horseman from Oare."

"Lovell I don't know, but Sharp I do."

"Said to be sharp by nature too?"

"In his cups he is. Nice man sober."

Grist lifted his hand and hailed his brother in law as he entered the drinking house.

The man hovered as if he felt we were not to be interrupted.

"No, please sit. You might be able to help me," I said.

"If you are sure, sir...."

A pint was put in front of the man and he downed almost half of it in one swallow.

"This is the constable for the county, Eth," said Grist, "Sir Aumary Belvoir, Warden of Savernake. So, you mind your manners. He's looking into the murders and such round about. Doesn't normally come to places like this, with us sort of folk. He knows the King, you know."

"Oh doesn't mean I don't enjoy being with folk like you, Grist" I said, smiling.

He snorted down his nose and took another sip of ale.

"What do you know about Sharp your colleague, then, Eth?" I asked. I assumed the man was named for the old Saxon king, Aethelred.

"All right. When sober. Devil when drunk, m'lord."

"Bit like you then, Eth" said Grist, wiping his sleeve over his mouth.

Eth glowered.

"Nothing like me. I don't get violent."

"Only yer mouth."

"Did he get violent two days ago, when it was raining a lot and you fullers were laid off?"

"Only the tenters were laid off. Us fullers were kept going."

"Ah, so you are an indoor man."

"Yes, m'lord. Erm... I weren't in here then, but I heard he had an argument with a man from outta town."

"Lovell?"

"Yeah him, sir. He's often in here."

"And it came to blows."

"It did... no real harm. Just a little blood-letting and then the landlord threw them out."

"Thank you, Eth, that is just the information I needed."

"You any closer to a solution m'lord?" asked Grist.

"I get closer every day, Bertrand. The more I speak to people the closer I get."

I looked carefully at Grist's brother in law. "Where do you live then Eth?"

"St. Martin's m'lord. Up the hill and...."

"Yes, I know where it is. Where exactly?"

Eth put down his mug and called for another.

"Over the river, past the tileworks, and a cottage on the left, just as you get to the big stand of trees."

I nodded. "Hear any hounds barking lately there?"

"Have I heard'em? Bloody things. Driving us mad. Begging yer pardon sir."

"Where do you think they are?"

"Back o' the tile works, sir, I'd say" Said Eth.

"Hmm. Do you know who they belong to?"

Grist and Eth looked at each other. Grist answered me as Eth's second drink arrived.

"Well, there isn't anyone out there but him and my sister and the brick works so I reckon it must be that fellow Tylor. The one who's been doing the mill roof."

"He has three dogs I'm told."

"More than that, sir." said Eth. "I reckon there's at least six a howlin' and a barkin' there. All bloody day and night."

"Then I shall go and find out," I said, "later."

More people came in through the door and the volume upped just a little.

"Why would folk need so many dogs?" asked Eth.

"Hunting, I suppose" said Grist.

"Not in my forest" I said.

"Aw no… course not" said Eth.

"Coursin' over the downs?" volunteered Grist.

Another man now joined us. I recognised him too.

"Hello Castleman. Finished your stint at the gatehouse?"

"Sir Aumary." He bowed. "Whatever are you doing here?"

"Listening to gossip. Pull up a stool and join us."

The other two nodded to him; they obviously knew him.

Soon he too had a pint of ale.

"We were talking about dogs, Castleman."

"Dogs sir? What kind of dogs… and how is the head, by the way?"

"Sore but mending. Thanks to you and Andrew."

"It was Simon really. He saw the bugg… beast."

"What kind of dogs Castleman?" I repeated, "Noisy ones." I guffawed into my ale which was nearly all gone. My! This stuff was very strong.

"We were wondering why someone would want so many dogs if they can't be used for hunting. They can't of course, as m'lord Belvoir has pointed out." said Grist.

"Forest Law prohibits dogs in the forest, all except mine and the king's.

Unless they're declawed."

"Yes. Well, the only other sport I know of where dogs are needed," said Castleman, taking a huge drink of his ale, and wiping the foam from his lips with the back of his hand, "is bears sir."

I sat up straight. "Bears, Castleman?"

"Yes, sir."

"How do you...?"

"I went to London once with the king. You remember sir, when we all traipsed...."

"Yes, yes I do... and...?"

"I went to a bear baiting. Dunno why. 'Cos the others did I 'spose. They tie the bear to a big stake and get it cross and then let hungry dogs at it. It gets a few of them before it's torn to shreds by the bigger ones. Sometimes the dogs win, sometimes the bear."

"This is for fun?"

"Wasn't much fun for me. I like dogs see."

"So do I, Castleman. I have several at Durley."

"Think this is why the dogs are there, sir?" asked Grist "Out in the shed?"

I put down my mug.

"Do you know, I think this is beginning to make sense a little now. Yes, indeed. Thank you for your company, lads."

I stood and they all stood with me.

"Yes... much more sense."

It was not until I got to the corner of Johannes' alleyway that I realised I had not paid for my ale.

*****

Serves me right. All night my stomach roiled and boiled. Not used to the dreadful stuff made by the landlord of the Green Man.

I have a delicate stomach even now you know, Paul, my scribe. I can't eat what I used to and even then... forty years ago, certain things would turn me to water. Oh no, you don't need to write that down.

So that meant that I was back and forth all night to the privy out in Johannes' yard.

There was no moon. The night was as black as the king of hell's cotte. I had to follow the wall with my hand or I would over shoot the building of the privy. It was late, after the midnight hour. I hadn't managed to get my night eyes and I peered about. No one was around.

On my third trip back, I heard a dog bark nearby, in one of the yards of the houses along Oxford Street. It was insistent and a man shouted out of an opened shuttered window, for it to be quiet. He banged the shutter closed again.

All was silent once more save for the snoring of the pig in the garden next to Johannes' house. It snuffled and grumbled and in amongst the noise was another. A slight slithering. A metallic clink.

I knew what that noise signified and keeping as close to the wall as I could I made at speed for the back door, at a crouch.

I slammed the door shut and bolted it.

Just as I did, a knife came whistling into the panel of the door. Then, the fastened shutters were rattled and the knife came through to try to dislodge the bar holding them but they were too sturdy and it failed.

In anger the person banged the shutters with the flat of his hand. This man had been waiting, simply waiting just in case I emerged. He'd definitely got his night eyes.

Johannes, in his shirt, was quickly downstairs at my cry and once voices were heard in the house, the person fled down the alleyway, with a pattering of feet.

I sat down feeling weak.

"There is no doubt, my friend," said Johannes, "that your life is in danger."

"Yes… and yours too and wee Agnes, if I stay here."

"I think from now on, it would be best if at night you stayed in the castle. They'll not get to you there."

*****

The following day saw me angrily stomping down Angel Lane to the fullers and into the office of Master Pounder.

I did not knock.

"Another murder, Pounder."

"Oh, m'lord?"

As I'd entered I'd seen his body stiffen but he soon recovered his poise. He did not ask whose murder. He slowly rose from his table.

"Your master in?"

"He's just left for Elcot, sir."

"You didn't ask who has been murdered."

"I thought if you wanted me to know, you'd tell me, m'lord."

I waited a heartbeat. "The tiler, Eustache Tylor, Pounder."

"That is very sad. Such a young man."

I faced him across his worktable. I wondered if he might pass the church on his way home.

"Where do you live, Pounder?"

"Me, sir?" He was momentarily flustered. "London Road, by the bridge, sir. Why?"

'Hmm,' I thought to myself, 'not too long a diversion from church to bridge.'

I put my hand on the pommel of my sword. "So, how did you come by the wound on your head and why didn't you mention it yesterday?"

"You did not ask me and it's such a superficial thing - caught myself on some riverside path brambles as I was going home the other evening. I should

161

have gone home the long way but... I often take the short cut along the river." He tapped his head. "Going dark; I must have been a fool to try that way."

"Might have ended up in the river."

"Aye, and me not being able to swim," he chuckled.

"Anyone see you going that way?"

"No," he stuck his thumbs into his belt. "No, I don't think so."

"Then we only have your word for it."

"I'm afraid you do, my lord," he said.

I turned on my heel and took myself off to the river bank at the rear of the fulling mills. There was indeed a very narrow path at the back of the buildings. I emerged by one of the the dyers' sheds close by the ropery and walked the boggy land at the back of the buildings, as I'd done before when examining the river bed. I reached the bridge and I clambered up the side of the weed infested bank and stood on the roadway looking along Barn Street.

I found no brambles.

I crossed the bridge and wandered a little way up London Road. No brambles here, on either side of the road. My head teeming with thoughts, I backtracked and made my way through The Marsh; so called because it was a street which was low lying and boggy; and up to the High Cross to fetch Bayard from Johannes' stable.

I was going to follow the fuller to Elcot.

*****

The mills at Elcot were a copy of those at Angel Lane, three sheds and a large tenting yard. Fuller, standing at the gate, saw me approaching, planted his feet wide and stuck his hands under his armpits as if to hug himself.

Today he was dressed in two shades of green. Still he wore the red hat and the red boots.

"Greetings, my Lord Belvoir, you are far out of Marlborough, your usual hunting ground."

'Hmm, an interesting turn of phrase', I thought.

"Master Fuller," I replied nodding as I dismounted. A tenterman came to secure Bayard. "I hunt where I must."

"Come in and take some wine."

He showed me to an office which was bigger and more comfortable than the one he used in the town. As he poured, I told him of the death of Eustache Tylor.

"Why would he be alone in the crypt without a key to open the chest?"

"I did not say he had no key."

"But I assumed that if I was not asked to accompany him, then he must not have obtained a key."

"He had taken the key from the priest's house to open the room but no other key was found on him, no."

"Puzzling."

"Why do you think he would go to the crypt, if not to open the chest?" I asked.

Fuller shrugged. "The only reason to go there was to open the chest, sir, surely?"

"Or perhaps to see someone who had asked to meet him there? He certainly knew his attacker, for he turned his back on them, suspecting no violence."

"Hmm."

"Or maybe he asked to see someone and things got out of hand." I ventured.

Warin Fuller took off his red hat, sat at his table and threaded it through his belt as he was wont to do. His head, I noticed, was unscathed.

"He did not ask any of the other councillors to accompany him?"

"I have not asked yet, but you were the councillor who had been with him before and you had a key to the chest. I thought that the same two people always went together."

"I have not been to the crypt, sir, since we found the shortfall in the Bible fund."

163

"I want to ask you about your man Pounder."

Fuller paused with his cup to his lip.

"What about him?"

"How long has he been with you?"

"He worked his way up from the bottom, sir. I have employed him these past twelve years."

"He did not join you as a very young man, then?"

"No, I believe he was apprenticed first and the place did not suit him."

"Do you know where?"

"No, I'm sorry, I don't remember, my lord."

I did not believe him.

I sipped my wine and let the silence run on. I find that if one does that, people often get jittery and nervous and fill the gap in conversation. This can sometimes be quite telling and revealing.

Fuller did not. He remained quietly unruffled.

"He has a querulous tendency, does he not? Even a violent nature?"

Fuller took in a deep breath through his nose. "I have not seen it, if he does, sir."

"Aw come, Fuller, I have seen him beat men for the wrong look."

The fuller put down his cup and told me patiently, as if I were a child, that sometimes hard discipline at work was necessary for the smooth running of an enterprise such as his

I laughed out loud. "Master Fuller, I employ four times the number of men you do, on my estate and in the forest. Do not talk to me about discipline."

For the first time Warin Fuller looked uncertain.

I stood. "I don't yet know quite what is going on here, Master Fuller but I have a feeling that you are the spider at the centre of the web, catching the little flies, the lesser men and binding them. I will have you out of your web, sir. Do not doubt it."

I left him with an open mouth.

*****

I joined Johannes for dinner and who should be there but my old companion Hal of Potterne.

"I took the liberty of calling for him, Aumary," said Johannes. "It's clear you can't be left to wander around the town alone. Someone is after your blood."

I smiled. "That's most kind of you. I must admit, as I was treading the river path this morning I thought, here's a good place for an ambush. Good to see you, Hal."

"And I you, sir. It was getting a mite borin' at 'ome, with all those babies and 'olding threads for the mistress and playing 'pick up sticks' with little Lady 'Awise."

"Nonsense Hal, you love the babies."

"I like 'em when they are sittin' up and giggling, sir. These are a mite too small for fun."

"Are all the Durley babies thriving, Hal?"

"Indeed they are, sir."

I smiled. Hal loved children but had never married. He was like a special uncle to most of the village children, especially Hawise, my daughter.

"So now we go dog hunting, Hal," I said.

"Beg your pardon, sir?"

"Up in St. Martins there is a shed, I am told, full of dogs."

"Oh. 'Oo do they belong to?"

"We aren't really sure but we shall go and look."

Chapter Ten

The tiler's workmen went on with their labours as if nothing had happened. They knew what they were doing. They'd had their instructions. The death of the master changed nothing. Someone would come and take up the reins, they thought, though they did not know who this would be. That no one would come and supervise them was unthinkable. They did not want to dwell on the fact that they could all lose their jobs. They never thought that perhaps, they would not be paid.

It took us a while to locate the shed for it was not exactly in the tiler's yard. Tylor's men pointed it out to us through the thick hedge. Finding the way to it was another matter

We followed the main road to Mildenhall, but there were no little lanes or passes through the thick hedge or the scrubby vegetation to lead us to it. We backtracked and started in the yard and walked the perimeter. We found no gate, no passageway, no lane. We stood outside the gate of the tileyard and looked left and right. The river Og wound its way around the boundary of the yard on its way north to split up into several small streams, only to join up again.

Here by the boundary and following the stream, we found a small well-trodden track through the bushes. It skirted the yard and came out in open country to the east of the enclosed brick works.

Sheltered by trees, there stood a shed from which, as we approached came growlings and whinings and a few barks. As we neared it a frantic and angry barking began.

High up at one end there was a small window, open to the elements. On my tiptoes, I peered into the shed. The smell which hit my nose was formidable. I withdrew quickly. "I can see in the gloom, I think, seven dogs. Five of them medium sized. Two small, one is lying down... perhaps dead."

"Bigger than 'Oldfast but not as big as Jocasta, Mildred or Ben?"

"The size exactly." I risked another look. "I think these might be called Alaunt Vautre by our own dear Plum, Hal." Plum was my houndsman at Durley. "Though there are a couple of smaller ones in there and I don't know what they are."

The shed was secured with a sturdy bar across the door fastened by a hanglock.

"If we are to get in, we'll need help. It would be death to just open the door and walk in. If I'm not much mistaken, these dogs are the type bred and trained for their aggression and kept hungry. The key to the hanglock must be here somewhere. Perhaps in Tylor's own shed."

"Nah," said Hal. "We don't really need a key. I gotta good look at the door. We could simply take off the 'inges, you know."

We made our way back to Tylor's yard. We searched but we could find no key.

"Must be in his purse, Sir Aumary."

"That's a possibility. Can you ride back to Durley and ask Plum to come and help us, maybe John too? If Hubert can spare some time, ask him to come and bring a length of chain and bring medium sized rope, Hal. Lots of it."

"Where will you be, sir?"

"At the shambles buying meat and calling on Gallipot. I might call in on old Wat Fisher too. And I'll look for the key. I'll see you at Johannes' house"

"Right you are, sir."

Back down the hill and into Herd Street I went and then turned right into Silver Street, the road where the Jews had their fortified houses. Master Gallipot's was a few paces up Kingsbury Hill at Chute Alley.

A little bell rang as I entered his dark and sweet smelling shop and his silver head popped around the curtain used to screen his preparation room.

"Master Apothecary."

"Sir Aumary." Coming into the shop he wiped his hands on his apron, leaving white powdery marks on the dark fabric. "Please do not say you are come to tell me of yet another misfortune. I cannot stand it... I am deputy for Nick for two...."

"No, Gabriel, nothing more has happened. I am in need of a harmless soporific which when applied to meat will make an angry dog docile. In fact, seven angry dogs docile."

Gallipot blinked. "You want to doctor some meat so that you might render some fearsome dogs harmless? Have I the right of it?"

"I have no wish to hurt them, but I must get them from a shed where they have been locked these few days. They are not in the best of moods. And they need to be fed."

Old Gallipot chuckled. This was the second time in a few months that I'd heard this usually dour man laugh and it made me smile.

"Does the owner know you are...?"

"The owner, I think is Eustache Tylor, Gabriel. He will not object."

"No, indeed not."

He put up a finger. "One moment, sir." And he disappeared into his back room. I heard some hushed voices and at last he came out with a pot in his hands.

"Valerian, Sir Aumary. DO NOT get it on your hands and ingest it yourself. Just a little, a little, mind, on some meat should sort your dogs. Not too much or the beast will never wake. It should really be done by weight of dog but since you do not know your dogs, that will not be possible."

"They are, from what I can see, yea big with two smaller ones." I held out my hands and measured the dogs in the air.

"Then we can put the smaller dogs to rest completely with a measure as small as this..." and he curled his forefinger and thumb around to show a circle. "And levelled. Just a few grains"

"The others?"

"A little more will render them sleepy but not put them out completely. Will this help?"

169

"Indeed it will. How long will it take to work?"

"Let the sun shift to the south fully, over the forest. That should give you time. Larger dogs, a little more. There must be plenty of water afterwards when they wake," said Gallipot, "they will have a raging thirst."

If they hadn't already, I thought.

"Thank you. Please send the bill to Durley."

My next visit was to the shambles where the animals were butchered. I left Bayard at Johannes' for he hated passing the slaughter pens and would buck and neigh.

In a large wooden crate supplied by Agnes, Johannes' housekeeper, I managed to stuff several pieces of bloodied meat, mostly pig and sheep. This I covered with a tied hessian cloth borrowed from Agnes. I would string this from Bayard's saddle, when the time to depart for the shed came around.

A quick walk down the High Street and along Figgins Lane and I stood in front of the Fisher house once more, though this time they were not at home. The Fisher family were old friends and had performed many tasks for me in the past. A neighbour poked her head from her own bothy and said that they had gone up to the Manton stretch of the river to fish today.

I did my own fishing in my scrip and came out with a coin.

"Madam, can you tell them that Sir Aumary Belvoir has borrowed their large net again? I will return it this evening."

She looked shocked as I put the coin into her hand and folded her fingers over it.

"Yes, m'lord. But there's no need to...."

"Thank you, mistress," I said, as I walked to the back of the building and pulled off a net drying on a rack. I folded it the best I could and marched back up the High.

Once again at Johannes', I made a detour into the church where Eustache Tylor was laid out on a bier covered with a black pall.

I pulled back the cloth. The man had been stripped and washed ready for burial. I searched round for a pile of clothes. Here they were, by a pillar, folded tidily with the purse uppermost. There were three keys: one I suspected to the outer brickyard gates, one to the master's shed and one to the dogs' shed.

I called in to Father Torold in his house, to tell him that I had raided the purse for the keys and he nodded with a mouth full of pottage. My stomach grumbled. Yes, I realised it was dinner time.

Now, I sat in Johannes' yard with a mug of ale and some bread and cheese and waited.

*****

My men came in a while later, just as I was beginning to doze and we quickly made our way up to St. Martin's and to the shed where the dogs had been imprisoned.

The first thing for us to do was doctor the meat and I did this, for I was the only one who possessed gloves with which to handle the valerian. Once done with it, I washed my gloves in the stream and laid them to dry on a bush.

We tossed the meat in through the window, hoping that each dog would obtain a piece. There was a terrible scuffling and yelping. It sounded as if the fiends of hell were fighting each other in there. Indeed the dogs were fighting and snarling. I watched through the window as each dog grabbed a piece of meat and gnawed on it, biting at any who came to steal it.

A smaller white dog, who was set upon by the others, cowered in the corner. I threw her a piece and she gratefully caught it. I could not be sure each dog had taken a measure of the valerian but hoped that if one had failed to eat enough, the net would capture him and we would be able to subdue him.

Hal fiddled with the lock. The third key unlocked the hanglock.

Whilst we waited, Hubert and Plum passed the time dangling their feet in the brook. John ate his dinner and shared it with Hal.

We waited and the sun grew lower in the sky.

171

The shed was silent.

Hal carefully opened the door.

The smell, which hit us like a punch, was atrocious. Faeces and urine and hot animals. It was worse than the tanner's yard and they used such excrement in their work process.

John and Hubert had strung a chain from two trees not far away and Plum and Hal and I went into the shed. We did not need the net.

Poor creatures. Locked up here with little food and water, they had fought each other and many dogs displayed the wounds inflicted by their companions. One dog was dead in a corner. The smallest dog had been killed. Gnawed and fought over. Her throat was torn and her leg dislocated from her body and partly eaten. Maggots crawled over the corpse. The dogs must have been so very hungry. This dog I suspected, was Tylor's old dog Fetch.

I picked up the biggest animal. Its head was pitted with old scars and the breast was almost bare of hair. Its eyelids flickered and it growled but was unable to move against me.

"That ain't bin done in there, sir," said Plum as we brought her into the light and roped her to the chain. "Them's old wounds."

All dogs were brought out and roped to the chain. We went to the yard for bowls and dishes and filled them with water from the brook.

Plum and Hubert said they would wait for the beasts to wake when we should then feed them again, this time with meat which was not tainted.

The dogs would remain here until I decided how to deal with them.

Hal and I returned to Johannes at the High Cross. John mounted his horse Fire, and turned his head for home.

"Isabella is doing nicely, sir" he said, before he left us. "She looks better every day."

"Please God we will be able to do the same for these poor beasts, John. They have been so badly treated."

"I have a feeling that it will be a harder job than the bear, sir. After all, these dogs are bred to fight."

I shrugged. "And if they realise they do not have to fight?"

John smiled. In that smile I could tell he thought me too soft and unrealistic. Perhaps I was.

*****

Hal and I spent the night at the castle in one of the guest rooms set aside for messengers and royal heralds.

Now I thought I knew in part what had been going on but I needed to sort my thoughts into some order. As usual, I sat at the table and scribbled all that I had learned in the past few days. It made sense in parts, but there were still gaping holes in my theories.

The best thing would be to take my ideas to Nicholas Barbflet and see if he might plug some of those holes.

He was hobbling about his room with the aid of two crutches, trying to exercise his knee when we arrived. He lurched from pieces of furniture to bed.

"Johannes told me I must try to get about as soon as I could bear moving, but to put no real weight onto my knee or leg. It's hard to do so, when neither legs will cooperate."

I smiled. "Well, you can rest now and listen to what I have discovered and see if any of it makes sense to you."

Hal helped Nick to his bed and lifted his legs for him, taking the crutches and putting them close by.

"I now know what some of those legless beggars feel like, Aumary," said Nick as he adjusted his seat for comfort. "No wonder they develop such muscles on their upper arms."

"Aye. They do."

"Never again will I pass one by without giving them a coin," he smiled.

"Speaking of coin, these happenings are all about coin, Nick. The coins in

173

the bear fund bag and the coin to be made at the fair in August."

"Ah, tell me."

"Tylor did indeed appropriate the money from the Bible fund. He cannot easily have managed it without Master Fuller seeing and turning a blind eye, as I have said."

"But how does Master Fuller benefit, Aumary, he's a wealthy man already?"

"I've said it before and I'll say it again," chipped in Hal, "rich men always like to be a bit richer. They get used to 'aving the money. I think coin corrupts in a way." He realised what he had said and squirmed a little on his stool. Nicholas Barbflet was also a wealthy man.

"Aye it does. You always have to be on guard, of yourself and others, Hal," answered Nick, unperturbed. "I can't tell you the number of times I have been offered coin and other inducements as the town reeve. The temptation to take it is strong, but the will to refuse must bite harder."

"Not all are as scrupulous as you, Nick. Our Master Fuller, for one, is not, I'm sure."

"Tell me."

"He and Tylor removed the Bible money and added it to the bear money. This is not about hiring a bear and handler for a week's innocent dancing and performing of tricks. This is about buying the right kind of bear for baiting with dogs. Hal and I have just set free seven dogs from a shed at the back of the tiler's yard. They are the kind bred for attack."

"Let free?" exclaimed Nick, "God's Cods, Aumary... you...."

"They are quite safe and secure for the moment. I'm unsure if we shall be able to turn them from beasts to beauties, Nick, but only time will tell."

"Ah. For a moment there I thought...," he chuckled.

"So this bear, to be procured from a relative of Eustache Tylor's in Bristol, will have been a beast and certainly no beauty. The bear was to have been exhibited at the time of the fair... somewhere out of the way. Word would go round to those who are interested in such things. Money would be wagered on the outcome. There would no doubt be a lot of money to be made on it."

"Foul," said Nick.

"There are men who like these violent things. More than you can imagine. They are thrilled by the bloody fight and tantalised by the wagering. Rather like the gladiatorial fights of old. No doubt other men would come from near and far bringing their own dogs to join in the fighting, either winning a considerable sum or losing their animals. It's unlikely the bearward would allow his bear to be too damaged by the dogs. Dogs are cheap... bears are obscene amounts of money. Particularly, if they are young."

"So if Tylor was plannin' this illegal bear fighting..." began Hal,

"The council would never have given its sanction to such a thing Hal," said Nick, "So you are right to say illegal. But it's not against the law of the land I think

" 'Ow come 'e ends up dead?"

"I cannot prove this as yet, but I think that he was witness to an event which had to be kept very quiet. Perhaps Tylor was not the totally unscrupulous man we have labelled him and he had some qualms about something. Some knowledge more deadly than about a bear. Yes, there is the matter of the embezzled funds but also there is another thread running through this mystery and I am only just now beginning to see it."

"I don't know how you do it, Aumary," said Nicholas. "You tease out all the facts from such a tangle as if they were each laid out in front of you in the warp and weft of a weaver's loom."

"Ah no, Master Barbflet" I said with a smile to my voice. "The cloth is already woven and I am merely unpicking it!"

Chapter Eleven

Hal and I sat in Johannes' yard and I thought about all the people who had died in this unhappy series of events.

The bearward, the two unfortunate millers, the poor dairymaid, the old woman Gytha and now Tylor. Out of the six, I had quizzed three of them myself.

The dairymaid Audre had spoken about seeing the bearward out on the river path. Gytha had spoken to me about the man she had thought she had smelled with the dead maid. Tylor had actually told me very little, but did someone think that he had imparted something of great importance to me? I felt uncomfortable. Did these folk die because I had spoken to them? Nonsense; I had been examining a great many people and they were still alive to tell the tale.

I looked up at the blue skies with the scudding white clouds hurrying on their way to Newbury and beyond. All these people were in my vision for a short time and then gone like the clouds. Just as it was difficult to recall the shapes of the clouds now passed, it was a task to recall exactly what I had said and what had been said to me, by the now deceased witnesses; for witnesses I think they were. I wished I had employed a scribe from the castle to write everything down for me.

Someone, as Johannes had said, was covering their tracks in a most brutal way. I tried to picture who might have seen me with each of the people I spoke to.

There were too many to count. It was a foolish exercise for there were many people I had spoken to who remained firmly alive. I had many suspects, particularly for the murder of the old woman, each of whom had what seemed like a perfectly good alibi or, as I saw it, no motive.

I must go back to the very beginning and examine again the death of the bearward. The death which had sparked the whole tale.

"Hal."

"Hmmm?" Hal had been leaning his head on the wall of the house gently snoring. "I think we must visit Master Cowper again."

"Again, sir?"

"There are a few things which have now come to light which we did not know when we last spoke to those artisans. I think the time has come to ask a few more questions. This time we shall write it all down."

*****

"Master Cowper. Good day to you."

Durwyn Cowper turned in the action of tapping, a metal band around the top of a barrel.

"Ah, my Lord Belvoir." He bowed and his leather apron creaked as he came upright. "Have you come to tell me who put the head in one of my barrels, sir?"

"I'm here to ask a few more questions, Durwyn, if I may."

I introduced my scribe, Harold, whom I had borrowed from the castle records office.

Cowper put his little hammer and the small metal tipped piece of wood he'd been holding into the breast of his apron.

"I remember you saying to me Durwyn, though I have to admit it did not register in my brain at the time...."

"Must'a done sir for you are remembering it now," said Hal.

"Ah yes... well... I should have made a connection then and I didn't. You said Durwyn, that someone had taken off the lid of the barrel, before you did."

"Must have done, sir, to get the head into it."

"It cannot be inserted any other way?"

"Not without breaking the head piece sir... smashing this piece here...," and he reached behind him for a round shaped piece of wood which had been made by joining four planks together and cutting it into a circular shape.

"This, see, is inserted before the chime goes on."

"The chime is the round wooden hoop at the top?"

"Yessir. Let me show you."

Durwyn Cowper took us into one of his sheds. Here his apprentice Drew was fashioning with some sort of adze, a piece identical to the one which Cowper had in his hand.

"Drew here is making a head."

Drew looked up and nodded to me.

"Four pieces jointed as close as can be, or you lose the liquid in the barrel, 'cos it will leak. In between each piece, we lay a rush, sir, and then tap them all together with these wooden pegs," said Cowper.

"And the rush gives you a watertight seal?"

"That's it m'lord. Now with all this effort going into making a head, we aren't going to want to smash it and make another over and over."

"No, I can see that."

"So if we want to open a barrel from the top, we...," and he walked over to his journeyman Easton, who was bending a piece of wood over the heat of a small pile of sawdust which had been set alight on the beaten earth floor.

"We take off this piece of wood which is a clevis, sir. It's secured with nails so we can snap them through and reuse it. Then we can tap off the hoop at the top which is the chime hoop, with this."

From his apron breast he took the metal tipped piece of wood he had been holding when we entered the yard. "With this hoop driver, off it comes, sir, and then we can bend the staves of the barrel to get at the head; this bit here." And he waved the round piece in the air."

"And all this must be done to open the barrel from the top?" I asked.

"It must, or you destroy your work, sir."

"Hmm; show me Cowper, if you might, how it's done."

The whole thing took the master cooper a few breaths. At once, there lay a barrel without a top. It took slightly less time to put it back together again.

"This is how we mend casks see. They have quite a long life, do our casks, and they're sent back to us to be mended."

"I can imagine that. So much skill and effort goes into making them, you would want them to last."

"Aye, sir." Cowper puffed out his chest. "Ours are the best. Why, there's some casks here made by my ol' Dad which are forty years old."

"There are no other coopers in Marlborough are there, Durwyn?"

"No sir, though, I expect when Easton here has had enough of working for me he'll be off and he'll start up on his own."

Easton smiled and went on with his work.

"Can the town stand that? Two coopers?"

"Oh aye. Town's growing. We can just about cope now. I expect more ale houses will spring up and we don't just make barrels you know. Troughs, buckets, pots, vats…

"Vats, Cowper?"

"Aye, the like of which Master Tanner uses over there." He pointed behind him beyond his wall to the tanner's yard.

"And the troughs I have seen being used at the fuller's yards?"

"Yessir, those too."

"Have you had any other apprentices, over the years, finish their training and go off on their own, Cowper? Say, to another town?"

"Seven years sir, a man is apprenticed for. Then he's a journeyman, then he's a Master. I've been here fifteen years, I suppose, so yes I have. One went off to Devizes. He's still there as far as I know. The other, sadly, died three years into his coopering. Why do you ask, sir?"

"Because whoever did this deed, Cowper, knew enough about the coopering trade to take off and replace the top of the barrel. And quickly."

Cowper went white. "But we established, sir, that it was none of us, didn't we?"

I nodded. "But someone who knew what to do."

"Aye, I see that now. He wiped his brow with his sleeve. "Well, I'll be blowed."

"It's a very skilled job that - cooperin'," said Hal when we were standing outside the gates.

"Yes, indeed."

"See the way that fella Easton was chopping that wood like it was butter, sir and never a stroke wrong, perfectly round and the perfect size that 'ead thing was gettin'."

I was staring at the old woman Gytha's house which was directly opposite the cooper's gates.

"Hmm, Hal."

"That cooper's adze, sir, mighty sharp."

"Hmm."

"And quite wide."

I turned to my old friend. "But the bearward's head was removed in the forest, Hal."

"Aye, but the doctor said there was evidence of choppin' "

I looked at the ground and my mind turned over fact over fact about this murder.

"A man who might have been a cooper, and still had his tools, you think?"

Hal shrugged. "Have to think about it don't we, sir?"

"Aye, and the other thing we have to think about is this - Gytha's house, is right opposite the coopers. Did she hear something that night, though when asked she denied it? Her's is the nearest house. See, that one there...." I pointed up to the house on the other side of the lane, "It has no windows to the rear." I pointed again. "That one at the other end of the yard, again no windows face this way. The next house along to Gytha's is the back door to Nick's house. He built this bit on a while back, I remember - new kitchen, he said. No one sleeps there at night."

"So Gytha was the only one likely to 'ear the rumpus that night in the yard when the barrel was being tampered with?"

"Just so, Hal."

"She 'ad to die then 'cos she saw the man at it?"

181

"Or he thought she had?"

"And she smelled the man who was with the milkmaid."

"Yes."

"Ah... sir... gates were locked."

I looked back to the gates now drawn to the side of the wall.

"Yes." I chewed my lip. "But a convenient tree, close by the wall there." I walked down the lane. "Give me a leg up, Hal."

Hal locked his hands together and propelled me upwards onto a forked branch of the elder tree which grew from the cooper's yard wall.

I grasped the top of the wall and looked over.

"Well, well. A pile of stacked wood. I could drop onto that as soon as spit, Hal." Down I came and dusted my hands and the front of my cotte.

"We know how 'e got in and out. We know 'e's a cooper...or 'as bin," said Hal

"I so wish my memory was better Hal, about those to whom I have spoken and when. I have a feeling that I have unwittingly let out a few facts which have enabled our murderer to understand what peril he is in and do something about it."

"Aw no, sir, it's not your fault."

The back of my head had begun to ache. I rubbed my neck. My injury was catching up with me.

"Come. Let's go and eat. It's been a long and eventful day, Hal."

I sent the scribe back to the castle.

*****

I despatched a message to Hubert and Plum, whom I'd left with the dogs at the tileyard. We would deal with them tomorrow. Meanwhile, they were to make sure they were fed and watered and made secure. They could then go home to Durley. Hubert would take a message to Lydia. I would be home as soon as I could tease out the threads of this tangled mess.

182

Imagine my surprise when Hubert trotted in to Johannes' house a while later with the little white dog under his arm.

"Sir, this one's not like the rest. Sweet as a nut she is. I didn't want to leave her because she was so afraid of the other dogs. Can I take her home?"

He put her down on the floor of the yard and she immediately started to tremble. She looked up at Hubert with such sad eyes.

"That's Tylor's dog, Aura," said Johannes as he fed her a piece of mutton. "The one that chased the chicken."

"The one he said was missing," I said.

"Aw, she's got a bite to her ear," said Johannes. "I have some salve for that." And he disappeared into the kitchen.

"Hubert, if you want another dog, you may have her but she is not to chase our fowl when they are out." Hubert's little old blind and deaf terrier Gregory had died in the early spring and he was rather lost without a dog.

"Aye sir. Thank you sir." He beamed from ear to ear and he held little Aura as Johannes bathed and salved her bitten ear. That done, man and dog made off down the lane towards the forest.

I sat back and contemplated the blue sky till a chilly little wind got up and we all retired to the kitchen, until it was time for Hal and I to make our way to our billets in the castle. It seemed the wind had driven people to their homes early and a few large wild droplets of rain splattered the roadway around us. We were leading Bayard and Grafton by the reins. It was unfair of us to ask Johannes to feed and house our horses for so long, when we were after all, on official business, so we were taking them to the castle stables.

I walked with Bayard on my right and Hal on my left with Grafton to his left. The skies were murky and though it was a while or so before dusk, the light was very poor. We had reached the end of the road before the houses petered out. Southfield, the grassy space where the fair was held, was to our left, the church of St. Peter was to our right.

Ours ears picked up a high whine followed by a dull thwack and Bayard

183

reared up screaming, as an arrow hit his right hind quarter. I pulled down on the reins and ducked behind him.

"Come on old boy... the gate is just there."

Running, with Bayard hopping on three legs and screaming in pain, we rounded the corner before the castle gate.

Another arrow hit the wet road just a foot from my exposed back. A third flew harmlessly over our heads and fell into the moat.

"Merriman!" I yelled, "archer in the church tower!"

We ran across the bridge and under the gate arch to safety.

Andrew's head popped out of the gate and his narrowed gaze flew up to the figure, just visible on the very top of St. Peter's tower.

He ducked back in as we arrived and I handed Bayard to a groom.

"See to him."

In a very little while we had found three soldiers to accompany us.

Six of us then flew out of the gate and I made for the nearest door to the tower of the church, on the south wall. A soldier followed me and waited there, sword drawn. Andrew went for the western door which was the nearest to the castle wall. There were only these two exits.

The other two soldiers covered the walls to the north and east.

I ran for the tower, closely followed by Hal and we clattered up the steps. The church had been built by the castle masons and the inner staircase was constructed in the same way as those at the castle, winding right.

I drew my sword from the scabbard at my left hip. There was little room here to manoeuvre but once out on to the top of the tower, I would be able to apprehend our archer with more freedom.

With great circumspection, I rounded the last bend in the stair and stepped up to the open trap door, the only entrance onto the roof. The light was fading fast.

The roof bore a very slight peak and the simple doors were double and folded back onto the leads.

184

I cautiously poked my head out of the opening. I faced north. No man here. Risking an arrow at short range, I leapt up onto the roof and scanned around. The roof was empty.

Hal came up beside me.

"By Beezelbub's bubbies, how can 'e 'ave got away? We were 'ere so quick."

I shook my head and caught my lower lip in my teeth.

Hal looked down and shouted, "Gone, Andrew."

Andrew shook his head. "No man exited this way."

We swiftly turned about and rattled down the stairs.

The nave was a simple block with unadorned round pillars marching down its length. The chancel was a smaller space at the end, through a large arch. Hal turned into the right aisle and I to the left and we walked carefully down its length.

One day there would be a proper fixed rood screen here to separate the nave from the chancel, but at this date, we simply had two free standing wooden screens, either side of the steps leading to the altar.

Behind one of these we found Father Columba hunched up and out cold. His brown outer robe was gone and he was left in his white shirt and braies.

Leaving Hal to minister to his hurts, I raced for the south door.

"A man in priest's robes?" I asked the soldier standing there, his thumb in his belt, his sword across his shoulder.

"No one has come out, sir," he said, "except Father Columba."

I sighed. "Which way, man?"

He pointed and was about to speak again when I pushed past him, vaulted the churchyard wall and ran up the road towards the main High Street.

In the gloom, I could see no one. Then the flash of a heel turned up into Chantry Lane, to the left and I followed. The man had his hood up.

I lost him on Back Lane and surprised a courting couple saying their last goodbyes before parting for the night. The girl shrieked. The man swore.

And so did I.

*****

Poor Bayard. It was not a bad wound but the arrow had to be extracted by the horse doctor at the castle. He would be laid up for a while. The stolen robe was found next day bunched up in a doorway at the very end of Back Lane.

I cursed, "We had him, Hal."

"'E's a quick'un, say that for 'im and 'e don't seem to care much what 'appens. Takes such risks he does." He chuckled " 'E's really got it in for you, sir."

"So now we are looking for a man who has been a cooper, can shoot an arrow...."

"To be honest many men can do that sir, maybe not well but...."

"Can you see Master Nick with a bow, Hal?"

"Ah no... not his kind."

"Someone who is fleet of foot, so not too old, who is handy with a throwing knife and who...."

"Has the cheek of the devil, sir."

"Aye, Hal, that he has."

*****

The next morning saw us at the cordwainer's. He hailed us as we passed his home on foot.

"Sir Aumary. I wonder if you could step in a while. I have something to show you," he said seriously.

I followed Gilbert to his back room. Here were kept some materials for his work and the tools with which he fashioned his boots and shoes. The larger amounts of hides were kept in store sheds in the yard at the back of the house.

I nodded and smiled to the two apprentices, Felix Castleman and Harry Glazer.

186

"We were coming to make some soft boots today, sir. You remember the sort we make for you and a few others? What you like to call indoor shoes?"

"Aye felted above and with a leather sole."

"Just so."

Gilbert picked up a length of felted wool, a bale of cloth of indeterminate colour, marled pale grey and brown.

"We were just coming to cut the felt when... we found this."

He unrolled the top layer of cloth. There in the middle of the material was a big brown red splodge.

"Blood," said Hal and I together.

"Aye, that's what me and the boys thought too."

"Where do you keep it?"

"The felts I keep in this room as I don't want the damp getting to it. Only the hide is kept out there." He gestured to his yard, through the open window.

"You can't account for the blood?"

"No accidents. No. Me and the boys are whole and unscathed. Someone else's blood, this is."

I fingered the beard of my chin. Goodness, it was getting too long for comfort.

"Where does the felt come from, Gil?"

"I get it sent over from Elcot usually but, they didn't have any, so this batch comes from Marlborough fulling mills. Came yesterday."

Hal, Gil and myself all locked eyes.

"Hmm," I said.

We had not walked five or six paces up the road when scurrying towards us came Father Torold from St. Mary's.

"I hear that you have been shot at, Sir Aumary."

"Aye but I lived to tell the tale. My poor horse took the brunt of it."

"No man taken for it?"

"None yet, Torold."

"Praise be you are unhurt."

"It was not for want of them trying, father."

"Poor Columba I hear, was hit about the head."

"He was. Are you going down to St. Peter's to offer him spiritual comfort?"

"I come to see how he is and if he needs my help at his church. If he is laid up awhile, he will not be able to minister to his flock."

"You hope they will all make the extra journey and come up to you at St. Mary's?" Torold looked at me under his auburn brows.

"No sir, I will sing mass here too, should it become necessary."

"Good for you, Father Torold," I said, chuckling. It was well known that the two churches, one at the eastern end and the other at the western end of town, enjoyed a friendly rivalry.

"God go with you," said the priest.

"And with you," said Hal and I.

Torold quickly turned back. "Oh sir, I nearly forgot. A lad, a small lad with white hair. He came into the church looking to find you earlier this morning. He had searched for you at the doctor's house but there was no one there. After me, his next stop was to be the town reeve's house."

"Where is he now, father?"

"At the Barbflet house, I think."

Osric was stepping from the door of the town reeve's house as we approached and he bumped into me.

"Oh sir, beggin' yer pardon."

I steadied the lad with two hands on his shoulders.

"Ah, m'lord Belvoir, you are just who I have been looking for this past...."

"Aye, we know lad," said Hal, "we met Father Torold."

"What news Osric?"

"Me Da wants you again, sir. Up at the camp. Something mighty odd." Hal and I looked at each other.

"Mighty odd, eh?" said Hal.

There was a definite familiarity about the next scene when Osric, up on Hal's saddle and I, not on Bayard this time, but on a horse from the castle stable, trotted up the hill to the glass blowers camp.

Aldo Swift came out to meet us and dispensed with his leather apron and the sweat rag which had been tied around his head.

He took up a tunic which was laid neatly on a nearby bush and shrugged it over his head. He'd been sweating profusely whilst working the glass in his workshop and the cooling breeze outside, whilst welcome, would soon chill him.

"Here, sir," he said, "if you'll follow me."

We threaded our way through the clearing, full of men prodding fires with long metal sticks and unloading a cart full of gravel. This was the raw material for the glass. The beech trees of the West Baily were being burned for their ash and the gravel sorted and refined for the sand.

Aldo took us promptly to the edge of the clearing, and we looked down into a cart in which lay a bolt of cloth.

Hal looked at me quickly.

"Looks mighty like the one Gil just showed us, sir."

Aldo pulled out a length. There on the top layer was another red brown splodge.

"I have been wondering how we can transport the glass we make more safely to its destinations," he said. "I learned that the fullers make a thick felt, most of which is the rubbish from the bits of cloth thrown away if damaged in the fulling or tenting process."

"Aye," I said. "I've seen it made. All the rubbish is thrown together and a thick felt made from the leavings."

"Makes a mighty fine padding for the glass and I can use it over and over. Straw is all right but tends to deteriorate. Felt is longer lasting."

"But when you took delivery of this...?"

"I found, well, look for yourself. There is, I think, a deal of blood there."

This bolt of felt seemed to have absorbed more blood than the one Gilbert

189

had shown us, though if you could not put the two together, I suspect you would be hard pressed to see the difference.

"I am right, m'lord?" said Aldo "It is blood?"

"I'd like to say that someone has spilt brown dye onto the fabric but this will never have been anywhere near the dyeing sheds," I said. "No one would bother to dye such waste stuff."

"It's blood all right," said Hal.

Aldo shifted uncomfortably.

"In the light of what you found the last time you visited the forest, sir? I wondered...."

"Aldo, you are quite right to tell me. This is no mean amount of blood."

I took hold of the bolt of fabric. "We didn't do this to Gilbert's, but Hal, take the other end and Aldo - pull."

We unwrapped the felt. Every twelve inches or so, the splodge was there, until gradually it faded away. We had unwound perhaps eight feet before it was seen no more.

"Where did it come from, Aldo?"

But I knew of course. We rewrapped the felt.

"The fulling mill by the river, in the town."

Hal started to pull his long forked grey beard, a sure sign he was puzzled.

"Sir... surely 'oo ever delivered this felt would not 'ave done so if they'd known it was stained so badly?"

Aldo flipped the felt bale over. "From this side it looks perfectly innocent. It's only when you start to unwrap it, it looks bad."

"Same for Gil's bolt, Hal," I said.

I replaced the cloth in the cart.

"When did you take delivery of it, Aldo?"

"Yesterday. I didn't look at it until this morning, early."

"Was it brought to you by cart here in the forest?"

"Yes. There were other deliveries on the back of the cart but no other felt

190

bales," said the glassman.

"One had already been delivered to the cordwainer in town," I said. "We saw that bale earlier this morning."

"Is the blood from the bearward, sir?" asked Aldo, his face serious and pained.

"I can't think of anyone else in this series of deaths who has died in a way which would produce so much blood," I said. "Beheaded in the forest, the head tossed into the back of a cart onto the bales and covered over with cloth, and the body hidden in undergrowth."

Aldo shook his head. "But why?"

"Ah now, that is a more difficult question to answer," I said.

We said our thanks and farewells and Hal and I jogged back to town. "We need to go up to St. Martin's and see to the dogs, Hal."

"I don't fancy that at all, sir. What are we going to do with them?"

"Perhaps I can ask Nicholas Barbflet, who in the town, might be in need of a couple of guard dogs. I think they would make admirable guards of, for example, working yards. Cowper's yard might not have been breached if he'd had a dog there."

"I see what you mean... but...."

"Dogs bark Hal. If they hear something strange, they bark. They don't have to tear a man limb from limb. Remember when we had our intruder on the stable roof at Durley. It was Jocasta who brought him to our attention."

"Aye, it was."

"They are more a deterrent than anything else."

"I'll take your word for it, sir."

But when we reached the chain by the shed at the back of the tileyard, the dogs and their ropes were gone.

*****

We questioned the tileyard workers. They had heard the dogs barking and snarling late yesterday afternoon, they said. They had assumed we had come to fetch them. A cart rumbled down the road and someone took the dogs across the fields, they thought, though they were far too busy to pay much attention. Someone must have loaded them onto a covered cart further up the Mildenhall road, through a gap in the hedge. That's all they could tell us. The only man they saw was the driver. No one recognised him.

I trotted up the road looking for tracks. There in the hedge, quite a way up the road were slashed and broken pieces of hawthorn, hazel and alder. Someone had forced their way into the field in order to recover the dogs unseen.

I was glad we had removed Aura. Heaven knows what was going to happen to the rest.

Were they removed to the town? No, I doubted it. They would be too conspicuously noisy. I put that puzzle aside and rode back to Hal waiting by the stream.

As we returned to the centre of town we heard a distant rumble of thunder. Riding down the Kingsbury Hill, I looked up at the sky. It was inky blue over the forest.

"I have a mind to go to the mill and see how they are getting on with the re-building Hal. You take the horses to the castle."

"Right you are, sir."

There was much activity at the mill. The wheel was being fitted at the eastern end and there was a deal of shouting, calling instructions, and answering from the inside of the building.

I stood back and watched for a while. The new wheel was huge and heavy and oddly clean, completely devoid of any weed or green moss growing on it. I wondered how long it would take for the thing to age. As I watched a small puff of dust emerged from one of the holes in the wall. Someone was clearing the blocked ventilation holes. I turned on my heel, pushed the re-hung door and stooped through the door hole.

The inner stairs had been repaired. Some new treads and handrails had appeared. I trotted upwards. There on the milling floor, I found those who were supervising the replacing of the wheel from the inside and young Milward, who was scraping out the clay mixture from the holes with a small knife.

He knuckled his forehead. "My Lord Belvoir."

"How goes the work, Milward?"

"Slow sir, this stuff is packed in tight and is very dense."

"Let me look."

He had been balanced on a stool by the outer wall, at the side of the mechanism, which was now a series of interconnected wooden spars and metal parts, the like of which reminded me of some of the tangled forest trees at Savernake.

I perched, as he had done, on the stool and stretching up, wriggled Milward's knife into the gap. Out came a lump of very pale dry clay. I stood looking at it in the palm of my hand for a while.

"Carry on lad," I said as I handed the knife back.

Hal now joined me and we both looked down at the dried lump sitting on my palm.

"Where have I seen this before, Hal?"

"I dunno sir. Looks like the sort of thing that the tilemen use."

"Hmm. Their clay is much more gritty. This is smooth, as smooth as I ever think you will get clay. There are no lumps in it at all. And it's very pale."

"No wonder it did a good job of bunging up the 'oles then, m'lord."

I stood for a while longer looking at my find, until the millers and carpenters decided we were in the way and politely asked us to move.

I stored it in my purse.

"It will come to me, I'm sure."

We exited just as there was another large boom of thunder but as yet no rain. I strode to the mill pond wall. The level of the water was back to normal. The plants which colonised the inside of the wall; the mosses, little ferns and ivy leaf toadflax, had been submerged by the extra water and they were visible again now.

I looked over the wall of the bridge. The water trickled at a lazy rate out of the gap left in the sluice into the river Kennet.

I looked back to the eastern wall of the mill. The wheel pit was emptied of water so the men could work. Some water inevitably trickled through the ill-fitting sluices at the river end but this was not enough to put the fitting at risk. The men stood on wooden boards.

Grist came up behind me.

"Good day, m'lord, though I don't know for how much longer." He looked up at the sky. "We shall have to abandon work if that lot comes down on us."

The blue black sky was directly overhead now.

"Things have moved on apace, Grist, since I last looked."

"We shall be able to begin work again next week, I think."

"Under your guardianship?"

"Aye, Master Menier has hung up his apron," he said sadly.

"Congratulations Grist," I said "Master miller, now."

"Aye, sir. Thank you, though I am unhappy about the way of it."

I watched the receding back of his bright yellow tunic as he went through the door.

*****

The Heavens opened just as we reached Johannes' kitchen door. The doctor was out. Huge drops of rain splattered the earth of the courtyard and stained the few flagstones he had laid there as a path to the stable and other buildings. The mill work would - *forgive the pun Paul* - grind to a halt now. The kitchen was warm and inviting and we sat down happily to a pie which Agnes had fetched from the baker's oven, after the communal bread of the town had been baked.

I took out the piece of clay from my scrip and toyed with it.

Agnes quizzed me with her mobile face.

"Found in the ventilation holes of the mill and partly responsible for the terrible blast they had there, two or so weeks ago. For some reason I think I've seen it before, or something like it and I cannot for the life of me remember where."

Agnes tutted. She took the clay from my palm and turned it over and over. Suddenly her face broke into a smile.

"You know what it is, Agnes?"

She nodded her head furiously as she gave the clay back to me and disappeared for a heartbeat or two into her little pantry like cupboard at the back of the kitchen.

She came out brandishing a piece of clay identical to the one I held in my hand. She took a small dish and crumbled some of the powdery stuff into it and pounded it with one of Johannes' pestles.

Her sign for 'wait' followed and then she dashed into the passageway and I heard her little feet pattering up the stairs and over the wooden boards up on the first floor.

She was back in an instant with one of Johannes' woollen shirts. On the front was a greasy orange stain, where some medicine, I suppose, had splashed up at him. She sprinkled the stain with a little water and then scattered the clay over it and yet again we saw the sign for 'wait'.

Agnes had once been a ladies' maid and she had learned how to care for fine clothes and other items of apparel, whilst serving the Lady Matilda de Neville.

We drank our wine, ate more pie, chatted about this and that and commented that the rain had stopped. Just as we were about to leave, Agnes tapped me on the shoulder.

She took the shirt, shook the powder into the dish and showed me the result. No greasy stain. It was gone.

I blinked.

"Well, I'll be buried in Burbage!" said Hal. "That's fuller's earth that is!"

Agnes nodded energetically.

*****

"We don't have enough evidence, Hal, that's the trouble," I said as we walked down the High Street.

"But sir, the scratch on the 'ead, the fuller's earth, the fact 'e has no alibi for the time the bearward was killed, nor the girl for that matter. The fact 'e owns a yellow tunic. And 'e deals with felt don't 'e? The fact he's just a nasty bas...."

"He may be nasty, Hal. He may indeed own a yellow tunic but for that matter, so do you!"

"It's saffron, sir, not yellow...," said Hal "much more, wearable colour." He sounded most affronted.

"I beg your pardon," I said, chuckling inwardly. "Well, we need a little more to fix on him before we can arrest him."

"Aw sir!"

"No doubt he would get a good lawyer to refute everything we put before him. He has access to the money to hire one."

"And there's me thinkin' it was just as simple as a pimple, sir."

I laughed out loud.

"We need to trap him, I think, Hal. Somehow. He's a slippery fish but there must be some way we can lure him into making a mistake and betraying himself."

I looked up to Heaven and a thought came to me.

"I had a soldier looking after the second mikmaid, Berewynne, Hal. Did I tell you?"

"You did, sir?"

"Let us go out to Preshute and see if we can put something to them."

"No need, market day tomorrow. She'll be 'ere with 'er milk, won't she?"

"You think she'll come?"

"Got to sir... cows don't milk themselves and what's she to do with all that milk?"

"Make cheese, Hal?"

"Ah yes... but my guess is she'll come with her soldier to sell it. Gotta make some money see, hasn't she? I 'eard she 'int bin in the town since... since her friend was killed."

"She may go elsewhere."

"Nah don't think so... damn long walk elsewhere with two pails 'a milk."

"You have a point, Hal."

"Shall we see her tomorrow then, sir?"

"Yes, Hal, I think we shall. Meanwhile I want to go and talk to Nicholas. I've a few questions for him."

Nick was sitting up in bed, tearing the meat from a leg of fowl as we entered.

"Sorry to interrupt your dinner," I said. "There are a few questions I want to ask you about the mill."

Nick gestured to the bench and swallowed. "Join me for dinner. There's far too much for me here. I'm not as active as I used to be and I think that Felicity thinks I need building up."

"You do need to eat the right things to mend your legs. I'm sure Doctor Johannes has told you that," I said.

"Aye," said Nick.

Hal reached for an apple, a rather wizened object from last year's picking.

"Fish, apples, beans, dried fruits," reeled off Nick.

"And...," I peered at the meat Nick was eating, "duck, eh?"

He shrugged, "Well, we live by the river...."

We all laughed.

"So what do you want to know?"

"Your millpond? I've had it from Grist but I'd like it from your own lips. How often do you top it up?"

Nick wiped his fingers on a napkin.

"When we have a big consignment of grain coming in from somewhere which doesn't happen often. Three times a year maybe."

"Other than that?"

"We must keep it at a certain level to grind the flour for the town's bread. We top it up when we need it."

"Answer me, true. Have you had any complaints from further down the river, that you are depleting the flow?"

Nick sat stock still.

"It's never for long."

"Have you?"

"Aye, Master Fuller complains now and again."

"And what do you do?"

Nick shrugged. "Not a lot we can do. If Master Fuller wants more water then he must dig a pond and store it himself."

"Anyone else?"

"Of course he has the mills at Elcot too, so he's doubly affected. But we were here first. This mill is fifty years old. His mills are only fifteen or so. Why site them there if you know that...?"

"And you are grinding corn for people to make flour. Their daily bread. More important than fulling cloth, I suppose?" I said sarcastically.

"Aye, put like that, I suppose it is."

"Master Tanner ever complain?

"No, he takes his water by hand when he needs it. Mind you, old Fuller has complained to Tanner about the quality of the water coming from his works."

"Oh?"

Nick sighed. "Nothing to be done really, but Tanner flushes his waste into the river at the back of his yard. You can imagine what the water looks like."

I had seen it myself, muddy with effluent from the tanning vats.

"It soon clears but if Fuller wants water for his cleansing after the fulling process, when the cloth must be rinsed... you can imagine the arguments there are."

"I can."

"So you and Master Tanner are not Master Fuller's favourite people."

"We rub along."

"I heard, I'm sure, Gilbert Cordwainer speak about a court case? Last time we were all together. What was that - you and Fuller?"

Nick sighed. "Yes it was. Four years ago. Fuller brought an action against me. I was kind to him and settled it amicably. I didn't have to. He lost his case. That's why we agreed that we would only fill the pond three times a year for large amounts. And there are stones placed along the river to gauge carefully how much is taken at any one point."

"Aye I've seen them. I thought they were just stepping stones."

"The Culverstones were originally measuring stones, Aumary. Before my time too."

"Ah, I see."

These were the large sarsen stones placed in the river bed at the back of the tanner's and fuller's yards. Folk used them now as a bridge across the Kennet.

"You are responsible too, aren't you, for keeping the records of the indentures of Marlborough apprentices?"

"Aye, in my cellar, with other Marlborough documents."

"How are they set out?"

"They are all different according to the trade. Each master has his own set but we have duplicates in case of damage from, let's say, fire. The council can be called upon to adjudicate if a man is accused of mistreating his apprentice for example, or for that matter, if an apprentice, treats his master badly. The indentures record by what conditions the lad is taken on. How much is paid to the master. Lodging, food, clothes, equipment, time off to see family. That sort of thing. It's a private agreement and rarely comes to law. We can usually resolve problems, the council and I."

"I remember when Giles Thatcher let my young Piers of Manton go because his asthma turned bad when learning the thatching trade, it was an amicable parting and a portion of the money paid out to educate and lodge him was paid back," I said.

"Not always the case but… mostly it can be resolved happily."

"So not everyone is delighted about an apprentice leaving before his final time?"

"No, not all. What's this about, Aumary?"

"Perhaps, though I'm not sure myself, a lad apprenticed some years ago to a cooper. Maybe in Marlborough, maybe not, who didn't finish his term and went off to apprentice himself elsewhere or not - I don't know. A man who bears a grudge. A man who has a violent nature."

Nick grimaced. "You want me to look into the records?"

"If you could."

"How far back?"

"Fifteen years maybe should do it."

"I'll see what I can do. I'm not sure complete records go back that far. Anything is better than lying here staring at the ceiling. Gabriel is so efficient, he leaves me little town business to do," he sighed.

"You chose him as deputy," I laughed.

"Aye, and it was for precisely that quality." He sighed again.

*****

Saturday market day came round again. I was up at dawn but the milkmaid did not show as early as she usually did. I had time to collect my willing scribe from the castle.

Eventually she came timidly into the mill yard, closely followed by her rather youthful soldier.

A few of the men standing around the workings of the mill wheel came up to purchase milk. Berewynne was quiet, contained and watchful.

Her guard stayed a few feet behind. I observed them for a little while before making myself known.

"Berewynne, good day. I was not entirely sure you would be here today."

The girl curtsied as best she could with the weight of her pails of milk.

"Oh sir, a girl must eat. I gotta milk the cows and me Ma says I gotta come out to sell."

Hal close by, coughed pointedly.

"We haven't seen you in a while."

"No, sir. I was too affeart and that be the truth." She looked back at her soldier.

"But with Jem here looking after me and time passing since... since... Audre died, I thought you might'a caught the devil, sir.

"I am sorry to say no, we haven't caught him, Berewynne, but I was very much hoping that you might help us do that."

"I don't know no more than what I told you before."

"Come. Let's go into the mill and sit comfortably in Master Nicholas' office. Harold here will write a few more things down for us. Won't you, Harold."

Once sitting in the quiet of the office, surrounded safely by four walls, Berewynne relaxed a little more.

"Tell me lass, how long have you been coming to the mill to sell your milk? I remember Audre telling me that you used to come together before the markets were granted.

"Aye we did. She were a little oldr'un me and she came first on her own."

"When was this can you remember?"

"Oh must be... ten years now."

"No, it can't be," I smiled. "You must have been a mere baby then."

Berewynne giggled. "Oh no sir, I'm older'un you think. Audre, she was fourteen when she first came so now she'd be...."

"Twenty four if still alive."

"Aye sir, and I'm twenty two."

"Never! And I had you both down as girls."

Berewynne simpered.

"I suppose you have seen a lot of coming and going in ten years, nearly?"

"Aye sir. More men at the mill now. The tanner's yard is bigger too. So's the fullers. And the castle. Now a course, we have the market too."

"You never met any man who took your fancy then, Berewynne, from all these men in the yards? Never walked out with any of them?"

The girl looked quickly over at the soldier Jem, who was lounging by the door.

"No sir. I don't want to marry a stinky tanner or fuller."

"Ho no, I understand that," I chortled. "A miller then?"

"No sir, I don't like the dust... I like soldiers, sir," and she smiled sweetly at Jem who returned the smile.

"Ah," I said rubbing my nose.

"You told me that Audre was a little too free with her favours. Did she favour one person above all others?"

Berewynne poked out her tongue and clamped it between her lips. "Not in recent years."

"A while back?"

"Aye."

"What happened, do you know?" I asked.

Berewynne pulled her mouth awry. "I don't like to say really... but now she's gone, I s'pose I can. He was bashing her."

"He beat her?

"So she dumped him. And then a while later, he left town."

"Good for her," I said. "Where did he go?"

"I dunno."

"What did he do for a living this man?"

"I can't remember."

"Berewynne, you want to help find this madman who killed your friend, don't you?"

"Oh yessir, more than anything."

"So if I ask you to do something for me, which might be a little bit... dangerous, you'd consider it?"

Berewynne looked quickly at Jem. "If I had Jem there to protect me, sir... I might think about it."

"Well, it's very important and if my plan works, we shall find the monster who killed Audre and the old lady Gytha. This is what I need you to do."

And I outlined my plan.

Her eyes grew as round as the heads of Master Cowper's casks.

"Not only will Jem be there, but we shall too. You'll be well looked after. I won't allow anyone to hurt you."

Berewynne took a heartbeat to decide. "I'll do it, sir," she said.

Chapter Twelve

Berewynne went on her way, her soldier Jem trailing in her wake.

"Do you think she can do it, sir?" asked Hal.

"Not difficult is it, Hal; spread it about town that she knows what went on the evening of the old girl, Gytha's murder?" She doesn't have to be specific; just intimate that she knows a thing or two."

"You think he'll bite, sir?"

"I'm almost certain. If he doesn't hear directly, the gossip will reach him by the end of the day. And if it doesn't, well, we shall have lost nothing."

"I 'ope she remembers to come back 'ere before she sets off for 'ome along the river track. We'll 'ave a devil of a time following if she doesn't."

"Jem will make sure she does as she's instructed, Hal. He doesn't want anything to happen to her."

"Ah no...," chuckled my man at arms. "Right little matchmaker aren't we, sir?"

"Now Hal... I wasn't to know she had a liking for soldiers."

We left Nick's office and sauntered up the lane. Level with Master Cowper's yard, we heard raised voices.

"I think you should tell him."

"But what if I'm wrong?"

"You aren't wrong, Cowper!" This was Mistress Cowper's voice. "You remember how it was, Durwyn. You were almost affeared to come to work or be at home for that matter."

"Oh, don't be hysterical, woman."

"I'm not. I remember how it was, even if you don't, you great dumb ox."

"What if I say something and a man is accused of murder because of me and he is innocent. Think of that!"

"Let the constable think of that. That's his job. You should tell him."

"Tell me what, good lady?" I said, stepping into the gateway.

Mistress Cowper almost jumped out of her clothes. "Oh M'lord Belvoir, you gave me a fright!"

"I am sorry to startle you so. I couldn't help overhearing you. What is it you think your good man should tell me, madam?"

A look passed between the cooper and his wife.

Durwyn Cooper sighed. "You asked me, sir, if I'd had any apprentices leave me and go to other towns?"

"I did. Two, you said."

"He forgot about the one that broke his indentures, sir."

"Ah...," I said, glad at last that my sixth sense was working perfectly. "It is as I thought."

Cowper was just about to open his mouth to speak when Waterman one of the younger millers, came running down the lane from the Barbflet house. He overshot the gate of the cooper's and we heard him skid on the stones. He backtracked.

"Sir Aumary Belvoir? My master thought you'd be at the mill but...."

"I'm here instead, Waterman."

The young man put a piece of parchment in my hand.

"With the town reeve's compliments, sir. This is the document you were looking for, he thinks."

I unrolled it. Cowper peered over my shoulder.

"I can't read nor write sir, but I can recognise my mark. That's it there...," and he pointed to the bottom of the document. "A circle with a stave running through it," he said.

"And this mark here?"

"'Twas what I was going to tell you, m'lord. I had an apprentice a long while back. He were a wrong'un, sir. I told him to pack his bags.

"He was violent and abusive, sir," said Mistress Cowper. "To his master and to me. And us giving him a roof over his head and food in his belly. And Durwyn educating him, sir, in the mysteries of cooperin'."

"He struck the wife, sir. Several times. He liked to hit women."

"I see."

"He left half way through his third year."

"Who, Cowper?"

"His name was Godfric sir. Godfric Farmer."

I frowned. This was not the name I had been expecting.

"Describe him, as you knew him," I said to Cowper.

His wife butted in. "He won't remember a thing like that, though I will," she said, and she began to describe the man who had left the cooper under a cloud.

"Stole the tools that Cowper had provided for him too. So he's a thief an' all." When she had finished, I glanced once more at the document in my hand. The indenture was made out for the man, Godfric Farmer.

But I knew what he called himself now.

*****

Berewynne returned to the mill later in the evening. We would wait a while until it was little gloomier and the river path was less frequented by folk. By now her pails were empty and she managed them more easily.

I would send Jem out to the river towards the castle mill. Here the Kennet was bounded by trees and bushes of all sorts. The girl would walk along the lane to Preshute, the first village beyond Marlborough. Jem was to hide in those bushes and trees and follow her, keeping parallel to her at all times, but as unseen as he could contrive to be.

Berewynne told me that she had spoken to all who would listen and some who had eavesdropped, that the constable, Sir Aumary Belvoir, had removed her guard and she would walk home alone tonight.

"Did folk not wonder why you were to be out later than the time you usually go home?" I asked.

"Oh sir, I said I was going to see my old grannie for a while, on Figgins Lane. That would make me late, wouldn't it, sir?"

"Then you had better do so, Berewynne. Jem will walk you there and then disappear onto the river path."

"I'll follow at a distance, sir," said Hal, "and wait... see who turns up."

"Please God he doesn't bring his bow," I said quietly.

"Berewynne, keep as close to the bushes as you can. Walk from side to side as if your buckets are heavy and you are tired. If you can, hold them to your back."

"Aye, sir... I can do that. But why?"

"Just do it please, my brave girl. I won't be far behind you."

I squeezed her shoulder. "Off to your grannie's now. I am off to organise the rest of the men. You will be well guarded."

I worried that I had put the girl in too much danger as I trotted to the castle to fetch a couple more men, including my friend Andrew Merriman who insisted on being included in the party. I explained what I had in mind.

"He might, as you say, use his bow... what are we to do then?"

"She will be a moving target, with trees, bushes and reeds between them. The river bends here and there. I'm hoping there will be no good sight line."

"Please God."

The light was fading now and we made our way down to the river across the bridge. One man stayed hidden at the bridge end, with instructions to follow our felon from the town. The others strung out along the path and had a command to follow only when the man appeared and had passed them. Berewynne was to walk the half mile to Preshute village. Please God the man made his move before the day faded to dark and she reached her destination. The most likely place for an attack, I thought, was the loneliest part of the track, where the river bent in an arc from Preshute village towards Manton Grange; the barn belonging to the castle, which owned much of the land thereabouts. This was almost exactly between the two villages.

I saw the girl trip lightly over the bridge, look back once to wave to Jem, who disappeared into the bushes as if he was returning to the castle via the moat path. Then she settled her buckets and marched down the river path.

At the back of the castle moat, the river split into many small streams. One of them of course, fed the Castle Mill. I waited at the mill bridge, then, hid myself behind the mill building, leaving one soldier behind. Once the girl was around the bend in the stream, I ran up to the little stand of bushes and trees which began at the river's edge and which eventually marched up the incline to form a hedge working its way up to Granham Hill. Berewynne walked on in her pale blue dress. Luckily it was a light colour and we could all see her; sadly so could our murderer.

I stopped to listen. No one followed me. The man from the bridge was still in place.

"C'mon... c'mon" I said to myself, impatient for my suspect to make a move. No one followed Berewynne.

Suddenly I heard a splash further up the river. An otter perhaps? No, it was a larger splash than that small river animal would make?

If our suspect had entered the river, he could have brought no bow for he would not be able to keep the string of it dry and so could not loose it. Here he could not wade across with it above his head; the water was too deep. One good thing, I thought.

We now had only three men with the girl, plus Andrew, Hal and Jem the soldier, for two men were behind me and had not followed. This was, I realised, because our man had not come from the town bridge as I had thought he would. He was ahead of us. He was not following Berewynne but heading her off.

"Damn" I raced for the river path. I could see no one. In a way this was good, for neither could my murderer.

Then I saw Berewynne as instructed, weaving from side to side of the track. Sometimes the vegetation grew right up to the path and it made the line difficult to follow. At other times, the trail was wider and clear of nettles and riverside plants. But Berewynne had travelled this lane often and knew all its twists and turns.

Suddenly a hundred feet ahead of Berewynne, a bevy of ducks went up as if scared by a water dog. She looked back for reassurance. Of course, she saw no one.

I saw her speed up.

"Damn!" I was running in spurts now to keep her in my sight. I imagined noises; footsteps, the rustle of clothing in a bush, the snap of a twig, a light scuffle. No, I had not imagined it; a water vole scurried in front of me and plopped into the river. My heart thumped as a barn owl flew low over the water, its ghostly face turned towards me in the half light.

Berewynne now turned to the bend at the edge of the village where she lived close by the path to the barn, stepping lightly over a trodden muddy puddle in the lane made by the feet who had walked it; those folk coming daily to and from the Grange.

I could not see her. I did just about notice Jem, in his dark blue tunic, a low light catching his sword pommel or some other metal part of his mail.

Good, at least he was close by.

I ploughed on, trying to catch up on the girl but not making myself too obvious.

All at once, Berewynne screamed. There was a scuffling noise and a metal rasp as a sword came from a scabbard.

Jem.

I heard Hal's voice "Belvoir, to me, to me." The war cry of my family.

I rounded the bend. Jem was on the floor, bleeding from a wound in his forearm.

"In the river, sir," shouted Hal as he slid down the river bank. "He's got her in the river!"

The light was extremely poor now but I could just see Berewynne's light apron bobbing about at the edge of the water.

Hal reached the water and plunged in.

"I'm after him." I yelled as I threw off my cotte and sword belt. "Merriman - the river!" I cried as Andrew came running up the bank from further up.

Moments later Hal pulled the girl up the bank in a froth of water and a snaggle of plants.

She was unhurt but shaken. I noticed her buckets were a few yards up the path and one had a huge rent in it.

Here the river was about twenty feet wide and as deep as this small and mostly shallow river was going to get. I struck out for the furthest bank following the figure swimming strongly for the other side.

I heard Andrew yell, "I'm with you Aumary," but did not hear him splash into the river and swim after me.

The other two soldiers at the side of the river had by now no doubt heard the cries and had come to tend to their wounded compatriot and help with the girl. Hal ran along the other bank keeping pace with our felon.

Andrew and I would follow the murderer.

Out of the water, he made for the stand of trees which bounded the village of Preshute. We heard his frantic and wet, slopping footsteps on the chalky ground. Clouds of midges danced about my head as I plunged through the undergrowth.

It was almost fully dark now and hard to see far ahead. I could see the flinty wall of the church come into view and the river bend around the graveyard. The flints shone white in the low light.

"Hal?" I cried out.

"Here, sir," came his voice from the other bank. "He's heading for the village across the fields."

Preshute was a very small village of some fifteen houses on the southern bank of the river, though there were other buildings; barns, outhouses, piggeries and of course, the church

"Please God," I said out loud, "do not let him take sanctuary in the church."

But I don't think it occurred to our arrogant felon.

After much running across open ground, he skirted the village, ran north, circuited the buildings and once more plunged along the riverbank. Good. I still had two men here one at the bridge and another at the mill. I could call them to stop him.

Once he reached the kink in the river where it began to straighten out and become shallower, he once more dived through the water, skirting the castle walls.

"Damn!" Now my men were on the wrong bank to apprehend him.

Andrew, puffing between words, came up at my shoulder.

"He's on the other bank. My guess is he'll swim the moat, avoid the bridge and go around the castle walls."

"You go to the bridge and find our men - one's at the castle mill, one at the bridge." I said.

"I'll swim the moat after him. If he's not going that way, you'll get him coming from the south."

"Glad you said that," said Andrew, his white teeth gleaming in the gloom. "I'm not as good a swimmer as you are." Then he was off.

Hal was a little way behind me, I thought, on the northern bank of the river. Soon he would be penned in by the castle wall.

I yelled his name again.

"Aye sir... coming to the castle moat now."

"I'm for swimming the moat and skirting the walls," I shouted. "Andrew is at the bridge."

"Right you are, sir."

"Can you meet our man coming round the northern side of the castle?"

"Providing he doesn't go west sir... to the Avebury road."

"Catch him before he can!"

"Right you are, sir," said Hal with a confidence I could tell he didn't possess.

At that moment our man splashed into the moat at the south west corner and I followed, now in almost total darkness.

His dun coloured tunic was not easy to follow and all I could see was the creaminess of the churned up water as he ploughed his way to the bank.

I was mere yards behind him now and he was tiring.

The moat side had been cleared of plants so that no man might have an easy hand hold should the castle should be stormed. The bank was slippery and he managed to gain a couple of yards as I lost my footing once or twice, trying to follow.

Round the western wall he went, vaulting the stanchions at the edge of the castle mound and making for the northern moat.

I heard the castle guard yelling that a figure had been spotted. Please they wouldn't loose arrows at us!

As I clambered over the barrier myself, our man reached behind him and a knife came out of a concealed scabbard. I heard him draw it and saw the gleam of it, in the faint light from a castle keep window.

I ducked, as I thought he had thrown it. But no, it was a feint to keep me at bay.

He dived into the moat again. I followed. My strength was ebbing. This time we were both slower swimmers.

He clambered out. I was yards behind him and legs pumping but now and again stumbling, he made for the town.

I yelled "Merrriman, Hal."

One answered me from my right, another from behind me. Both were quite distant. "He's by St. Peter's."

My felon and I had made better time than either of them, for Hal had had to negotiate the bend in the river, a longer passage on his side and Merriman had to run the length of the castle wall on its eastern side.

"He's a slippery bugg...."

"Aye, Hal, he is. If I know him, he'll make for Back Lane. Andrew along the High as quick as you can to the other end of the Backs."

Andrew sped off.

"Hal with me."

We ran, I squelched, in front of the few houses at the side of the church and up Chantry Lane. Our man could only hide in one of the two courts there or run on along the lane which had the open country of the Common on the left side and the backs of the houses of the burgage plots of the High Street on the other. One or two courtyards opened out onto the lane and there was a plethora of small plots for people to grow crops. Once or twice an outbuilding made a narrow corridor between the houses and the darkness might conceal a man with a knife.

Once more we launched ourselves into the pursuit.

A woman was coming out of her house at the back of Neates Yard as our felon passed though we did not see her, and there was a clang of a metal bowl dropped, a screech and a curse. Now we knew where he was.

We apologised our way around her.

At Chandler's Yard, the man fled down the track and came out on the High Street only to slip north once more through Ironmongers Lane a few yards further on.

At last a moon came out of clouds to help us and we saw the man leaping high over the crops at the back of houses between that lane and Kingsbury Hill. He was heading for the main road and eventually, the High Cross.

"Damn." I had asked Andrew to place himself at the very end of Back Lane, a few dozen yards up the hill. He would miss him.

However he did not miss him. He had not yet reached the lane.

We came out of Back Lane and ran down Kingsbury Hill. We heard a tussle and an oath.

Andrew had managed to get the man into a difficult position on the steps of the High Cross. His arm was across the man's throat and he leaned on the upright of the stone. Andrew was banging the man's wrist, the hand holding the knife, on the stone of the cross.

Sadly pressure on the fragile stonework made the cross base crumble. The whole thing wobbled and then toppled. Andrew fell forward as we watched and our felon rolled and ran free, down the High towards Angel Lane.

Hal went to Andrew's aid; I ran on again. My legs were aching and felt like whippy saplings. They would not obey me, but I stumbled on.

I risked one look back and saw Hal take Andrew into the doctor's house, close by the cross. He would follow me soon enough.

With great circumspection I entered the top of Angel Lane.

My fugitive was limping now, for the fall from the cross had damaged his leg. There he was hobbling down to the bottom and into the fuller's yard.

I gathered up my remaining energy and followed, closing the gates quietly but not barring them. I would want Hal to follow me in. For the first time, I drew my knife and regretted my sword left lying on the riverbank.

"C'mon. I know you're here," I shouted and my voice echoed strangely around the walls and tenting frames.

"You're tired and injured. How far do you think you'll get now?"

I heard a low growl from the rear of the furthest tenting frame nearest the back wall. I pictured in my head how the yard had looked in the daylight.

"You can't possibly hope to succeed against me. I'm a trained fighter. What are you? A bully and a murderer of old women and young maids." I was trying to bring him out into the open, to pique him to temper. Prod him into action.

"I was a soldier once too," came a voice. "We are evenly matched."

He had moved. He was now one tenting frame nearer.

"Ah... so that is how you learned to kill so efficiently, eh? I wondered about the missing years after you left the cooper's."

The murderer laughed. "I found it surprisingly easy to kill."

I stepped forward slowly, inch by inch. "Harmless bearwards, young girls, old ladies. Your speciality, eh?"

I reached the first tenting frame. Nothing was strung onto it.

"Milkmaids a strong point, is it? You tried to kill Berewynne tonight. First, to strike her down and then you tried to drown her. Would've been just another

215

sad accident, eh fuller?"

"You set me up."

"I did."

"Bastard! I hate you, Belvoir."

"Not so fond of you myself, fuller." I rounded the edge of the frame.

Suddenly he came at me. I ducked to avoid a blow. A cooper's axe. Narrow and long, the blade had been sharpened to a glistening hardness.

I spun round. In his left hand, he carried a thinner bladed adze with a curved handle. That too came whirring towards my head.

Where had these come from? Left concealed somewhere in the yard? No, the adze had been on his person. I remembered the milkmaid's split bucket.

The axe carried through and stuck into the wood of the tenting frame.

"Oh dear," I said. "What a miscalculation."

The murderer lurched towards me and kicked me in the chest. I fell back onto the outer frame which buckled under my weight. The pins which fixed the lengths of cloth to the wood dug into my back, for I'd abandoned my gambeson at the riverside.

I tore myself and my shirt from the pins and rolled onto the splintered frame, catching my hand on a further set of pins.

All I could see of my assailant was his open mouth grinning and an absence of teeth.

One more pass with the adze and he turned and fled the open space for the nearest fulling shed. I heard the yard gates open and Hal shout, "Aumary!"

"Here, Hal!"

"What?" said Hal as he took in my bloodied state. He held a flare high. "Thought light might be a good idea. What's 'appened?"

"He pushed me onto the tenting pins of the frame. Superficial only." But I did not tell him that they stung like fury.

"Andrew?"

" 'E's fine," said Hal. "Just a bit of an 'eadache."

"Our felon's in that shed," I pointed.

"How many exits?"

"I don't know. Windows big enough to drop to the river path maybe."

"Right. Be prepared then, for more running, eh?"

I doubled over and put my hands on my knees. "Oh, I do hope not."

After a moment's silence when we'd heard no noise of a man exiting the shed, we followed.

The door squeaked as it opened and a thrown knife came out of nowhere and hit the door post. I'd ducked sideways just in time.

"One weapon down, fuller. Tut... not a good idea."

The smell in the shed was overpoweringly acrid.

Hal found a place to secure the flare and it flooded the shed with light but it didn't reach into the furthest corners for, it was a large room. At least now we were not outlined by the light but it did throw outlandish shadows. Hal prised the knife from the door.

"Thanks for the present!" he yelled.

We split up. I went right, towards the offices and work benches. Nothing here. Hal worked his way over to the fulling machines.

The machines with their wooden paddle feet were silent now. The water wheel which powered them was inactive.

We searched under and around the machines. Nothing. All windows were on the water side and about six feet up. There was no other door. The light from our flare, flickering and unreliable, showed up the spars of wood and metal, all the moving parts as if they were some giant insect.

Suddenly we heard a grinding. Then a swoosh, as the paddles of the great wheel outside began to turn.

We spun around. Our felon was starting up the water wheel. As yet no moving parts of the fulling equipment were in motion, then one by one, the fuller flicked each lever and they began to clatter with the noise I'd heard when I'd been in the sheds asking questions. The noise was deafening and unnerving.

That is exactly why the murderer had started them up. It momentarily distracted us. Hal started for the door, believing the felon had capered in the torchlight for the exit. Shadows could be deceptive. I turned round. Behind me was our grinning and toothless fuller.

One pass with the adze and I gave way, moving towards the nearest machine. The paddles were now stamping up and down, dancing like so many little devilish feet in a disgusting mixture of urine, faeces and perhaps, fullers earth. No cloth was being danced on though.

He swiped at my middle and again; I moved back. His reach was longer than my knife but I was quicker and fitter and, dare I say it, cleverer.

I ducked another blow and brought my knife up to his thigh, slicing a good chunk from his wet tunic and hose and wounding the skin beneath.

He yelled and went for me again with little thought of where his blow would land.

I stepped backwards, felt the lip of the fulling tray and the reverberations of the machine in the middle of my back, then ducked under the legs of the frame.

The fuller came on with the momentum of his blow and fell head first into the noxious mixture.

I quickly jumped up behind him and held him there. His legs thrashed. He managed to turn around and attempted a kick to the cods which only partly made contact.

But he did make enough contact with me. I doubled up as the fulling hammer came down on the felon's head and there was an audible crack as it broke his cheekbone and nose. Quickly I threw him on the floor, where he gasped like a fish. Had I left him in the machine his head would have been mangled like a ripe peach.

Gasping myself and still doubled up I shouted, "Hal, turn off the machines."

"Tryin' to," he yelled. "Dunno which one's which!"

Eventually the machine and all its fellows stopped. Hal had found the lever to the outer water wheel.

I fell to my knees feeling very sick.

"God's cods, Aumary," said Hal. "Them's horrible things," pointing to the fuller's paddles. I looked over at my now semi-conscious felon.

"Never mind God's cods… Hal… what about mine?"

"Get yer did 'e?" he chuckled.

I nodded.

Hal turned the villain over with his foot "Well, we got 'im."

"Eventually." My breathing steadied at last and the pain died, "To the castle with him, I think."

I threw him in the gaol and asked the gaoler, a dapper man called Peterkin Gayle, to fetch the castle doctor. I would not have my prisoner dying of complications to his wounds before I could have him tried.

I turned at the door. The murderer was coming to his senses a little more now. Phew. Did he stink!

"Well. You led us a merry dance."

The felon spat at me.

"Thought you said you couldn't swim. What a lie. Seems you were born to it. Ah well."

The man sat up straighter. His left eye was beginning to close up and blood had streamed from his nose. His ugly face was even more ugly with the swelling of his cheek.

"Good Night Farmer," I said, "or should I say, Pounder. Sweet dreams. See you tomorrow."

And I went to get my own hurts seen to by a much better doctor up the street.

Chapter Thirteen

I was spread out over Johannes' workroom table, the wounds in my back being tended, when Andrew, lying on a pallet in the corner, came to.

"Christ's Bones Aumary!" he said. "That was some chase."

"Aye, almost three miles by my reckoning. You all right?"

"What happened? Did we get him?"

"We did. He's in the castle gaol getting his hurts seen to... ouch... by a much kinder doctor than this one, I think."

Johannes smirked. "Lie still and pay attention then!"

"What happened to me?" asked Andrew. "I don't remember."

"The High Cross gave way, the top fell onto you; a glancing blow, knocked you senseless. Pounder got away and ran down Angel Lane."

"Ah, so it was him as you thought. God's teeth, I feel so sick."

Andrew had attempted to sit up.

"Still, sit still and it will pass," said Johannes dabbing at my cuts with vinegar.

"Hal and I got him. He'll hang."

"The young lad Jem?"

"A cut to the arm. Not too bad. It was Pounder's cooper's adze. Had Jem not been wearing his sleeved hauberk, he would be minus a hand."

Andrew laughed. "He'll be a hero to young Berewynne, now."

I joined his laughter, "Aye, he will."

"Do you think he'll tell you what this was all about... Pounder, I mean?"

"Who's to know?" I got up from the table and pulled an old linen shirt belonging to Johannes over my head. "I think I understand most of it, but not all."

"Good luck getting him to speak then."

I shrugged. The action hurt my sore back. "He'll hang anyway. For the attempted murder of Berewynne. My own ears heard him say he found killing easy. I've some witnesses, some evidence. That will be enough to damn him."

I tried to tuck the shirt in to my damp braies. "Tssst! Ouch.I think I'll leave it loose." Johannes turned back to me from washing and wiping his hands.

"Aumary, be still. I haven't finished. I've got some salve for that."

*****

Next day, I managed to shrug into a woollen gambeson dug out from the castle armoury, much like the one that Jem had been wearing under his mail. My back stung abominably but I was happy that this was all the hurt I had sustained.

Johannes kept hold of Andrew for he wanted to make sure that his head was not more severely wounded than it appeared. Andrew slept on the palliasse in the workroom, the whole night and late into the morning.

Hal and I walked down the High to the castle and reported the injury of its major officer to one of its senior soldiers. Another took Andrew's place at the gatehouse for the time being.

Gayle let us into the gaol and we walked down the few steps and confronted Godwine Pounder, who had been Farmer, who seemed to have shrunk to half his size and he wasn't a large man anyway.

Harold the scribe set up his little table by the door, lit a candle, sharpened his pen and waited.

Farmer sat hunched up on the stone ledge which ran around the outer wall, a blanket around his shoulders. His hands were manacled and his feet fastened and the chain passed through a ring on the wall. His clothes were still damp from his swim. The light caught his bruised face as he looked up and saw us coming through the door.

He attempted a sneer but his ravaged features only produced a grimace.

The doctor had cleaned him up. The nose bone had been put back in place and a linen band tied tightly around it and fastened at the back of his head. He looked slightly ridiculous.

The damaged nose made his speech sound as if he had a head cold.

"Welcome to my humble abode, my Lord Belvoir. Sorry I can't offer you any refreshment."

"I wouldn't take it from your hand anyway, Pounder," I said.

I stood against the wall and folded my arms across my chest. Ouch. No, I couldn't lean on the spiky flint wall. Hal stood in the doorway, open for the scribe to write in the light.

"So, tell me, Pounder. Why?"

"Why what?"

"Why the bearward, the old lady, the dairymaid, Tylor, the mill?"

Pounder too folded his arms as best he could with his manacles and pressed his lips tight shut.

"You are guilty, as guilty as Cain was of killing Abel."

"Who are they then? Do I know 'em?"

"Not a churchgoing man then, Hal," I said, looking back at the door.

Hal scoffed. "Can't imagine it, Sir Aumary, 'e's apprenticed to the devil."

"Devil maybe, but you were apprenticed to Master Cowper all those years ago, weren't you, Farmer?"

"My, you have been doing your job," said Pounder, once Farmer.

"And he was rid of you because you were... shall we say... a most unpleasant apprentice."

"I hated coopering, that's all."

"And yet you learned enough in thirty months to take off the head of a cask and reset it."

"Must have been paying attention that day," said Hal.

I walked about the small room. There was just enough light coming in from the high window, a barred space at the base of the castle keep, and the door, for me to be able to see my prisoner. The gaol was dug into the top of the mound.

"So by your own admission you then went off and became a soldier. Where was this then?"

"Wales. 1191. Joined Old Henry's lot. Baldwin of Exeter was recruiting for the next crusade."

"You never made the crusade?"

"Nah... too much fuss going all that way. But I did fight in France."

Thus far, I was convinced this was the truth.

"Ah. And there you learned to fight and to kill?"

"I'm sure you have done your fair share, m'lord."

I laughed. "Actually Farmer, would it surprise you to hear that I have never killed a man in my life? God willing, I shall never have to."

Farmer scoffed and wiped his hand over his mouth. His manacles rattled. "Would've killed me though if you'd had to."

"The Lord Belvoir saved your petty little life, Farmer," said Hal with venom. "Those paddles would'a cracked your 'ead open like an egg."

I sat on the very end of the stone bench and rested my legs which ached from all the running of last night.

"Then what? You came back to Marlborough?"

"Had family here then."

"No longer?"

"No. Me brother died."

"Master Fuller took you on?"

"Aye. Learned the trade from the bottom up."

"But he would not make you his apprentice?"

"I didn't want to. Been there once. That was enough," sneered Farmer.

"Did Master or Mistress Cowper not recognise you?"

"They had no cause to come to the fuller's yard. I lived away from them down by the bridge. My appearance after years had changed. Why would they?"

"And naturally your name changed. People see what they expect to see, don't they? So here you are, happily working at the yard. What happened to change everything?"

There was no answer.

"Shall I guess? You met the bearward. What was he to you, Farmer?"

"No one."

"You did meet him."

"I saw him about."

"Which is more than most people, for he shunned the town."

"Ah, that was Tylor's doing."

"Why? Tylor was not an intimidating man. Why should the bearward be frightened off by him?"

"You know that Tylor had a plan to hire a bear for the town fair? He didn't want the council to see the old performing bear and decide it would do and spend the money on it."

"Aw c'mon Master Farmer!" I laughed. "You expect me to believe that? Yes, I know that Tylor had plans to hire a fighting bear to be baited with dogs. That would have to remain a secret. The dead bearward was another issue entirely, surely."

Farmer sighed "He was going to get the bearward for the fair with a quarter of the money collected and use the rest for the fighting bear." He looked up at me. "You know of course he stole the money from the Bible fund?"

"Aye, I know that."

"He contacted the bearman through his brother who knew about bears. The man used to winter in Bristol and he asked him to come for the fair but the stupid man came too early. He told the bearward to stay away till the fair. Go up to the forest. No one should see him."

"So how did his head get into the cooper's barrel? That was not Tylor's doing." I could see that Farmer was thinking quickly.

"He..."

"Whatever you are about to tell me is a lie, Farmer. The tiler was a simple man, no more capable of taking off a head than my daughter. He certainly didn't know how to open and mend a cask."

"It was an accident."

"An accident?"

"Aye, we argued and the bearman fell, hitting his head. So that no one would know him I took it off."

"Would it surprise you to know, Farmer, that there were no wounds to the bearward's head save the chopping of his head from his neck?"

"He was alive when you did that, you bastard. And you knew it," said Hal running his hands along his forked grey beard.

I saw Farmer swallow.

"So why did the head have to go into the cooper's barrel and be delivered to the mill?"

Farmer chuckled, "You tell me."

I rose. "All right. I will, as I see it."

I turned my back on him and looked up at the small window. A flock of starlings went noisily by.

"Your master, to whom you owe everything it seems, had an ongoing feud with the mill. It's all about water, isn't it? Water taken from the river. He failed in a court case four years ago to prevent Master Barbflet from filling his pond to capacity and so he thought he'd give them all a nasty shock, if not a nasty dose of poisoning."

"A warning, that's all."

I shook my head.

"Then there's the mill blast."

I turned back to him. "How did you learn about that, Farmer? Did you work in a mill too, in your long career?"

"You learn a lot of things... travelling here and there," he said, smiling.

"Indeed you do. I learned about dust blast for the first time when the mill was destroyed. I also learned that fuller's earth is the most dense kind of clay there is and that it was used to block up the ventilation holes of the mill. Now I wonder, who had access to fuller's earth?"

"Plenty of people."

226

I shook my head in disgust, once more.

"You killed two perfectly innocent and unconnected people in that mill."

"People die all the time."

"The mill will be rebuilt - would you then destroy it again and again?"

"When my master becomes town reeve, there would be no repairing of the mill."

"How was that to benefit the town, Farmer? People would starve without bread."

"My master would build a new mill."

"Ah... I see. A rival mill. No, not a rival... the only mill. Were you somehow planning on forcing Master Barbflet out of business?"

Farmer smiled.

"Or maybe Master Fuller would take over the town mill as town master?" I said. "Well," I added, "Hell will freeze when that happens. So now we come to the dairymaid. What did she see?"

Farmer had lapsed into silence again.

"You were out early in the mill yard. Did Audre see you at the eastern end of the mill at your work with the clay?" I looked at his face. "No. Perhaps not. At your work with the poor old lady Gytha then?"

A tick began by Farmer's good eye and would not stop. He lifted his hand to rub it and the other followed, being manacled together.

"She must have seen you go into the old woman's house."

"No!"

"Did she see you come out of the mill perhaps after stealing the key? I saw you too, you know. After the blast. Making your way back to the fuller's yard. You threw the key into the river and I recovered it. You have a particular way of walking, do you know that?"

Farmer looked quite shocked at that and once more his Adam's apple bobbed.

"A cocky little strut, on your bandy little legs. Your shoulders go up and down like the paddles of your mill. I saw you with your hood up but you looked back once. Bad move Farmer."

"The Lord Belvoir saw you and recognised you," said Hal. "Not a good move, looking back."

Farmer swallowed again. He wasn't to know this was a lie.

"So now we come to Tylor."

"Tylor was an idiot."

"Perhaps he wasn't the keenest arrow in the quiver, Farmer, no. His only crime was stealing the money. He murdered no one."

"He killed the old woman"

"Why?"

"Because she saw him with the dairymaid."

"Again Farmer, you have no idea about the people in this sorry tale. She could not have seen him. She was almost blind. And why would he want to murder his great grandmother?"

"His...?"

"Aye. You didn't know that, did you? I thought he might have told you."

Farmer went pale.

"However, the old woman had the keenest sense of smell and she smelled you, Farmer. Smelled you for the piece of dung you are. A fuller was with Audre when she died. She could not see you, but she smelled you. Others reported a yellow tunic was worn by the culprit. So many have yellow tunics. Even Hal here owns one."

"Saffron, sir."

I smiled.

"You wore yellow and you were spotted that night arguing with the tiler. What did you argue about?"

"I told you he was an idiot."

"Did you tell him things were getting a bit too difficult? Did he put cart and horse together to make an equipage, and realise that you had murdered

228

his grandam?"

Farmer sniffed.

"Did he tell you that he was going to the authorities and you said... ' You will not!' Am I right Hal? "

Hal nodded.

"No one heard me... no!" cried Farmer. "They can't have heard me. We were so...." He tailed off as he saw Harold scribbling furiously.

I tutted, "Undone by a little girl, Farmer. A little girl. She heard you. She saw you make to strike Tylor but he fought back, didn't he, and he ended up on the floor with a gashed head." I shook my head slowly. "He knew you'd followed his grannie into her house and killed her. She wounded you with the end of her distaff. Scraped you with the point." I chuckled, "And don't spout me the rubbish you did last time; the brambles at the side of the river got you on the way home. There are none! I've looked."

Farmer was sitting stock still.

"It isn't true."

"So now let's start at the beginning again." I nodded to Harold.

"Why did you kill the bearward?"

"I didn't."

There was a slight silence. Harold's pen ceased to scratch. The wood pigeons who often pecked for spilled grain in the bailey cooed to their mates from the roof tops.

"Come Farmer. If you tell me the truth I can make it easier for you. You'll hang anyway, of that there's no doubt; but I can ask that they drop you so you die quickly, or I can have you throttled for a few minutes. It's up to you."

I let that lie for a moment.

Farmer licked his lips. "He knew me."

"Knew you as Farmer?

"Aye. He was going to tell. I had to stop him."

"Tell what? That you were back in Marlborough? That you were trouble?

A violent man. A thief. That's hardly worth killing for."

"I knew him years ago. I...," Farmer licked his lips once more, "before he became a bearman, he was a leather worker."

"Ah... hence his clothes."

"I tupped his wife," he said, smiling.

"Well, why am I not surprised by that?" I said. "Where was this?"

"Out Gloucester way."

"When you were on your travels?"

"He got just a bit angry. She said she was leaving him, see, and coming with me."

"Had you encouraged her in this?"

"Nah, don't be daft. She was just another woman. I told her so." He laughed. "Stupid bitch came at me."

"And you killed her?"

"What do you think?"

"How?"

"I strangled her. The bearman caught me at it."

"He didn't raise the hue and cry?"

"Oh aye, he did. But I was gone before he came to his senses."

I passed my hand over my eyes. This man would murder for a word out of place.

"You met again?"

"On the river path - quite by accident. Tylor was with me. That's when he told the bearward to hop it."

"And he goes up into the forest, afraid of you. You follow. So the bearward dies nastily and you remove his head."

"Did you get pleasure out of 'is murder, Farmer?" asked Hal. "Watching 'is face as you 'acked off his 'ead."

"Knowing full well the man couldn't move to defend himself," I added.

"Wicked," said Hal, shaking his head. "Knowing that every blow could be felt by the poor sod."

"And I really don't believe this nonsense about the head in the barrel being solely a warning to Master Barbflet. So what's the truth about it?"

"The truth?" Farmer began to laugh hysterically. "Ah well, you'll have to ask Master Durwyn Cooper about that."

"Rest assured we shall, when we have finished with you," I said. "You aren't quite right in the head are you, Master Farmer?" I said, standing over him. "You have always been a little too easy to anger. A man who was eager with his fists, with any weapon to hand. A man who enjoys inflicting pain on another."

Farmer stared at me, his one good eye wide. He bunched his fists.

"You beat mistress Cowper didn't you? You liked to beat Audre the milk maid, I hear. Oh yes, we know you walked out with her some years ago and that she ended it."

"Little trollop! How dare she just drop me. Just like that. How dare she? Me?"

"Ah yes... anyone who does you what you see as an injury must suffer, mustn't they? And when you saw her that day talking to me, telling me things, you imagined that she must know something."

I sat again on the bench.

"You know, I wondered if she knew her attacker because of the words her friend Berewynne used when she saw her. She said that she looked shocked when she walked round the end of the mill building. She was. Shocked to see you again. Perhaps you hadn't made yourself known. Perhaps you'd kept out of her way. Your appearance was quite different anyway."

"You should've seen her face when I grabbed her and told her who I was," he chuckled. "She never came into the yard, see. The fulling yard men would go out into the lane to buy milk. She hadn't seen me, not for years, but I'd seen her."

"So you pulled her to the back of the mill on the river path and thrust your cooper's adze into her neck. One blow. And you tipped her into the mill pond which was conveniently high in water. She floated round the leat and her friend saw her. Naturally you were away then by the water path and back in your yard in minutes."

Farmer smiled the most unpleasant smile.

"Berewynne found her just before I did. Oh, and no, before you ask. She didn't see anything. This was just a story we put out to catch you, Master Farmer. And you so willingly gobbled our hook."

So quickly and without warning, not a drop of malice showing in the eyes, the felon was on his feet. He threw the manacles over my head and pulled tight. Hal made a lunge for me but I'd already kicked the feet from under Farmer and he fell to the floor.

"Get up, you pathetic apology for a man," I said, disentangling myself from the chain.

He dragged himself up to the bench once more.

"Try something like that again and I might forget my aversion to killing. There would be no inquiry, should you be found dead in your cell, would there, Hal? After all, I am the law here."

Hal shook his head, "Oh no, sir. Unfortunate accident, I'd say."

I heard Harold cough but when I looked back at him, he just smiled.

"I ought to break your miserable neck. Three attempts on my life, Farmer. Bludgeoned in Church Alley, then an attempt to knife me at the doctor's house and as Hal here will attest, an arrow in the back by St. Peter's church. Getting too close, wasn't I? You felt threatened. Unsafe. I'd crossed you. My poor horse. What had he ever done to you?"

"I hate you, Belvoir."

"Not very fond of you either, Farmer.

"Bastard!"

"So anyone who crosses you must suffer. In your world, Audre had crossed you; Tylor had crossed you too. He was going to tell all. He suspected that you had murdered the old lady. Gytha knew that you had been with Audre shortly after the girl had helped her draw water from the mill pond. She knew, because

232

she smelled you. She knew that you had climbed over the wall of the cooper's yard. It was dark. You didn't see her. Her house is mere paces away; she smelled you then. Naturally she didn't see it was you that dark night, but she knew your voice as you called to Audre on the day of her death. Heard you as you talked to her. She knew you, for you had been unkind to her when you were apprenticed to Cowper as a younger man, and in those days Gytha had her sight. She remembered you. She would remember a man who beat her."

"She was a stupid old woman."

"Everyone who crosses you is stupid, aren't they, Farmer?"

"You think you are the clever one," said Hal "when all the time it was you being stupid. Jumping to conclusions. Imagining everyone knew something."

"Me... stupid? Pah! Me?" spat Farmer.

"So you lured Tylor to the crypt. Did you tell him that Master Fuller wanted a word? That would have brought him running."

"Stupid bastard. He really was soft in the head you know," said Farmer, with a slight giggle.

"So now, we come to the head. Oh, you have waited so long for this opportunity, haven't you. To get even with Master Cowper and his wife?

"He deserved it."

"But no, you weren't going to kill him. That was too quick. You wanted him to really suffer."

"He told me I would never make a cooper. I didn't have the patience required, he said. I was too sloppy in my work. Coopering is such an exact art. I didn't have the art in my bones, he said. How dare he! His wife told me I was an arrogant bastard with a high opinion of myself. Well, I'd show them. I could make a cask. I could take it apart and put it back together so they wouldn't know it wasn't their own work." He started to giggle again. "A severed head in his own barrel. Haha! I wanted him to be taken for the murder."

"He had an alibi. I know that a wife cannot testify for a husband but still...."

"Ah, but if you had prodded you would have found out that he was in the

Green Man as he said… yes but that he had plenty of time to do the deed. His wife lied for him. He wasn't at home as early as midnight... oh no. He was dead drunk on the river path for a long time before he sobered and went home. A long time to do the deed. Put the head in the barrel. I know because I carried the drunken man there and left him. He had no idea who was with him."

"So you put your childish plan into action. Frame Durwyn Cowper for the murder. The head is in his barrel. It must be him."

"Childish? Childish? I wanted him to be taken for it." Farmer began to blubber. "I wanted to be there when you strung him up and hear his bitch of a wife screaming and crying. I wanted to watch as they dropped him and I wanted to hear his bloody neck snap!"

"We knew he wasn't the felon. He had no motive."

"You gotta hang him. I want you to hang him." Farmer was incandescent with rage "I want to hear him draw his miserable last breath!" He was crying in fury now. "I want the town to know what a fool he is. I want him to lose his good name. I want him to hang. He MUST hang!" he sobbed between clenched teeth - those he had left.

"Just because you want something in this world, Farmer, it does not mean it will happen. In your perfect world, you get your own way. That is not true of life. This is about personal vengeance, isn't it, and it's also about the will of your master the fuller."

Farmer drew his arm over his eyes, dislodging the band over his nose. "He hates Barbflet."

"So you did his dirty work for him."

"I was well rewarded."

"You'll be rewarded all right," said Hal, "it'll be your neck that's snapped, not the cooper's."

*****

We left Farmer blubbering and repeating over and over, "He must hang,

234

I want him to hang."

Poor Harold looked shocked.

"Go and write up what he said please, Harold," I said patting him on the back. "And don't worry about it."

Yes, Paul. My poor scribe was upset by what he'd heard, but like you he was a young man with little experience of a wicked world. He had spent his life so far, secluded in the keep of the castle with other men of like mind, scribbling lists of supplies and copying dry legal depositions. This was a real awakening for him.

Hal came out into the light and Peterkin Gayle locked both the cell door and the outer door with his bunch of keys. Hal thrust his arms above his head and yawned.

"All done then, sir," he said. "We'll be stretchin' 'is neck within the year's end."

"Not quite done, Hal.

"Oh?"

"When Harold is finished and we have had our dinner, we shall all go down to the fulling mill and confront the man who is at the centre of all this. The spider in his web."

"Warin Fuller?"

"Aye, our upright councillor. We'll see what he has to say."

"Surely now we 'ave 'is right 'and man in the gaol and blubberin'...."

"Ho no, Hal! Don't underestimate our wily councillor. I'm sure he has a lie or two to be plucked from nowhere. But before we do anything, we must send a party out to the Elcot mills. We are missing some dogs somewhere, you remember?"

The men who kept the king's hounds and de Neville's as well, at the castle were more than happy, for a little silver, to go and bring the lost dogs back. They were used to such beasts. I thought this the easiest solution. Armed with sticks, muzzles and a warrant to search the place and apprehend the dogs, the men trotted off the mile or so to Elcot, chatting as if this was all in a day's work for them. I told the houndmaster that if they met with resistance they were to come back and armed men would go back with them. They were on the king's business and any man who did not cooperate was guilty of treason. That would be enough to ensure compliance.

The dogs were as I had thought, at the mill, once again locked in a shed far enough away from the main buildings to be kept, in part, at least a secret"

*****

Fuller was at his mill in Marlborough and as yet knew nothing about our raid on his mill in Elcot. He did however know that Pounder had been arrested. I took Gallipot with me as a representative of the town council. He stood quietly at the back. Harold once more acted as scribe.

Fuller's face was pasty and sweat beaded his brow when he saw us enter.

I nodded. "Master Fuller."

"My Lord Belvoir." He returned the courtesy. "Gallipot," he nodded.

"I have my scribe here, Fuller. I hope you do not object to his presence?"

Fuller licked his lips.

"A cool day, Master Fuller, for you to be so warm that you perspire. Are you ill, sir?"

"I am a little discomforted, yes. I hear you have my man Pounder in your gaol. Explain if you will, what he is doing there, sir?"

"Oh I will, Master Fuller. You may like to be seated."

Fuller looked at my smiling face. He knew the smile was not a sincere one.

"You know the man as Pounder then?"

"His name I believe is Godwine Pounder, yes."

"And yet when he was apprenticed to Master Cowper in Crook's Lane, some years ago, his name was Farmer."

"Fancy that," said Fuller, sitting slowly in his chair. "I had no idea."

"You do not ask me why he saw fit to change his name?"

"If it is his will, he may do so. It's not a crime, is it, my lord?"

"No, but the act of changing a name may *conceal* crimes."

"And with which crime do you accuse my man, sir?" he asked.

"Ho ho, Fuller. There are many, spanning quite a few years."

"You have evidence, I hope?"

"Better than that, a confession."

"No doubt obtained under duress. I will have a lawyer...."

"No duress, though that in itself is not illegal. I could have had him tortured, Fuller, even though it's frowned upon, but it's not my way. No duress, save that I told him when he hanged, I would ensure that his neck was broken - a swift death. I would not leave him to throttle. Have you ever seen a man throttle to death, Master Fuller? It's most unpleasant."

"I do not indulge in the bloodthirsty pastimes of the masses, my Lord Belvoir. I stay away from that sort of thing."

"Ho ho. But you will allow a bear to be tied to a stake and worried by dogs. Dogs, which more often than not, end up with horrendous injuries. Dogs which die of those injuries, Fuller."

"I most certainly do not."

"We found 'em, sir," said Hal. "At the back o' the mill at Elcot."

"If you found dogs there, they were not held there at my will." I reached into my cotte.

"I beg to differ."

I placed the parchment very deliberately on his table.

"This is the sworn statement of one of your men at the mill sir. He tells of you asking to take the dogs from St. Martin's by cart, to your mill at Elcot."

"He lies."

"I am sure we can find the cart. We might find evidence of the dogs being in it. I don't know, but it's possible."

"It is a lie. Whose mark is this? Let me question him myself."

I shook my head. "So that you can have him... erm... removed, sir? I think not."

I heard Master Gallipot behind me shift his feet. It was clear he was shocked by what he was hearing

"A fierce bear was to be procured by Tylor, was it not, with the money the two of you stole from the Bible fund."

"No sir. I know nothing of the bear fund."

"No doubt the bear would be housed out there in that lonely place, Elcot. Maybe the fighting too would take place close by. There's a deal of money to be made, Fuller. And you love money, Master Fuller."

"No more than the next man."

"No, I cannot see a man of your nature there at the bear pit, with goggling eye and slavering mouth, betting on the dogs. Yours was a more... pecuniary interest, wasn't it? You would send out your man and your faithful servant would bring back the money you would make from it all. Nothing more."

I decided to sit in front of him. He had not asked me to be seated but I pulled up another chair which had been set against the wall.

"You have very discontented workmen, sir."

"I do not. I dispute it."

I tutted. "It's so difficult isn't it, to make a man work hard?"

"That is what my overseer Master Pounder is for, m'lord," said Fuller, clenching his teeth. "And you have removed him from his work."

"Forever I'm afraid. You'll be needing a new man." I saw Fuller's lip quiver. "No, your workers are very unhappy. They do not like to be forced to tread the cloth themselves when the river is not high enough to turn the wheels of your machines. I don't blame them. I do see your point though. It isn't your fault that the river isn't high enough. It's Master Barbflet's fault, isn't it?"

Fuller took a deep breath through his nose and his nostrils flared. "It is, sir."

"You lost your litigation. Why was that? Corn is more important than

238

cloth? No?" Fuller sat back in his chair. I could tell he was worried about what was coming next.

"I looked up the records, Master Fuller. Nicholas Barbflet agreed to limit the number of times he took a deal of water from the river. You agreed that you would dig a pond of your own and keep it for emergencies when Barbflet was compelled to use more water. I see no evidence of a pool, sir. Neither here nor at Elcot."

"These things take time, m'lord. And money."

"Aw come, Master Fuller. Four years? That's time enough. You have plenty of money. You are buying the old chandler's house. That will not cost breath and spit, sir."

I crossed my leg nonchalantly over my knee. Gallipot just behind me crossed his arms over his chest and cleared his throat.

"Best you tell the truth, eh Warin," he said shakily.

Fuller looked up at his fellow councillor.

"This is all complete rubbish, Gabriel. And a misunderstanding."

"Your man misunderstood your instructions when he stole the key to the mill, fixed the mill wheels and blocked up the air holes with fuller's earth then?" I said.

Gabriel Gallipot started and unclenched his arms. "No! Not the mill!" He wiped his brow with a shaking hand. "I remember a conversation," he said, "some time ago. A proud Barbflet telling the council that he had made the mill safer for his workers and for the town by inserting holes into the wall. I remember you quizzing him most explicitly. Oh yes sir, I do. Most explicitly."

"A misunderstanding, Gabriel," threw out Fuller. "It's true that relations between Master Barbflet and myself have soured of late but that does not mean I would wish to ruin the man."

"You began with the head in the barrel. Pounder tells me that was your idea," I ploughed on.

"He lies. It most certainly was not. Why ever would I wish to do such a thing?"

"He tells me it was a warning. A bit of fun. An attempt to poison those at the mill. When it failed, and you realised that it had been intercepted and would not now reach the mill, the building had to go, didn't it? Of course you knew that Farmer had reasons of his own to frame the cooper."

"I most certainly did not, m'lord."

"Frame the cooper... my lord?" asked Gallipot, "Durwyn Cooper?"

"Yes, Gabriel. Years ago, Farmer, alias Pounder was his apprentice and they had a nasty falling out. Earlier today, Farmer yelled to the rooftops that he was desperate to get even with him and have him hanged for the murder of the bearward."

Fuller's eyes narrowed. He wanted to know what else his man Pounder had said. "Why would he wait so long?" he asked.

"Oh you mean a cosh over the head in a deserted alley, a knife in the ribs in a dark yard, an arrow loosed from the top of a tower. Yes, more his style I agree, but he wanted the man to suffer the ignominy of knowing that the whole town saw his mortification, his shame. And he wanted to see him hang. Killing him was not enough."

"Oh dear me... oh dear, dear me," said Gallipot.

"His master, Fuller here, was becoming a power in the town and with it Pounder was a rising star. He waited for just the right opportunity. So, both of you had a hand, if you will forgive me, in putting the bearward's head in the barrel. Your idea, and Pounder's execution."

"Why did the bearward die?" asked Gabriel, running his hand over his forehead once more.

"Another old feud. Pounder is good at those, Gabriel. The bearward whose name was Godfrey Barend met Farmer years ago and recently recognised him as the man who had killed his wife. He had to go."

"Oh... this is most distressing," said Gallipot in a faint voice. I offered him my seat which he accepted gratefully.

"So now we come to the death of the tiler. Tylor was getting a little jittery, wasn't he? I'd found him out. He didn't like that. Came to you jibbering. He had to go."

"No, Warin. Tell me that it wasn't you…," said Gabriel Gallipot.

"Of course it wasn't me, Gabriel. This is a parcel of lies!"

"He wanted to confess about the bear fund and he wanted to implicate you and Pounder. That couldn't happen, could it, Master Fuller?"

Fuller's hands were flat on his table and suddenly they clenched. "I have had enough of this stupidity. I know nothing about any of this. If my man Pounder has broken the law he shall hang. Just because he works for me does not mean I knew about his affairs."

"You knew it all. You paid him well. We have been to his house. We have recovered his thirty pieces of silver, sir. The money you paid him to bribe and threaten and murder and betray. We found the bow too, which he used in his attempt to murder me. Naturally the weapon he used to murder his victims, I found on his person last night. It's a narrow bladed cooper's adze. Perfect for the blow to the neck or spine. He tried it on me."

Fuller blinked. "I did not know him when he was a cooper."

"No, but you had him working in your mill many moons ago… oh no, not here, but in Elcot. That's why he was rarely seen in the town in the early days."

"No employer can possibly know the truth about the history of every man he employs."

"No, I will agree and I have reason to know this but his temper and his willingness to undertake, shall we say… unsavoury tasks for you, was why you kept him on."

"Rubbish!"

"He has confessed to save himself a painful hanging. He has implicated you. You are guilty, oh not of the actual murders, but you planned them, or ordered them. Pounder alone murdered Barend, the girl and the old lady, but the death of Tylor, the two masons and, had he succeeded, me, were your conceptions,

Master Fuller."

Fuller's nostrils flared once again.

"I refute it entirely."

"Ah... I forgot... Hal, do you have our piece of parchment ?"

"I do, sir." Hal took the parchment from his gambeson. It was a tiny slip of a thing.

"The first rule of thumb, Master Fuller. Never put anything down in writing but that you destroy it afterwards."

I read the piece of parchment. "It's a mere strip of course, but it is in your hand and bears your signature."

"What is it, m'lord?" asked Gabriel white faced.

"It's the note sent by Master Fuller to the bearman in Bristol requesting a fierce bear to be reserved for the town council, for August."

"NO!" shouted Fuller trying to grab the letter. Hal was there immediately pinning him back in his seat.

I read, "A fierce and angry bear so that we might entertain the town with a goodly spectacle. A bear to be baited with dogs."

Fuller glowered under his brows.

"I did not write that."

"Master Cordwainer's brother in law is a wine importer in Bristol. I merely had him look around for a buyer of bears there and question him. It was not difficult to find your request, sir."

"Pounder swore to me that he had destroyed that letter. He could not read. He....would not have left it. Damn the man and his stupidity...," he tailed off.

Fuller watched as Harold's pen scratched on the parchment.

I was silent.

I put the paper down on the table in front of Fuller. It was one of Master Gallipot's prescriptions.

*****

Fuller glowered. "You seek to hoodwink me, sir."

"Warin, tell the truth," said Gallipot, wiping his forehead with a small cloth. "It can do you no good now to lie. We have all heard you."

"Heard me what Gabriel?" Fuller pursed his lips.

"Heard you admit to ordering a bear when it was not your job to do so. Heard you...."

"I merely wrote a note for Tylor since he could not write, requesting a bear to be procured for the fair. You have no evidence to suggest that I am involved in the moving of the money, nor the setting up of the illegal fighting."

"Sadly sir," I sighed, "it's not illegal. What you do on your own land is your affair."

Fuller smirked.

"And I'm sure that whatever monies were made from such an enterprise would be recorded so that tax could be levied by the king's tax gatherers."

Fuller blustered. "There would be...."

"Done this sort of thing before, have you, Fuller?" I asked.

"Certainly not."

"Then you will have no objection to my men at the castle, the clerks responsible for recording the taxes paid by the town, looking through your records? You can have nothing to hide surely, Master Fuller."

Fuller stared at me and went bright red. Almost as red as his hat.

"I can have my men prepare...."

"Oh no, Master Fuller. No mill employee will touch the records. In fact, I have had soldiers secure your home at Elcot and the mill office there and I will do it here too. I would not like to think that things could go... astray."

I saw Fuller's hand shaking.

"Hal can you organise that please. Ask Andrew Merriman."

"Right you are, sir," and the door banged.

"What else might we find as we search your home, Master Fuller?"

"Nothing that should not be there, I can assure you. And do not worry my wife or my son and daughter. I shall not...."

"Ah yes. They live at the Elcot mill, don't they? It is always so sad when a great man falls and his innocent family must fall with him."

"What do you mean by that, sir? Explain yourself!"

"You know how small towns are, Master Fuller. Gossip will be rife. It will soon become known that we are investigating your businesses. Speculation will build upon speculation. Unsavory tidbits will be shaken out like so many fleas from a beggar's clothes. All those little secrets...."

"I have no secrets from my family, sir."

"No? Then I must be wrong when I learned that you keep a mistress out at Preshute. A lady by the name of Edith, I heard. So much more convenient when you buy the house on Chantry Lane in Marlborough. Adultery is a sin, yes, but not yet a crime, of course."

"Many men of worth keep mistresses," said a flustered Fuller.

"But not an upright town reeve, Fuller," said Gabriel Gallipot forcefully. "They must be, like Caesar's wife, beyond suspicion."

It was then that the outer door opened and a young man entered. The family resemblance was unambiguous. He looked to be in his twenties with a shock of dark hair and deep brown eyes.

"Vyvyan," said Fuller with a quaver in his voice. "What do you do here? You should be at the mill in...."

"Aye I know but something has come up, father." He glanced at me and nodded. Then he saw Gallipot. "Master Gallipot."

"Do not bother me now. I'm busy."

"You know Pounder's in gaol?"

"Yes, these good gentlemen have come to inform me." Fuller recovered a little poise. "Where are my manners? This is my son Vyvyan. He manages the mill at Elcot for me. This is the constable, Vyvyan, Sir Aumary Belvoir, Lord of Durley and Savernake warden. He has been investigating the terrible murders

244

in the town."

I nodded. He bowed.

"And the dogs have been removed."

Fuller winced. "Yes I know that Master Tylor's dogs have gone."

"Tylor's? I thought they were your dogs which you...."

"VYVYAN! Go back to Elcot. You are not needed here," yelled Fuller.

The young man folded his arms over his chest. "What's going on?"

"Master Pounder has been taken for the recent murders and now lies in the gaol, Vyvyan. It seems he tried to murder the cons...."

Vyvyan Fuller laughed. "I told you not to trust him. You knew he was violent. Whyever you kept him on, I don't know."

"Vyvyan! Be quiet!" but the admonishment didn't touch the young man.

It was obvious there was no love lost between father and son.

Fuller's son uncoiled his arms and walked round the table to stand behind his father.

"Useful to you though, wasn't he?"

Fuller turned and glared at his son.

"I said, return to Elcot. You must have things to do there."

"Plenty," said Vyvyan, not making any effort to shift himself.

"So, Sir Aumary, what evidence do you have that Pounder committed these crimes?" he asked.

"I'm not yet at liberty to divulge too much. Suffice it to say we can put the blast at the corn mill down to him and other killings."

"Master Barbflet's place? I heard it had gone up in smoke." Vyvyan looked at his father. "Got your wish at last then, father? I often heard you joking that you'd like to torch the place." He chuckled.

Fuller gave his son such a look that Vyvyan stepped back.

"A joke, father. Just a joke. Like your own."

"A joke or not, Master Vyvyan, it seems your father paid Pounder to block up the ventilation holes of the mill and tamper with the wheels. The result was the destruction of the mill and the death of two of its millers," I said. "And the injury to many others, including Nicholas Barbflet."

Vyvyan Fuller went white.

"No. No. Father wouldn't do that. It was all wishful thinking... a joke. Wasn't it, father? You were angry, but you wouldn't do such a thing. After Master Barbflet beat you in court...." He tailed off.

Master Fuller was rigid in his chair. Then he put his elbow on the table and his head in his hand.

Vyvyan distanced himself further. He moved around to the front of the table.

"You wouldn't kill for it... no, I can't believe you'd kill," he said leaning over his father, white knuckles pressed against the wood of the table.

Fuller looked up at his son with such venom, that had he been able to bite like a venomous snake, the young man would have been dead.

"My God... you did, didn't you?"

"His hand was not the one that wielded the weapon but his was the brain which planned it, Vyvyan," I said.

Vyvyan almost staggered back. "No, I can't believe that. He was angry but he would never...."

"When the words are committed to parchment, Master Vyvyan, perhaps the constable will let you read what Pounder has said," suggested Gallipot.

"Aye, I can do that," I said sadly.

Vyvyan looked at the floor.

"Never, never did I think it was anything other than the wishful thinking of an old man thwarted in his ambitions."

Warin Fuller turned his face away from his son. "Go home, Vyvyan," he said quietly, "Go home to your mother."

*****

After a little while, Hal returned to the mill and we accompanied Master Fuller to the castle gaol.

In deference to his status as a town councillor, I allowed him to be incarcerated in one of the tower keep rooms.

Hal came out from the room after he and Peterkin Gayle had settled him there. I told him the part of the story he had missed when running up to the castle and organising the search party for the fulling mill in Marlborough.

"Still no confession, but damning evidence then, sir."

I shrugged. "It will depend on the judges. If they accept that Pounder is merely being malicious in implicating his master, we may lose him. I doubt we'll get a word from the close lipped Fuller himself."

"We can hang Pounder at any rate."

"Aye, that we can, or the justices can. But Fuller? He can pay lawyers to refute our arguments against him."

"Damned by his own son... now there's a thing," said Hal, shaking his head. "Who'd a thought it?"

"You should have seen his face." I said. "There was such anger in it, I thought he was going to grab young Fuller by the throat."

Later that day, my words became an actual event.

Vyvyan Fuller came to see his father at the castle, bringing clothes and items he would need for his prolonged stay.

Peterkin Gayle stood outside the door as the Fullers stood face to face. He heard part of the conversation.

"Mother is beside herself, sir."

"Take her and your sister to your grandam's in Newbury until this is over."

"I have instructed the lawyers to come and look to your case."

"I will be out soon enough."

"I have read the deposition of Godwine Pounder, sir. I... I... think...."

"What you think, boy, is of no import. Your duty now to me is to rule the mills and look after your mother and sister until I can come home."

Gayle said there was a silence before the young Fuller said. "I would like to believe in your innocence sir, but... I do believe you guilty."

"My guilt or innocence is not your affair. My lawyers will...."

"...Have a hard time proving your innocence, sir."

"Not a shred of actual evidence comes back to me. Nothing. I am a careful man. I guard my tongue... unlike you, you little toad."

"I cannot stand back and let what you have done go...."

"You are my son, your loyalty is to me."

"No sir, my loyalty is to the truth and to justice. Six people died and were several injured. Are lives worth so little to you? Ah... I should be able to answer my own question there."

"How dare you!"

"Lives are nothing to you, are they? Money is all. Money and power and status. I have known this since I was a child. Mother, me, Frevisse... we were all pawns to be used in your game and we are family. How much easier was it for you to sanction the death of...."

Gayle then said that young Fuller was cut short and through the door he heard a shuffling and gurgling. When a body hit the door, Gayle burst in to see the elder Fuller had pinned his son by the neck to the wall and was throttling him.

Afterwards, when Vyvyan Fuller was extricated from his father's grip and the door had been locked, Gayle asked him if he would like to press a charge of attempted murder or at the very least striking him with intent to wound him.

Vyvyan, shaking his head and rubbing his bruised throat said, "No. My father's present sins will see him out. I do not need to add to the list."

At last I was able to return home.

Chapter Fourteen

I returned home to the thorny problem of what to do with the bear, Isabella. Lydia and I sat and discussed it with Hal, Crispin, John, Peter and Walter Reeve. We were all agreed, even Peter, who had grown to love her, that we could not keep her at the village. She was now cured of her wounds, her mangy fur was beginning to grow again, her eyes were bright and her ears perky, in spite of the fact that she was not a youthful creature. We were all worried that whoever took her on, would not treat her properly and that she would fall into disease and suffer ill treatment. None of us wanted this.

The problem was solved in the simplest way. On May 4th 1206 when the village was basking in bright sunshine and the cow parsley was nodding in the lanes in the breeze, the King's party rode into Durley. He was on his way, he said, to Freemantle in Hampshire and since this was in his path, he might as well stop and sup with me. The baggage train was far behind him and he travelled with a few men. John was a traveller with a restless energy and had an amazing stamina for riding around his country, visiting his royal mansions and castles and those of his subjects.

After a good dinner of capon in a ginger sauce and some of my fine Bordeaux wine, John relaxed and began to open up about his failure to keep hold of his lands on the continent. I told him of our recent murders and the solving of them.

We were alone in my office when suddenly the subject changed.

He threw his leg over the arm of the chair.

"So, shall I hear this case of yours in person, Aumary? I can if you like."

"My Lord King, surely that would mean you'd be delayed here and...."

"Nonsense, we can do it and have it out of the way in no time."

"My liege, surely you have better things to do?" It was well known that John enjoyed the law. Had he not been King, I think he would have made a superb lawyer. As it was, he was a superb organiser.

"Make a change from 'send this money here, buy arrows there, find horses from there, build another ship'...," he laughed.

"Such is the lot of a King, sir."

John chuckled. "Pah! I'm on my way to Aquitaine. I'll not have my mother's lands in the hands of that arrogant devil, Philip. You know of course I had to abandon my last attempt at Poitou. Bloody man threatened to invade us here! This island. HERE!"

"Yes, I remember. We were all ready for them in Marlborough," I smiled.

John grinned. "Aye, no doubt you were. De Neville had things under control too, I hear."

"He did, my lord."

"Hmmm. Watch him Aumary. I don't entirely trust him

I was staggered and said so. "But my lord, he is your old friend. One you have trusted with many roles in your government. What has changed to...?

"Things do change, Aumary." John looked sad. "How many people have I trusted, whom I now have cause to mistrust?"

I knew that he was talking about one of his long standing friends and supporters, William Marshall from whom he had become estranged.

John sat up straight. "No, it's just a feeling in the bones but I don't trust him."

"Is he with you sir, at the castle?"

"No, I sent him on ahead. So what say you? Shall we examine these fullers of yours?" I could not say no.

*****

John and I returned to Marlborough castle later that day and the fullers were brought before him. I smiled to see all confidence go from Warin Fuller when he saw that his monarch was to be his judge.

It was brief and fair. John heard all evidence, heard every statement read out, asked for witnesses to come forward. How could they not obey their King?

He ruled that Pounder be hanged in Marlborough, for there was no need to send him to Winchester since John himself had pronounced and these were Marlborough crimes. Marlborough should see the end of such a felon, said John. The man was dragged out screaming and kicking, still insisting that the cooper be hanged in place of him.

John looked long and hard at Warin Fuller, who quaked under his stare.

"You are guilty, Fuller, of that there is no doubt. If Sir Aumary tells me you are found out, then sir, you are found out."

He looked down at the notes that had been made for him, on a waxed tablet. "He owns the mill here in the town?"

I nodded.

John furrowed his brow. "Profitable?"

"The clerks tell me, very much so, sire."

"Then I'll have a fine. Sell the mill at Elcot- I will have the profits. I'll leave the town fulling mill for the son who will also send me yearly, upon the anniversary of the day of this trial, an amount which I have yet to decide. Is that fair Sir Aumary?"

I am, in general, averse to capital punishment, for I do not think it works to deter crime, but my tongue itched to say to John that I thought this man should hang. I know John was ever mindful of money gathering and to be truthful, the fuller was a broken man. It was a good solution.

"It's fair, my liege."

John rose, as did we all.

"And the man?"

"He may rot for all I care," and he went off to his supper.

*****

The following day he passed by the manor again on his way to Hampshire, having stayed overnight at the castle. In the early morning he and his retinue clattered into the yard. John bounded up the steps.

"Well, Aumary, a good day yesterday."

"Yes, sir, a very good day."

And we fell to chatting about the legal minutiae of the case.

After a while, John prepared to leave. He turned back.

"Your last letter told me you had a son."

"I do, sire. He is but a few weeks old now."

"I'm glad for you. I'm yet to get one you know. But I will. In time. Not that I haven't proven myself with others, you understand."

"I am convinced of it, John." I said, smiling widely.

The King and I were old companions from boyhood. I was allowed now and again to give him his given name but I had to carefully pick my day.

"Where's that perky daughter of yours... she must be what... six now?"

"Hawise is seven just...." and before I knew what I'd said, "she's out in the meadow with her bear."

John laughed out loud for a moment or two.

"I thought for a heartbeat you'd said 'her bear' then, Aumary!"

I scratched my head. "Hmm I did, my King."

"This I must see," said John striding down the hall.

On our way to the meadow, I explained that I had rescued the performing bear of the murdered bearward, Barend and that Peter was now her keeper. Hawise and he were Isabella's especial friends.

"Isabella!" roared John. "What a name for a bear!"

"Aye John, named after your wife." I did not tell him it was his first wife, for his second was also called Isabella and he doted on her.

He chuckled all the way to the meadow where Peter, with his back to us, was putting Isabella through her paces.

"And so Isabella, how are you today? Are you well?"

The bear nodded.

"Well enough to dance for us?"

Peter touched the bear lightly on the leg with a stick and she began to caper.

John roared some more. Peter turned quickly. It took him a while to realise who was standing by me for the sun was behind us. Then he dropped to his knees. Hawise, who was with him giggling, shielded her eyes from the sun and peered. Then she too made a wobbly curtsy.

"Hello King," she said.

"Hello Hawise," said John, approaching and leaving me behind. "What have you here?"

"This sir, is our pet Isabella. She does all sorts of tricks."

"Then...," John sat down on the grass cross legged, "let us see some more."

No one would have credited it. The ruler of this little island realm of ours and a few other places besides; a powerful man, with the right of life and death over his subjects, as we had seen yesterday, burdened as he was by loss of land, a French enemy and recalcitrant barons, sitting on the grass roaring with laughter at a performing bear, controlled by a young man of fifteen and a girl of seven.

I stood behind him and laughed too.

"This is marvellous!" said John, dusting down the regal backside when he sprang up from the grass.

"You wanted a home for her Aumary, you said?"

"Aye sir, a friendly, kind and caring home."

"Then let me take her. She shall have her very own place at the Tower, good food and plenty of it, grass to run on, people to see to her every wish. I promise she will be kindly used."

I looked at Peter and Hawise with my eyebrows raised.

They looked stricken but managed a smile. What could they say?

John went fearlessly up to the bear and stroked her brown fur.

"Come up any time to see her. You shall see her whenever you wish."

*****

Later next day, Isabella waited for the royal baggage train to trundle by and we lingered at the end of the lane for a man to take her from us. I watched as the creature lumbered away led gently by the harness which Judd Sadler had made for her. Peter and I then sadly turned for home.

And that was the beginning of the menagerie which John kept at the Tower in London, which grew, I'm told, under his son Henry.

We never saw Isabella again.

What happened to the fuller, did you ask, Paul? Why, he disappeared back to Elcot and after the sale of that mill, he was someone else we never set eyes on again.

He was replaced by another man at the next election of councillors in July and Nick retained his position as reeve. Pounder was hanged on Gibbet Hill.

Everything jogged along nicely for a while. After a while a rhyme grew up and circulated in the town... "Marlborough rare, Marlborough fair, sold the Bible to buy a bear." Everyone was humming it. Though it wasn't entirely a true version of events - it took the town's imagination.

Until, of course, we had another murder.

Ho No! Paul. That is for another day. You must go back to the priory now. Off you go. You don't want to be too late travelling through the forest. There might be ghosts and demons lurking... like there are in our next tale.

Oh no Paul... I shan't tell you. That as I said is for another day.

~~~

Author's Note

The story of the bear actually belongs to the town of Congleton in Cheshire and not to Marlborough. I hope the inhabitants of that northern town will forgive me for stealing their legend and moving it back three centuries and down south.

Congleton became notorious in the 1620's when bear baiting and cock fighting were popular pastimes. For some reason when they were unable to attract the numbers of people they wished to the sport and because they couldn't find the money for a new and more aggressive bear, they used the money they had saved to buy a Bible. Eventually they managed to replenish the fund with the income from the increased number of participants to the sport.

After 1204 when King John granted Marlborough its charter, the town was able to govern itself. Previously it had been governed by the monarch. Much trade was accomplished between Bristol and Southampton and the downland town. This is why my bear comes from Bristol.

In the early thirteenth century, towns like Marlborough were becoming more organised. Naturally we have no idea quite who was on the governing body (until some details were recorded in the later 1200's) but the town reeve (later the Mayor) would be the person elected by the inhabitants to see to the running of the place. Artisan guilds were growing up at this time and it was possible that the reeve's helpers were drawn from members of, for example, the tanners, dyers and fullers guilds. Marlborough was a place built on and prosperous with, cloth and skins, and so these occupations would have been important to the town. It's not unlikely town councillors were drawn from these trades and others of similar ilk.

Dancing bears, cock fighting, bear baiting and dog fighting had not quite yet gained the popularity they did in later centuries but I'm sure that there was a market for such pastimes even as early as 1200. Some people, I'm sure, would have frowned upon them.

It is true that King John began the menagerie at the Tower of London. The first record of wild animals at the Tower is in 1210 when they were kept for the amusement of the royal court. Ostriches, lions, tigers and elephants were all kept at one time. Perhaps Isabella the bear was the first of these in 1206?

In this book John is becoming progressively more worried by his lords and barons. About this time, he began his feud with Earl Marshall and other men of influence, culminating in the Great Charter of 1215. His wariness of some of his companions is well documented and over the years some men were in and out of John's favour, losing and regaining offices bestowed on them by the monarch. We don't really know why, though we might guess that perhaps John did not think them as trustworthy as everyone else believed. The close rolls are littered with removals and appointments and men were removed from office only to appear again when they had regained the monarch's favour. As time progressed this state of affairs worsened.

Now to Aumary. He is a minor lord, not terribly wealthy and more a businessman than pure aristocracy. As warden of the forest he has quite a practical job and needs to know about the forest and its trades. He is a knight, yes, but first and foremost, a forester. I have made him a sympathetic character as so many folk of his class in novels, are portrayed as proud, haughty and nasty. I fail to see how many of them could be so. They were dependent upon their peasants for their livelihood. If the peasant didn't prosper, neither did they, at this level of society. Grander folk perhaps could be less amenable. Aumary takes every man as he finds him and isn't averse to rolling up his sleeves and getting on with it.

I have tried to follow the The Patent Rolls (in the form of the *Rotuli Litterarum Patentium*) by Thomas Duffus Hardy of 1835, to show where King John was known to be on certain days in his reign. If I say he was in the vicinity of Marlborough, then it was very likely he was.

Glossary

Adze - a tool similar to an axe used to shape and form wood.

Assoil - forgive.

Bearward - bear keeper.

Bliaut - A roomy over garment worn by both sexes (but mostly women) and pleated to the waist or under the bosom in women.

Braies - men's underbreeches.

Chime - The wooden rim of a barrel.

Clevis - top metal rim of a barrel.

Cordwainer - shoemaker.

Coroner - sometimes called the Crowner. The man appointed by the Crown to deal with unexpected deaths. The coroner was the man who drew up the jury of twelve men to decide the cause of death and if need be, impose fines.

Cott - Cottage.

Cotte - A long sleeved or sometimes sleeveless shift or tunic. A coat.

Distaff - A stick or spindle on to which wool is wound for spinning.

Fulling Mills - fulling, sometimes known as tucking or walking, is a process in woollen fabric making where the cleansing of cloth to rid it of oils, dirt, and other impurities, takes place. This often has the added bonus of making it thicker. The worker who does the job is a fuller, tucker, or walker, all of which have become common surnames.

Gazehound - a dog rather like a small greyhound.

Gyves - foot restrainers wrapped around the ankle.

Hanglock - padlock.

Hue and Cry - A loud cry calling for the pursuit and capture of a criminal. In English law, the cry had to be raised by the inhabitants of a hundred in which a crime had been committed, if they were not to become liable for the damages suffered by the victim.

Journeyman - a man just out of his apprenticeship.

Palliasse - mattress.

Paternoster - The Lord's Prayer.

Pottage - a thick soup or stew made by boiling vegetables, grains, and, if available, meat or fish. Food of the peasant class.

Rood Screen - a screen of wood or stone, separating the nave from the chancel of a church.

Rouncey - an ordinary, all-purpose horse. They were used for riding, but could also be trained for war and it was not unknown for them to be used as pack horses.

Sippets - milk soaked bread.

Skep - beehive.

Stanchion - a support or barrier.

Tally stick - an ancient device for recording information on a piece of wood or bone.

Tenteryard - an area used for drying newly manufactured cloth after fulling. The wet cloth was hooked onto frames called tenters and stretched taut on tenterhooks, so that the cloth would dry flat and square.

Town Reeve - the man responsible for the governing of the town. In later times the mayor.

Valerian - a plant, an extract of which induces sleep.

Vatmen - Men who worked the vats to full the cloth.

About the Author

Susanna, like Aumary Belvoir has known the Forest of Savernake all her life. After a period at the University of Wales studying Speech Therapy, she returned to Wiltshire and then moved to Hampshire to work, not so very far from her forest. Susanna developed an interest in English history, particularly that of the 12th and 13th centuries, early in life and began to write about it in her twenties. She now lives in Northamptonshire with her husband and two small wire haired fox terriers called Delphi and Tabor.

TITLES IN THIS SERIES

Belvoir's Promise
She Moved Through the Fair
Down by the Salley Gardens
I Will Give my Love an Apple
Black is the Colour of my True Love's Hair
Long Lankyn

Please visit the website for further information
https://susannamnewstead.co.uk/

Printed in Great Britain
by Amazon

47966116R00149